"Do you think I would lead a maiden astray?" Chris
asked.

"Frankly, yes," Jacqui replied, feeling a knot of
apprehension unravel.

"I've been waiting all evening to get my arms around
you," he murmured as he held her gently to the
length of his body, burying his hand in the flaxen
fall of her hair.

"You're not wearing anything under your robe,"
Chris observed.

Jacqui willed herself to prolong the moment, to
absorb each new sensation of his closeness. She
was shocked by her own wanton desire for him not
to stop as he blazed kisses down her throat to the
cleavage between her breasts, and reached for the
sash of her robe at her waist. . . .

Dear Reader,

It is our pleasure to bring you a new experience in reading that goes beyond category writing. The settings of **Harlequin American Romance** give a sense of place and culture that is uniquely American, and the characters are warm and believable. The stories are of "today" and have been chosen to give variety within the vast scope of romance fiction.

Jane Bierce has the working knowledge of all of the elements necessary to build a city. For her first book, *Building Passion,* she called on the expertise of her husband, a construction worker. Having been born in an oil town and raised in a mining town, Jane has seen the birth of first ideas come to reality.

From the early days of Harlequin, our primary concern has been to bring you novels of the highest quality. **Harlequin American Romance** is no exception. Enjoy!

Vivian Stephens
Editorial Director
Harlequin American Romance
919 Third Avenue,
New York, N.Y. 10022

Building
Passion

JANE BIERCE

Harlequin Books

TORONTO • NEW YORK • LONDON
AMSTERDAM • PARIS • SYDNEY • HAMBURG
STOCKHOLM • ATHENS • TOKYO • MILAN

Published July 1983

First printing May 1983

ISBN 0-373-16015-1

Chapter One

Jacqueline Belpre hung up the telephone on her littered desk and stared at the man who was standing before her, splendid in his navy blazer and pale gray slacks, his black hair waved gracefully back from his broad, tanned forehead. He smelled of expensive, sensuous cologne which was at the same time characteristically discreet. Handsome enough, she appraised, and obviously not poverty stricken. He was a refreshing change. Most of the men his age who came into her office at Osprey Builders were dressed in tattered blue jeans, dirty T-shirts, and work boots, layered with grime and reeking of sweat and surreptitious beers.

"I'm Christopher Warden," he introduced himself, unsmiling, as though she should already know his reason for being there and possibly his life story. He placed a long cardboard carrying tube on her desk and tugged nonchalantly at the collar of his pale blue shirt, which was open at the throat, showing a wisp of curly black hair.

"Jacqui Belpre," she said, eagerly extending her hand across the space between them as she got to her feet. As president and chief salesperson of Osprey, it behooved her to appear outgoing and friendly, even if this character showed all the cordiality of a prickly pear.

"Leisure Discovery," he said, barely touching her hand with his. "We would like you to bid on our latest project."

"Oh, yes," Jacqui said, picking up the tube, reading the label and putting it down again. "The luxury cottages on your Egret Island property. I've heard people talking about that, and I'd like to bid, but I just don't have the time to devote to a presentation before your deadline. If you'll excuse me, I have to get out to my model house at the Shelter Cove development."

"Miss Belpre, I also have a personal matter to discuss with you," Christopher Warden said, a note of urgency in his clipped Bostonian tones, quite unexpected on the west central Gulf Coast of Florida, north of the Tampa Bay area.

"I beg your pardon?" Jacqui asked, studying his serious gray eyes, cold and immutable as granite.

Christopher Warden cleared his throat and commanded her attention. "I could have had a messenger deliver these specifications, or ignored your firm completely, Miss Belpre," he said, with growing agitation, drawing himself up to his full height, which was an impressive six foot two or three, she judged. "But there is the matter between your brother and my sister."

Jacqui froze midway in reaching for the case that held the plans for the house she was going to inspect. "My brother—and your sister?" she asked. "I certainly was not aware they even knew each other. I have heard of Leisure Discovery, of course, Mr. Warden, but I have never before heard of you or your sister, or a matter between her and Kyle. And with all due respect, I have no time to discuss anything now."

"I must insist!" Christopher Warden said, his square jaw set.

"Then you'll just have to come and we can talk in my car, because if I don't get out to Shelter Cove in ten minutes, I'll miss two important appointments," Jacqui said, slinging her leather bag over her shoulder. "In this business, time is money, and I am not one to waste either."

"Miss Belpre," Christopher Warden protested, "I don't have the time to—"

"Do you want to discuss the so-called matter, or not?" Jacqui asked, tapping her blueprint tube against her desk impatiently.

"I think it is of the utmost importance," he said gravely, his Bostonian accent becoming even more pronounced.

Jacqui reached for her father's hard hat, which had hung on a hook in the office for the past three years since he and her mother had been lost in a boating accident in the Gulf of Mexico. Unceremoniously, she dusted its chipped red paint with the palm of her hand and then wiped her hand on the seat of her blue jeans. Forcefully, she thrust the hat at Christopher Warden and grabbed her own hard hat from the top of the filing cabinet.

Striding past him, Jacqui paused at the desk of Yvonne Halpern, her secretary, who occupied the front room of the office, itself a model home. "Yvonne," she said, "I'll be out at Shelter Cove to see Dorothea Grace and the landscaper, then I'll be right back. Call Ted Marks back and tell him that the Simpsons can have this place in two weeks."

Yvonne Halpern, a heavy-set widow who had worked for Osprey Builders for the past five years as an indispensable asset to its operation, sagged backward in her swivel chair. "But what are we going to do for an office until the other house is ready?" she asked, looking up at Jacqui, frowning.

"We'll just have to get the other model ready in two weeks," Jacqui told her, reaching for the front door. "I have no other choice."

Jacqui was already making a mental list of the phone calls she would have to make when she returned to the office after her rounds. Outside in the woodchip-covered lot, Jacqui's four-wheel drive wagon sat high on its all-terrain tires, its body color barely discernible under the dust on its sides. She made it clear to Chris-

topher Warden that it was not necessary for him to hold
the door of the driver's side for her, and there was
never a question of who was going to drive "the
Beast." She switched on the ignition and muscled the
vehicle into gear.

"Now," she said, backing out onto the street, "what
is this terribly earthshaking matter about my brother
and your sister?"

"Well," Christopher Warden said, clearly intimi-
dated by her driving, "it seems that your brother has—
ah—befriended my sister, and I would rather their relationship not go any further."

"Any further than what?" Jacqui prodded, looking
both ways at an intersection, and then turning left.

"She assured me that they are just friends," Christopher Warden said, bracing himself in the seat, his
chin showing definite tension.

"But you don't trust Kyle?" Jacqui asked, coming
right to the point. "Or your sister?"

"Really, Miss Belpre!"

Jacqui glanced at him again, then back at the palm-
lined street ahead of her. "Your sister has a name, I
suppose?"

"Alaine," he said, taking pains to be distinct. "With
an *A*."

"I see," Jacqui said, raising her chin so that the glare
of the morning sun would not blind her as it bounced
off the dusty brown hood of the car. "How old is she?"

"Seventeen," he said. "As I understand it, they met
when she fell while she was jogging past a house where
he was working."

"A likely story," Jacqui laughed, appreciating his
discomfort. "Are you going to tell me you think that
Kyle tripped her?"

"No, of course not," he said arrogantly. "He merely
went to her aid. She sat there and rested for a while, and
he brought her over to the hotel on his lunch break."

"On his motorcycle?"

"Yes," Christopher Warden said, with obvious distaste.

"I take it this was when he was working on Sullivan Drive about a week ago Saturday, I think it was," Jacqui said, after some quick reviewing of Kyle's recent schedule.

"Yes. The next day they went to the public beach to swim, Saturday evening they went to a place called Purple Popsicle, and swimming again the next day."

"And you just assume that wedding bells are in the offing?"

"I should certainly hope not!" Christopher Warden snorted derisively.

"Seventeen is too young for marriage," Jacqui agreed, sympathetically. "However, I can't see where you have anything to worry about."

"Miss Belpre, Alaine has only been here a month," Christopher Warden said, his facial muscles tense under their even bronze tan. "I have gotten her into a high school, but she has not made many friends there yet. I realize that she doesn't meet many people her own age living in the hotel with me, but—"

"She is living in Leisure Discovery with you?" she asked, with incredulous disapproval.

"Yes. Our parents are getting a divorce," he sighed, with the shame he might have expressed if he were confessing to an ax murder. "Alaine chose to leave both of them and come to live with me. It's the type of flighty thing she would do."

"Hm! I think she was pretty smart," Jacqui appraised, knowing that Christopher did not want her to make any judgments about his family and would resent anything she said on the subject with some justification, but she could not resist. "I can't think of anything more depressing to a young girl than having to listen to two smug, self-righteous Bostonians argue over who is at fault for a break-up. Why not come to Florida and live with a brother who works in a plush resort hotel complex with a golf course, tennis courts, two pools, and all sorts of exciting performers coming in to entertain?"

"It is not that simple," Christopher interjected.

"Of course not," Jacqui agreed.

"Mother wanted her to stay home, finish her last year of school—"

"At a proper girls' school, no doubt?"

"Of course. She certainly is not ready to associate with a—"

"I want to caution you, Mr. Warden," Jacqui said, taking the sandy short-cut road to Shelter Cove. "I think very highly of Kyle, not only because he is my brother. But if you were to get to know him, you would find him to be every bit the gentleman you might choose for your sister in Boston or Cambridge or any other good address in New England."

"Hardly!" Christopher spat out, angrily. "A masonry worker!"

"And a darned good one!" Jacqui defended. "There is nothing wrong with honest work, nor an honest worker."

Christopher Warden brushed dust from the cuff of his blazer. "Nonetheless, Miss Belpre, I want you to tell your brother to leave my sister alone."

"Oh, you do, do you?" Jacqui scoffed. "Well, I make it a point not to interfere with my brother's affairs of the heart, and he reciprocates. I told him and my younger sister Janice when I had to take over the family three years ago that I would not meddle in their lives so long as they didn't go outside the rules our parents had set up for us. I will discuss the matter with Kyle for my own information, and give him advice if he wants it. But I will not presume to order him to stop seeing your sister, and that's final."

"I should have known that you would be too wrapped

up in your business to do anything decisive about Kyle,'' Christopher accused.

"If that is the attitude you are going to take," Jacqui said, fighting to control both her temper and her vehicle as it traversed the worst of the undulating track, "I suggest you pack up your sister and ship her back to Boston, where she can at least be miserable among people she knows."

They had reached Signal Drive, the main street of the Shelter Cove development. Jacqui had counted herself lucky to have gotten the fifth lot on the left, which had a large live oak tree in the back to shade the house's patio, and a few straggling oaks clumped in the front yard.

There was feverish activity all along the street, where houses were being readied for the opening of the Parade of Homes four weeks away. Among the bungalows that copied the popular Spanish style with red-tiled roofs and wrought-iron trimmings, the colonials with quaint little shutters, and the contemporaries with angled redwood siding and handset stones, Jacqui's model stood out with its distinctive scaled-down half-timbering reminiscent of Elizabethan architecture.

She pulled into the drive behind a dry-wall finisher's van with every available door left standing open. Clamping her hard hat onto her head she grabbed up the plans for the house and jumped out of the car. "You may as well have a look around," she told him. "I have to talk business with some people before I head back to the office, but I won't be very long. Ah! There are the landscapers down at Chesterfield's."

Christopher Warden seemed reluctant to move, even to put the hard hat on his head. At last he got out of the car and followed Jacqui across the uneven bare dirt yard to the dooryard of the house. She vowed to ignore him as she pulled a notebook and pen from her purse and began her inspection of the dry-walling in the living room, dining room and kitchen. "How am I going to have this

place done in two weeks?'' she mused aloud, looking out
the dusty kitchen window at the ravaged backyard.

"Miss Jacqui!" a heavily accented voice called from
the front door.

"Manuel?" she replied, returning to the living room.
"*Que pasa?* I'm so glad you're here. Let me show you
what I want in the front yard."

Manuel, grinning with straight white teeth under his
luxuriant black mustache, pulled a small notebook
from his hip pocket and followed her out into the small
dooryard that was formed by the walls of the garage on
one side and the front bedroom on the other. "I've got
lots of ideas for you," he said.

"Good," she told him, "because I have to move
into this house in two weeks."

Manuel grunted and glanced at his calendar in the
front of his notebook. "If I can talk one customer into
waiting a day or so, I can do this house two weeks from
today," he said, scratching the stubble on his chin.
"Best I can do, unless I hire an extra man."

"Good enough," Jacqui agreed. "I want square
stepping-stones with white stone chips through the
dooryard, then stones over to the driveway."

"In a nice curve?" Manuel asked. "You have so
many angles in the house."

Jacqui agreed with a nod of her head. "Along the
sides, woodchips and low-spreading junipers and some
of those little shrubs with the gray-green leaves and
white margins—"

"Pittsoporum?" Manuel supplied, knowing that Jacqui did not have a grasp of all the landscaping names
yet. "Chesterfield is using a lot of pittsoporum," he
warned her with a wave toward the Spanish-style house
on lot eight.

"How about azaleas?" Jacqui asked, biting her
thumbnail.

"Not compatible with junipers, Miss Jacqui," Manuel shook his head. "But I could put them in containers and take them out later. This is a fairy-tale house, and I see roses, daisy chrysanthemums, and pink hibiscus there to hide the down-spout."

"But the money," Jacqui cut in with protest. "That gets expensive."

"You'll make it up when you sell the house, right?" he asked with a wide grin. "I have white azaleas, red roses, pink hibiscus, and a couple torgolusa junipers, the ones that grow upright and branch in pretty curves."

"Ah," Jacqui sighed in appreciation of the mental picture she was getting of his plans. "All right, then, and sod the front yard, and clean out under those little trees, take off a limb here and there."

"A few shrubs in front?" Manuel asked, making more notes in his book.

Jacqui nodded, thinking that each notation he made was costing more money, but the house had to look showy so that she would get as much business as possible from displaying it. She picked her way carefully past Christopher Warden, who was standing in the doorway of the house with his hands in the pants pockets.

"Now, let's look out back," she said, crossing the living room and dining room to the sliding glass doors that led to the patio, which would be screened and carpeted with outdoor carpeting. "How about continuing the azaleas out here, and grooming under this tree?"

"Is that all you want?" Manuel asked, checking the notes he had made.

"That's not all I want," she laughed, waggling a finger at him. "That's all I can afford."

"Ah, maybe I have some petunias I can throw in," Manuel suggested.

"Can you drop an estimate by the office in a day or two?" she asked.

Manuel laughed. "You never trust me, do you? You sure are Ol' Jack's kid." He turned to Christopher

Warden, asking, "Is this lady building a house for you?"

"Oh, no!" Christopher said, raising his hands defensively and shaking his head, as though it was the last thing he would do. "I'll never hire a woman to build a house for me!"

"Well, if I could have a house built for me, I'd come to her," Manuel told him. "She does the best job for the money of anybody around here, and I see all the builders."

"Don't try to sell him a house for me," Jacqui said, checking a corner by running her hand along the place where pieces of dry-wall were joined. "I don't need the aggravation. I've got four houses going up right now," she told him, conscious that she was trying to impress Christopher.

"I have to get back to work over at Chesterfield's," Manuel told her. "I warned him that it is almost too early to put flowers in, but he wants color pictures taken tomorrow for the advertisement tabloid in Sunday's newspaper."

"Busy, busy," Jacqui said, watching him leave. She was relieved to see Dorothea Grace driving into the yard.

The interior decorator was a tall, slender woman in her late forties, her blond hair helped a little by the hairdresser she frequented. She was highly respected in the area, and as a businesswoman she had an impeccable reputation. Jacqui sighed and lowered her voice. "Dorothea is one of the few people I know who can make that denim skirt and cotton blouse look absolutely elegant."

"Jacqui, darling," Dorothea's broad Atlantan drawl called, as she came into the house. She immediately took off her dark glasses and smiled with warm brown eyes. "Surely you don't need me any more."

Jacqui adjusted her hard hat, which was becoming uncomfortably sweaty. "I have my doubts about what I'm doing here," she explained. "Last year it was just a tremor, but everything I've been looking at in the decorating magazines has changed so radically, I really feel that I need to ask your advice."

Dorothea looked around the rooms attentively. "What do you have in mind?"

"Briefly," Jacqui said, taking a deep breath, "blue, pink, and romance."

"You clever girl!" Dorothea crowed, proud of her former protégée.

"Manuel is carrying the romantic idea of a little Elizabethan cottage in the dooryard with pink and white," she explained, reaching into her enormous purse for her bundle of swatches. "I'm using this light neutral carpet, and slightly lighter walls, drapes in a pastel blue, and this floral print for the upholstery."

"Um! So far, I love it," Dorothea approved, fanning the samples in her manicured hand and fingering the swatch of carpet.

"What I really want to ask you about is the master bedroom," Jacqui said, leading her through the family room. "Joe! I thought I heard you back here. Don't you usually start in the living room?"

The dry-wall finisher looked up from the thin plaster he was mixing and grinned toothlessly. "The tile man called me last night and said you had him scheduled to come in today, so I told him to hold off until noon and I'd be out of his way. He had another job he had to do this morning."

Jacqui pantomimed tearing her hair. "If it weren't for these housing shows, there would never be any excitement in this business, would there?" she asked them.

Dorothea and the plaster-spattered Joe laughed. "What would we do for overtime?" Joe asked.

"In here I'm planning on this dark blue-gray shade of paint on the walls, these drapes, and this print bedspread," she showed Dorothea.

Dorothea's brows furrowed. "I'd go a little darker with the paint, Jacqui," she advised. "The idea is right, but you need to be just a little bolder, a little more dramatic.''

"Good! That's what I wanted you to tell me," Jacqui said, pouncing on her words. "That was what I thought in the first place, but I—"

"Always go with your first instinct!" Dorothea dictated, implying that her statement covered more than decorating. "What about the other bedrooms?"

Jacqui turned toward the center section of the house. "I'm going to have to scrap my plans for them, because they are going to have to be office space. Look, would you do me another favor?" she asked.

"Besides giving you all this free advice?" Dorothea teased.

"Could you take on Janice like you did me?" she asked. "She's sixteen and she needs a job, part-time, after school."

"Is she as intense and impatient as you were?" Dorothea asked, smiling a bit wistfully. "Send her over after school tomorrow and we'll have a talk. If she is anything like you, I can give her the business and retire in three years."

"I'll see that she comes over," Jacqui promised. "Thanks."

"Look at the time!" Dorothea said, glancing at her watch. She fumbled with her sunglasses. "I have another appointment here. Jacqui, I'm anxious to see this place when it's finished."

"You're not the only one!" Jacqui laughed. "Will you be at the Builders Association meeting Monday night?"

"Yes. I'll see you there," Dorothea said, and waving, hurried away.

Jacqui looked around for Christopher Warden and discovered him standing in the archway which led to the bedroom wing, his arms crossed on his chest and his gray eyes watching her every move with an intense speculation she found distinctly unsettling. "I have a few more notes to make here,'' she told him, squinting at a ceiling joint, "and we'll be going."

She took a deep breath before venturing past him to continue her inspection. If he had blocked her way, she did not know how she would have reacted.

"A very clever bathroom there," he told her, sliding the dividing door closed and open again.

"In our house, there never seemed to be enough sinks, so I split the bathroom and put in two sinks," Jacqui said, proudly. "I build my houses for families, not just for retired people."

"I see," Christopher Warden said, dusting his hands with a fine linen handkerchief.

"I'm sorry if this was a bore for you," Jacqui said, feeling a pang of contrition for the way she had treated him, as she led him back to her four-wheel drive wagon.

"On the contrary," he said, taking off the hard hat, which he clearly detested. "It was in the way of an education."

"How to go out of your mind in one easy lesson?" Jacqui asked, putting her key into the ignition. "Well, everything came loose this morning, starting with the Simpsons wanting the house so soon, but it is something that can be managed. Shall we use the paved street, or take the overland route again?"

"Please use the pavement," Christopher said. "I am not in so much of a hurry to get back to my office that you must take your short-cut again."

"That's what I thought," Jacqui said. "Of all the times of the year, this is the busiest and, I guess, the part I like the most." She rambled on about some of the problems she was having, conscious of talking to fill up the time, to take away any opportunity that Christopher might have to criticize her. It gave her a sense of power to know that she had forced him into a situation where he was totally unfamiliar with the surroundings and at a loss, especially because he had been so critical of Kyle. Of all people, Kyle had to be the best possible person for Alaine Warden to meet.

She chided herself fleetingly for the streak of vengeance that had been unleashed in her to cause Christopher Warden his discomfort and then gloat to herself about it, but there was something in the firm line of his slightly cleft chin that told her he would survive her little game, one she had never played before and vowed she never would again.

"So what are the specs for your Egret Island project?" Jacqui asked, trying, by allowing him an opening into the conversation, to make amends.

"I'm sure you'll get a much better idea of the situation from the papers I left in your office. It's merely a matter of quoting figures," Christopher told her.

"Then why not just hire your own subcontractors?" Jacqui asked.

Christopher sighed. "We tried that once, Miss Belpre. Things are never so easy as they at first appear. Perhaps when you look over the materials, and we could talk—"

"Mr. Warden, I really don't intend to bid on that project," she told him forcefully. "You can see the bind I'm in. I have three other houses in various stages right now. So long as I have Kyle farmed out learning the trades, I'm the only one to ride herd on my subcontractors and look for new business."

"Explain what you just said about Kyle," he demanded, a puzzled expression crossing his face.

Jacqui steered the four-wheel drive wagon into her parking place. "Kyle is not old enough by state law to receive his builder's certification yet, so when he graduated from high school, I started farming him out to the best of my subcontractors. First he learned building materials from a wholesaler. Then I had him learn electrical wiring, plumbing and carpentry. Now he'll work at masonry for another month or so, and go on to dry-wall for the summer. In the fall he'll work for roofers. Then, he'll be old enough to start builder's school and learn contracting, the legal end of it. He's already had bookkeeping in high school."

"So there is a pattern to his not keeping a job over six months?" Christopher Warden asked, his dark eyebrows raised.

Jacqui opened her car door and jumped out. "If you thought he was shiftless because he wasn't keeping a job very long, you are totally wrong," she told him. "There is definitely a method to this madness. And he has not worked for a single employer who has not told him that he would have a job with him if he ever needed it. But that is not our plan. Kyle will take over Osprey Builders in about two years, and I'll just sit around the office and yell at the county inspectors."

"There is a possibility that I misjudged your brother, Miss Belpre," Christopher Warden said, and Jacqui realized that it was as much of an apology as she was likely to get from him.

"There is every possibility in the world, Mr. Warden," she said.

He handed the hard hat to her. "Should you decide not to bid on Egret Island, may I have that set of specifications back?" he asked.

"That's standard procedure around here," she told him, taking off her own hat and fluffing out her long, honey-blond hair. "Besides, I have so many sets of my own, why would I want to clutter up my office with someone else's? I might get confused and build a multimillion-dollar leisure complex instead of a three-two somewhere."

"Three-two?" he asked, his gray eyes quizzing her.

"Three bedrooms, two baths," she told him, flashing fingers. "Nice meeting you, Mr. Warden. I'll speak to Kyle, but I don't give him orders. And I'll send the specs back after I take a look at them. Just because I'm busy, that doesn't mean I'm not curious."

Christopher Warden backed away toward his sleekly gleaming maroon town car, one that would be immediately bogged down in some of the sandy, remote places Jacqui took the Beast. The closest thing to a smile crossed his face, and Jacqui wondered if he was smiling at her or at the relief of leaving her presence.

In the office, Yvonne looked up from her account books and grinned. "How did you manage to tear yourself away from him so soon?" she teased.

"He's all show and no substance," Jacqui called back over her shoulder. Going back to her office, which would probably be the breakfast area when the Simpsons moved into the house, she carefully hung her father's hat on its hook and replaced hers on the filing cabinet. She tossed her tube of specifications back into its slot and tentatively picked up the tube Warden had left.

Christopher Warden had been an interesting diversion in her day. Handsome. Cultured. Perhaps even spoiled. Definitely class-conscious.

There was something about him, though, that struck her as fundamentally appealing, something that would attract her even if the wealth, the refinement, perhaps even the physical perfection of him were stripped away, something indefinable. It struck a responding chord in her own being, almost as she had seen harmonic strings in a piano quiver when a related key had been struck. Through the years, she had steeled herself against reacting to the men whom she met, but Christopher Warden had appeared at a time when her guard was down and there was no avoiding the impression he had made on her.

She felt again a little sorry for treating him as wretchedly as she had, but he should have known that she would not have welcomed criticism of her younger brother with gratitude. Besides, he had made her feel plainly inadequate.

She looked down at the blue chambray shirt and blue jeans that she was wearing. They were functional, practical clothing for a woman who never knew what swamp or palm-thicket her work would be taking her to.

Taking a deep breath, she grinned devilishly to herself, then slid the Egret Island papers into an empty slot in the rack. So much for Christopher Warden.

"Yvonne? Can you come here a minute?" she called. "We have to make some plans."

Chapter Two

There was the inevitable quiver when she finally turned off the ignition of the Beast in her own driveway late that afternoon. Jacqui sighed and pulled the key from the slot, then dropped the heavy ring of keys into her satchel-sized purse. Almost forgetting the tube that lay across the passenger seat, she reached back to get it, then walked along the cement paving stones to the patio door of the house that her father had built seven years before.

"Is that you, Jacqui?" Janice called to her from the kitchen.

"What's left of me," Jacqui replied without humor, walking slowly to the kitchen. The wide white counters did not give the usual clues to what Janice was fixing for dinner. "What are we having tonight?" she asked.

"There's a slaw in the refrigerator," Janice answered, turning from the oven and laying down the bright yellow holder, "and I just now put a potato casserole into the oven. You just can't smell it yet."

Jacqui reflected that it was becoming increasingly like looking into a mirror to see those bright blue eyes, the long, waving honey-blond hair, only a shade lighter than her own.

"What are you doing?" Jacqui asked, noticing that Janice was fussing over their mother's deep-fryer which had been tucked back into the hard-to-reach corner of the kitchen cupboard for several years.

"Well, it's a surprise," Janice said, loving the opportunity to tease, to draw out suspense as long as possible. There were times when she was maddeningly effective at it, and this was one of them, Jacqui realized wearily. It was almost as annoying as her overuse of makeup.

"I've had enough surprises today, Jan," she said with a heavy sigh. "How about a straight answer?"

"Lisa's mother brought me home from school today," she started, glancing up at the clock. "She was telling me about getting some eating shrimp from one of the trucks that park in the plaza, and how good they were going to be. So, one thing led to another, and I asked her if she would mind taking me to get some, and showing me how to fix them, because I'm so tired of all the ground beef we have been eating lately."

Jacqui felt her eyes widen and her jaw drop. "Shrimp! Where did you get the money?"

"I hadn't spent any of my allowance," Janice said, with an offhand shrug of her shoulders, "so I thought I'd splurge."

"Well, I can pay you back easily enough," Jacqui told her, dropping her purse to its usual place on the counter and picking up the mail.

"Lisa's mother came in and showed me how to clean the shrimp, and she made the batter to dip them in. I wrote everything down as she went along," Janice rambled on. "So when Kyle gets home, all I have to do is heat this oil and dip them into the batter and fry them. I hope it's all right."

"If it works, it's more than all right," Jacqui told her, dropping the mail back onto the counter and giving her sixteen-year-old sister an affectionate pat on her back as she made her way to the hallway which led to her bedroom. "Got an idea for you, if you're interested in making some money."

Janice left the stove and followed her. "Interested? Fascinated!" she exclaimed eagerly.

"I thought you would be," Jacqui said, sitting down on the edge of her barely made double bed. "I was talking to Dorothea Grace about you today. She said for you to drop by tomorrow if you want a part-time job."

"Eh. Decorating?" Janice said, with a frown crossing her fresh, oval face.

"That's where I started," Jacqui reminded her, kicking off her shoes. "It's not something you have to stick to for the rest of your life. It's fun and Dorothea is great to work for."

"I'll talk to her," Janice told her, very apparently not overjoyed with the prospect. "But I'm not going to promise anything."

"Money is money," Jacqui said. "Look, I'm in desperate need of a shower. I have had about the worst day ever. I'm in a basically lousy mood, so just humor me, huh?"

"What do I always do?" Janice asked. Then she glanced at the tube Jacqui had brought into the bedroom and dropped beside her on the bed. "What's that?"

"Just a project that is out on bids," Jacqui told her, getting up and rummaging through her dresser for fresh underthings. "I don't intend to bid on it, but I just thought I'd look it over to see what it was all about."

"It's a good thing you don't intend to bid," Janice spouted. "You're working six and seven days a week as it is. I hardly ever see you. When was the last time we went anywhere together just for fun?"

If Jacqui had taken over the job of breadwinner and boss of the family, Janice had taken on the duties of mother-hen. She was constantly fretting over their sleeping and eating, their aches and pains.

"How would it be if I promise, in blood, that we can do something soon?" Jacqui asked, heading for the bathroom that was adjacent to the bedroom. She still felt very tentative about the room, which had been her parents' and now served as both a bedroom and a home-office for Jacqui.

"When?" she demanded.

"The weekend after the Parade of Homes," Jacqui said, thinking ahead.

"That'll be six weeks from now," Janice wailed, then her mood instantly changed. "What will we do?"

Jacqui closed the door between them, anxious for the solitude of the shower. "Maybe go down to Sarasota and look at the museums."

She heard Janice groan and walk away. Then there was the roar of Kyle's powerful motorcycle as it entered the driveway. Janice would go tell everything to Kyle, and she could have a few minutes of sweet, warm, perfumed peace in the shower.

But her thoughts went back to the morning, first to Ted Marks, then skittered off immediately to Christopher Warden, and she felt herself become tense and angry all over again. How dare he look down his elegant nose at Kyle, who had been raised to have every bit as much respect for womanhood as any stiff and proper Bostonian. So they were not rich. That did not really matter. Alaine Warden obviously needed to talk to someone who understood an irreparable loss of both parents. There had been a special love in their family that was no longer there, leaving them emotionally stranded. Jacqui had swallowed all her grief, taking charge of making all the arrangements, taking over the home-building company, and seeing that the houses under contract had been finished, while studying for her own builder's certificate. By the time she had reached a breathing space, Kyle and Janice had themselves back under control, and Jacqui pushed her feelings far into the background. Grief had a difficult time settling onto a moving target.

Now as she lathered herself with rose-scented soap, one of the few extravagances she allowed herself, she was dismayed that the force of the shower slackened. She knew that Kyle was in the other bathroom, and no matter how badly she needed her shower, Kyle undoubtedly needed his more. She quickly rinsed herself off and stepped out onto the thick bath mat.

Jacqui took her time, though, drying herself, tying up her hair, and getting into one of the light robes that were her trademark at home. She intended to sit down and look over the specifications for Egret Island, but the aroma of Janice's potato casserole and the deep-frying shrimp reached out to her, drawing her to the kitchen, and then to the breakfast area, where Janice was setting the table.

"How's dinner coming?" Jacqui asked, straightening a teaspoon on the table, and then feeling guilty that she had possibly insulted Janice.

"Just fine, I hope," Janice said, and returned to the stove to peer down into the deep fryer and wait.

Kyle appeared in the doorway, bare-chested, wearing only fresh but well-worn jeans, droplets of water still clinging to the tight blond ringlets of his sun-bleached hair. He was a handsome man, well over six feet tall, muscular from the hard manual work that he was used to. His face had long ago lost all its babyishness and taken on the angularity of adulthood, softened by his ready smile and warm blue eyes. Jacqui considered herself the ugly duckling of the three of them, but only because she had neither the time nor the inclination to fuss over her grooming.

Without a word, Kyle went to the stove and studied the contents of the fryer. He took the slotted spoon from Janice and stirred patiently. "Got a platter ready?" he asked. "Did you make a sauce?"

"Sauce!" Janice demanded. "You're lucky I made all this."

He gently poked her in the ribs with his elbow. "The cook has to taste it first," he reminded her, lifting a dripping golden blob from the fryer and shaking it off onto the paper towel on the platter Janice held. "They all look done, don't you think?"

Janice nodded and watched as he turned off the electric element and finished taking all the shrimp out of the boiling oil. "It's really not awfully hard to fix shrimp," Janice said, carrying the platter to the table, "once you get past cleaning the little dickens."

"Well, it's a very fitting meal for the occasion," Jacqui told them, as they all sat down around the round table. As was their custom, they bowed their heads for a few seconds, and then raised them again. "Ted Marks sold the old model today. The only problem is that we have to be out of it in two weeks."

Janice filled her plate from the various dishes before attempting the first bite of shrimp. Suddenly Kyle speared one of the shrimp with his fork. "If you're not brave enough, kid," he said, "I sure am. I hardly got any lunch today."

Janice took a tentative nibble at her shrimp, then a larger bite. "Needs something, don't you think?" she asked Kyle. "Something—"

"A sauce is what it needs," he told her, his blue eyes teasing as he managed to talk while he chewed.

"Well, next time, you can do it," Janice said, almost pouting.

Kyle, sitting at what was considered the head of the table, reached out with his big hand, placing it behind Janice's slender neck. "It's really delicious," he said, then grinned. Then he turned to Jacqui. "Can you get into the new model house so soon?"

"I'll have to," Jacqui said, dutifully cutting one of her shrimp in half with her fork and preparing to bravely bite into it. "I called around to some of my subcontractors and they were willing to try to juggle a job here and there," she told Kyle. "But next Sunday, we're all going to end up painting the place, because the carpet has to go in Monday. That's the only day they can install it."

"*We*'re painting?" Kyle asked, frowning, a forkful of slaw halfway to his mouth. "We?"

"I know that will cut into your swimming schedule," Jacqui teased.

Kyle shrugged, and Jacqui wished that he would have shown some surprise that she knew what he had been doing the last two Sundays.

She debated with herself for a long moment whether to go deeper into the matter of Alaine Warden, or whether to let everyone enjoy Janice's unexpected culinary triumph and bring up the subject later, when they could be alone. When Janice launched into a discussion of how she could keep Jacqui to the promised weekend excursion, and where they should go, the matter was settled. There would be plenty of time to corner Kyle when Janice had gone off to struggle with her geometry.

WHEN DINNER HAD BEEN CLEARED, Jacqui spread out the specifications for the Egret Island project, weighting down the corners of the survey of the land with a couple of glass paperweights from her mother's collection, still on display on the buffet.

"What's this?" Kyle asked, shrugging his shoulders into a blue chambray shirt indistinguishable from six others he owned and only larger than four hanging in Jacqui's closet.

"The specs for Mr. Warden's project on Egret Island," she told him and detected a flicker behind his blue eyes. "He delivered them in person first thing this morning—well, first thing after Ted Marks sold the house out from under me."

Kyle rubbed the cleft between his lower lip and his chin with one blunt forefinger. "Something tells me I'm about to find out why he delivered them in person," he said slowly.

"Sit down," Jacqui said.

"I guess I'd better," Kyle sighed. "What did he have to say?"

"He doesn't want his sister associating with a cement-block layer," she told him simply.

"She could do a lot worse," Kyle said, his fingers absently running over the edge of the survey.

"That is the essence of what I told him, among other things," Jacqui said, turning her attention to the summary of the contract. "I had to ask what her name is. To him, she is just his sister, not Alaine."

"From what she has told me that's symptomatic of the way she has been treated since she was a child," Kyle said. "The unexpected baby, the inconvenience to what was already supposed to be a perfect arrangement."

"And now that the arrangement has fallen apart, she feels—"

"Like she caused the divorce," Kyle said. He leaned back in his chair and crossed his arms on his chest. "She's hurting, Jacqui, and if I don't care about her, who will?"

He recounted the story that Christopher Warden had only sketched for her earlier. Jacqui shook her head that neither Kyle nor Christopher Warden had seemed to notice that Alaine was very much in control of the situation, and whatever anyone else did, Alaine had made her point clear. She was lonely, and she wanted a friend.

"I took her to the beach and to Purple Popsicle because I thought I could get her to meet other people," Kyle concluded, "but she does not want to be interested in anyone but me."

"And how do you feel about her?" Jacqui asked.

"Like I would about a sister, I guess," he told her, looking at her levelly with his sincere blue eyes. "She has been in private schools, very sheltered, very proper, all her life. I guess they have money. Of course, they have money! She is so small and helpless and—pretty—"

Jacqui raised her eyebrows at the word "helpless."

"Kyle—another one of your strays?" she asked, trying to keep from being too serious.

Kyle smiled sheepishly. He had been the one in the family to cart home the strays, and there had been times when the family had been afraid their home would turn into a pound. Luckily now they had only an independent female cat who appropriated a corner of the garage and drifted in and out of their lives at will, asking nothing more than an occasional handout of dry cat food and all their table scraps.

Jacqui shook her head again. "Have you met Christopher Warden?" she asked him.

"Oh, yes!" Kyle pounded the table with the palm of his hand. "He is a cool one. There I was, covered with cement dust and mortar, and he was in a three-piece gray suit and a striped tie. The second that he felt the callouses on my hand, he recoiled like a snake. I am not acceptable to be even a friend of his precious sister. But she does have a defiant streak in her. Alaine told me that she doesn't care what her brother thinks, she wants to go out with me anyway."

Jacqui shuffled papers around in front of her. Should she ask Kyle if he felt that Alaine was using him to rebel against her family, or should she let the whole thing work itself out at its own speed? she wondered. "I don't want to get mixed up in this," she told him, "but Christopher Warden asked me to talk to you about it. I've already told him that we have an agreement that I don't interfere in your affairs of the heart and you don't interfere in mine."

"And when was the last time you had an affair for me to mess in?" Kyle teased, leaning his elbows on the table.

"That has nothing to do with it," Jacqui said at first insulted then feeling herself smile.

"Only half as long, I'd bet," Kyle spouted, "as it has been since Warden had one, if he has a heart to have one with."

"Kyle, calm down," Jacqui said, thinking momentarily of what Christopher Warden would be like if he were in love. His gray eyes would smolder with passion, and the deep round tones of his voice would very matter-of-factly proclaim his undying adoration. A woman wouldn't have a chance when he put his arms around her and held her to his broad chest, when he began to kiss her with his classically sensual mouth. She swallowed quickly and brought herself back to the matter at hand. "Are you sure you are not in love with Alaine, just a little?"

"I've kissed her a few times, experimentally, you know," Kyle confessed. "But it didn't mean anything, not to me, at least."

"Want some advice?" Jacqui asked, with a sigh.

"I don't know," Kyle said.

Jacqui turned her attention to the papers spread out before her. She had no business even offering advice to Kyle, in view of her limited experience, she told herself.

"Oh, all right," Kyle said. "What do you think I should do?"

"It depends," Jacqui told him. "If Alaine is bothering you, and you want to get rid of her, as Christopher Warden wants you to, the best thing would be to reverse your psychology. There is one very good way to discourage a romance. Forcefeed Alaine on your presence, with proper chaperoning, of course. She needs family, so we include her in ours. Jan can distract her, since they are closer in age than you are to her. I need painters Sunday. Maybe—"

Kyle's face brightened. "You are so clever! Only someone who is a step back from the problem can see it clearly, though."

"I'm just your common, garden variety super-sister, dear Kyle, and don't you forget it," she said, then laughed with him. "Seriously, you work out the details. You can use 'the Beast' anytime you need it, because I think Christopher objects to the cycle. Count on me to chaperone, or take Janice along with you. Just be very obvious to Christopher with what you are doing and where you are going, and Alaine will soon tire of us and you."

"Guaranteed?"

"If it doesn't work, I'm going to forget I ever mentioned it," she said. "Look at this! They want to put six cottages on that island. Ah! They have no idea of the elevation they need to keep the units from being swamped by heavy seas. And—"

She scooted her chair aside a little to give Kyle a chance to see the plans as they had been drawn up. He moved papers around with his mortar-roughened hands. "Well, how would you do it?" he asked.

"I'm not even going to bid on this," she sighed. "Why bother to waste my time on it?"

"Just in case you ever want to do something like this," Kyle reasoned. "Look, Jacqui, the way these cottages are facing each other, no one would feel they had any real privacy."

"If they were clustered," Jacqui mused, "using common walls, and the natural contour of the terrain—Kyle, could you bring me my drafting board? I may just sketch out a few ideas."

She and Kyle were both good at drafting. It had come naturally to them, it seemed. But Kyle was more adept at visualizing structures from bare blueprints and specialized schematics, which Jacqui was wary of.

"All right!" Kyle exclaimed, when he comprehended what Jacqui was sketching. "But Leisure Discovery wants six units, and that is only four."

"What if we excavate this lower area behind these four, put in a service and storage area, and perch two units on top. Now, with landscaping and decking, all six units have views of the Gulf, and all the privacy they could want. With the common garden, really well-planned, exotic plantings, it could be like six little, private paradises. We could have a footbridge here to connect with the cart-path, and a service road here, out of sight. Even space for six cars, under a carport—"

"Do a front elevation for it," Kyle suggested. "What style do you see it in?"

"I see stone, angled wood panels. No, that would be too much upkeep. Stucco and stone, some redwood decks and walkways," Jacqui said, then turned to a fresh page in her sketch pad and drew quickly.

They worked together, trying one idea after another, spurring each other into better and better ideas, until Janice, in night clothes, came shuffling over to the table. "What are you doing?" she asked.

"Messing around," Kyle said, barely looking up from the table.

"Well, it's almost eleven, and you both have long days tomorrow," she scolded, then yawned.

"Mother-hen!" Kyle countered. "Is there any iced tea left?"

"It'll keep you awake," Janice said. "What's that? A house?"

"Six resort units," Jacqui said. "This is what the specs are, but I didn't like that concept, so we got to fooling around with the idea, and this is what we came up with."

Janice held the final sketch off at arm's length and made faces as she studied the rendering. "I guess if you have to mess up Egret Island, that's the best way to do it," she commented at last.

Jacqui sighed and slumped in her chair. "Well, that was a perfectly good evening wasted," she said.

"Just because I don't like it, that doesn't mean that Leisure Discovery wouldn't buy it," Janice said, flipping back to a previous sketch.

"I don't think it was a waste," Kyle was saying, rummaging through the refrigerator. "I learned a few things, didn't you, Jac?"

"Yes, I think I did." She flexed her back, then began straightening up the table and her drafting board.

"How long do you have before you submit this?" Janice asked.

"I'm not submitting it," Jacqui told her.

"You mean that you are going to let someone hack up Egret Island this other way?" Janice demanded. "Really, Jacqui—"

"She's right," Kyle said. "Looking at the alternative, this is a great plan. The cluster makes very good sense in a lot of ways. You really ought to finish this and take it to Christopher Warden to show him that we Belpres have something other than cement in our heads."

"I don't care if I never see Christopher Warden again," Jacqui told him.

"Come, come," Kyle chided. "You've always told us that business is no place to let personal feelings color your judgment."

"I didn't know you were listening," Jacqui said.

"Jacqui, if you presented this," Kyle said, spreading one hand across the work she had completed that evening, "and got the contract, think what it would do for Osprey Builders. It would make our year."

"That's easy for you to say," she told him. "I don't want to have anything to do with—"

"To say nothing of the reputation you would get from it," Kyle was going on, ignoring her protests.

"It seems like a waste of a night's work," Janice said, always the pragmatist, as she compared the two designs.

"Oh, yes, as though I had something else to do," Jacqui said. "It would take me three or four nights of hard work to prepare a proper presentation."

Janice looked at her intently. "What can I do to help?" she asked.

Kyle's eyes were their most serious blue. "I say let's go for it," he said, with a cautious urgency in his voice.

Jacqui rubbed the back of her neck. "Really—"

"From here, it's just drafting and estimating, Jac," he said. "You make a watercolor wash of each elevation, and some proposed interiors, and it's as good as done. I'll do the drafting and the estimating. Jan can make the iced tea and pick out the style of swimming pool we are going to have installed here when it's done."

"Your mother had one pushy kid," Jacqui said, pointing to Kyle, then she pointed to herself, "and one fool for work." She got up slowly. "Let's leave everything right where it is, and eat at the counter for breakfast. Agreed?"

Kyle nodded, then placed his hands on Janice's shoulders. "Bed!"

Janice nodded. "You too."

He immediately had a faraway look in his eyes, then he turned back toward the project on the breakfast table, but Jacqui knew better than to ask him what he was thinking. "Check the doors, Kyle," she told him. "I'll get the lights."

Chapter Three

The wind woke Jacqui from a heavy sleep seconds before the alarm was to ring. The walls of the house shook and she heard the rustling of leaves, straining to cling to the oak trees outside.

Then came the first spattering of raindrops against the roof.

Yawning, she turned off the alarm and sat up on the edge of the bed. "Janice! Get up!" she called out, but Janice's radio had already clicked on to a rock station, the only noise which assured that Janice would be fully awake and on the school bus by seven o'clock.

In the kitchen, the telephone rang, and a few minutes later, Kyle came to the door of the bedroom as Jacqui was putting on her velour robe. "That was Cletus Garwood," Kyle told her, scratching his mop of blond curls. "He says that this wind is from the south, which means that we're going to have rain until nine or so, and there is no point to going out to the job until then. I thought, since I have a little time, I might work on the bid for Egret Island."

"Be my guest," Jacqui said, around a yawn. "Look, how does Garwood always know exactly how long it is going to rain, and when to report for work? He's hardly ever wrong."

"He says that when the wind is from the south for more than four hours, we'll get rain," Kyle said, then shrugged. "If I work with him long enough, he'll tell me all the lore he knows, besides how to get the stress cracks to go where we want them."

Jacqui shoved her feet into her thong sandals and got to her feet. "All I know is that he is one of the best cement masons around, and you can learn a lot from him. Now, if you want to work on that bid, it might be a good time, between eight and nine, to get the quotes on the materials. Most of the offices are open at eight."

"You're not planning to get this thing together to give Mr. Warden on Sunday when I pick up Alaine to come paint, are you?" he asked, following her to the kitchen.

"I don't see how I can have it done by then, do you?" Jacqui asked him, drawing water into the kettle. She glanced across the room at the breakfast table, still cluttered with two nights' worth of work.

"No," Kyle agreed, getting the bread from the refrigerator. "So it will be Monday night before we finish it, and the deadline is the next Friday. He sure didn't give much warning to the bidders."

"Well, it seems to me that Leisure Discovery does not know how to conduct their business very well yet," Jacqui said.

"Come on, Jac," Kyle said. "You know why he brought you that set of specifications. Just to bug you about me. To see what kind of person you are. He had no intention of asking for your bid. Those specs were probably a set that someone returned to him, and he just used them as an excuse."

"And we are submitting a bid as an excuse to—" Jacqui caught a glimpse of a dangerous look in Kyle's blue eyes.

"What I was wondering was," Kyle said, turning away to start his toast, "who is going to take this bid in? You or me?"

"Personally, I don't care if I never see Christopher

Warden again in my life," Jacqui said, and promptly
felt a twinge in her shoulder, a twinge which she
claimed was an old volleyball injury, but in fact, was a
reminder of conscience. "I just remembered, Kyle,
that I won't be able to work on it Monday night, because I have a Builders Association meeting."

Kyle nodded. "I was thinking, maybe I should make
a scale model, to show how the positions of the units
will be varied by the use of the terrain. With the extra
night to work on it—"

"Kyle, why are we knocking ourselves dead on
this?" Jacqui asked. "I don't want to win this bid. I
don't want to have anything to do with Leisure Discovery or Christopher Warden. We're learning a lot on
this, but if I won this bid, I would be scared to death. I
would hate to accidentally get the dumb thing, and then
default on the contract."

"If, by some dumb quirk of fate," Kyle said, searching for the strawberry jam in the refrigerator, "Osprey
gets the contract, I'll foreman the job, so you won't
have to go near the place."

Jacqui rolled her eyes heavenward. "Now, that would
really give Mr. Warden something to think about, you
hanging around Leisure Discovery for the months it is
going to take to make this project come together."

Kyle laughed. "You make it sound as though I'll be
hanging around the pool or the golf course. Believe me,
I'd rather do that than—"

"You'll learn dry-wall this summer, and that will be
that," Jacqui said.

Janice shuffled into the kitchen, yawning. "That
wind is awful! What if it's raining this hard when I have
to get the bus?"

"Is this a hint that you want a ride to school?" Jacqui
asked her.

"How'd you guess?" Janice asked. "Hey, when are
we getting the breakfast table back?"

"Next Wednesday morning," Kyle told her, taking his toast from the toaster and trying not to burn his fingers.

YVONNE HALPERN was late for work, trudging into the office with her raincoat and umbrella dripping, apologizing that her electricity had been out and her alarm had not gone off. Jacqui did not particularly care whether Yvonne was late or not. A widow in her early fifties, Yvonne was a hard worker whose loyalty was unquestioned. She had worked with Jack and Sandy Belpre, and had almost become a member of the family.

"What are you doing with all that trash?" Yvonne asked, looking at the pile Jacqui was accumulating in the middle of the floor.

"I thought while you weren't here, and the phone wasn't ringing," Jacqui said, "I'd start throwing things away. Would you happen to have any moving boxes?"

"No, but I'll bet some of my neighbors do," Yvonne replied. "I'll ask around. Do you want me to help paint Sunday?"

"No," Jacqui said, after a moment's thought. "I think I'd rather you help with the moving the next week. I don't want to impose on you."

"It's not an imposition," Yvonne assured her. "I think of it as part of my job."

"Moving, maybe," Jacqui said, making a decision to throw away an old Christmas decoration. "Painting, no."

"You're the boss," Yvonne said, adding an old scratch pad to Jacqui's growing pile of junk.

"Yvonne, make a note that I have to talk to the bonding company this morning," Jacqui said, digging out some bent file cards from the back of a drawer. "I need a bid bond for the Egret Island project."

Raising an eyebrow, Yvonne made a note on her calendar. "So-o-o?" she drawled. "You're actually certifying that bid?"

ALAINE WARDEN was as charming as her older brother was formidable. She entered the model home gingerly, her eyes wide and inquisitive. Her small frame, refined, almost classic face, and black hair was a sharp contrast to Kyle's height and blondness, Jacqui thought, seeing them together.

"So this is it?" Alaine asked, her accent definitely Bostonian, her manner somewhat as Jacqui had always imagined Alice in Wonderland had had when she had fallen down the rabbit-hole. Her gray eyes were inquisitive and curious, showing that she was open to a new experience. She wore old jeans and a T-shirt that showed off her slender figure and her even tan.

"Alaine," Kyle said, a note of pride in his voice, "my sisters, Jacqui and Janice."

Without a flicker of restraint, Alaine reached for Jacqui's hand, which was already paint-spattered. "My brother told me quite a lot about you, Miss Belpre," she said.

"Jacqui, please," Jacqui admonished, imagining exactly what Christopher Warden had told his sister about her.

"Jacqui. And Janice, Kyle has told me a lot about you, all nice things. Where do I start?" Alaine asked, pushing her black hair back over her shoulders.

"Well," Jacqui said, "there's a bandana over there for you to tie up your hair. Then why don't you take a look around the house?"

"Oh, good," Alaine agreed enthusiastically. "By the way, Chris is bringing us our dinner when he comes to collect me later. He thought that it would be imposing on Kyle for him to take me back home."

Jacqui shot Kyle a look, but he had not reacted to the implied message.

Janice put down her paint roller and said, "Come on, Alaine, I'll show you around," and she led the girl away.

"So," Jacqui said, lowering her voice, "big brother doesn't trust you to get little sister home safely after dark?"

"He is trying to cramp my style," Kyle said, with a grin.

"Did you explain your strategy to him?"

"Didn't get a chance," Kyle said, pulling off his T-shirt and hanging it on a doorknob. "Besides, I don't think I'm going to. That way there is one less person who can sink the whole plan. If he knew, he might not react the way we want him to at times."

"Absolutely right," Jacqui said, after some thought. "Do you want Alaine to work with you or with Janice and me?"

Kyle picked up Janice's roller and loaded it with paint. "There is safety in numbers," he said. "Let's do everything together, the whole day."

"I'm glad we already hung wallpaper in the bathroom then," Jacqui laughed.

Janice and Alaine returned to the living room, giggling about something. Quickly Alaine put the spare bandana around her head. "Jacqui, this is a lovely house," she said. "So much room! We've always lived in townhouses.

"Janice told me that she started working for an interior decorator," she continued. "You all have such great plans for your lives, and such interesting work."

Janice pretended to be choking. "Actually, you can have my job any time you want it, Alaine. Somehow, Jacqui thinks that there is nothing in the world besides building houses and decorating them."

"Oh?" Jacqui said. "I thought you like working for Dorothea?"

"It's all right," Janice said, with a noticeable lack of spirit.

No, it's not, Jacqui thought to herself. She had assumed that Janice would like the job because she had found it so engrossing herself. It could be that Janice had heard so much about building all her life that she did not feel the excitement of watching a house take shape on an empty lot. Jacqui had not foreseen this trouble in her paradise.

She brooded about it, especially when they moved on to the bedrooms and Janice took the opportunity to criticize the colors Jacqui had chosen for them. The first was a pale pink and another pale peach. When they got to the master bedroom, and Janice saw the dark blue-gray paint, her tongue clacked in her mouth.

"This is really going to be horrid," she assayed, shaking her head as she studied the first stroke of her roller.

"It will dry lighter," Jacqui told her.

"I still think it is a big mistake," Janice said.

"Well, Dorothea thought it would be very striking," Jacqui defended.

"Precious Dorothea!" Janice exploded.

"You can go outside," Jacqui told her, pulling rank. "Or you can go paint the dining room all by yourself."

"What do you think, Alaine?" Janice asked.

"I like blue, myself," Alaine said, and from the look on her face, Jacqui could see that she was trying to be diplomatic.

"I think," Kyle said, pouring paint into a roller tray, "that it is about time we have a little break. What do you say, ladies? Let's go for a walk around the neighborhood and check on the other houses."

"You all go," Jacqui told them. "I'll finish up with the paint that has already been poured and then I'll take a break."

The longer she looked at the blue paint, the less she liked it herself, although she was as enthusiastic about her decorating scheme as ever. "It's got to look better when it's dry," she told herself when she was alone.

CHRISTOPHER approached the house on Signal Drive with an attitude of cautious anticipation. He had not been altogether convinced that Alaine should spend a whole day with the Belpres, although it was better than having her mope around all day, telling him how bored she was. But he could not have manufactured a better excuse to see Jacqueline Belpre again.

He entered the house, knocking at the front door first and looking around the living room, putting himself in the place of a prospective buyer. Impressed by the change a coat of paint made, he smiled to himself.

No wonder no one had responded to his knock at the door! Everyone was in the dining room laughing over a mock argument as they picked up their painting paraphernalia. Jacqui Belpre, dressed in an old chambray shirt with sleeves rolled above her elbows and the front shirttails tied high on her midriff, was banging the lid of a can tight with the handle of a screwdriver.

"Oh, Chris!" Alaine greeted him, by now splattered with all five of the shades of paint they had used. "What perfect timing! We're all finished except for cleaning up."

"Good," Christopher said hoisting the picnic hamper he was carrying. "And you're all hungry, I suppose?"

"Famished!" Alaine said. "Oh, this is Janice, Chris."

"How do you do?" Christopher said, then turned to Jacqui. "Miss Belpre, do you want to eat here, or should we take our dinner over to your home?"

"Er—" Jacqui said, quickly looking over at Kyle as though asking for help. "We—ah—have a project on our breakfast table at home—I—ah—"

Kyle put a roller into its empty pan and crumpled up the last of the paper. "Jacqui, the girls and I will go over to the house and set up dinner, and Mr. Warden can bring you over when you've cleaned out the rollers and brushes."

"Good idea," Jacqui said, wiping her hands on the seat of her cut-off blue jeans. "Take everything out to the utility sink in the garage and I'll be right there."

Christopher caught Jacqui's azure blue eyes with his own, wondering fleetingly if anyone else had ever appreciated them as he did. "How are your schemes for your master bedroom coming along?" he asked.

"Janice doesn't like the shade of paint," Jacqui reacted, sighing, then turning to lead the way through the family room.

"Perhaps she will like it better when everything is in place," Christopher encouraged, "or perhaps her concepts are a bit immature—"

Jacqui laughed as she entered the room in question. "Janice's concepts are rarely immature these days." The last rays of the afternoon sun slanted through the master bedroom. "In this light, I still can't get a good idea of how it looks," she sighed pensively.

"I think it looks quite—restful, yet—romantically exciting," Christopher said, "and after all, that is the purpose, isn't it?"

Jacqui looked up at him with surprise at his boldness. "Yes, I suppose."

"Blue is a favorite color of mine," Christopher told her. "The most fascinating women I have ever met have all had blue eyes," he said, lowering his voice and aiming his words directly at the azure eyes that watched him. He could not be certain, in the reddish light of the sunset, that she blushed slightly, but only that she was the most fascinating of all the creatures he was lumping together.

"Oh," Jacqui said, trying to appear preoccupied with inspecting the walls closely, trying to see if any spots had been missed and should be touched up before the brushes had been put away.

"We got off to a bad start, didn't we?" he asked, standing in the middle of the room. Jacqui could feel him watching her, could hear in his tone and inflection that he wanted her attention.

Jacqui looked up at him quickly, then sighed. "Yes, we certainly did."

"I am very grateful for your inviting Alaine to help you today," he continued. "I can see what you are trying to do."

"Oh?" Jacqui asked, wondering if her strategem was so transparent that he had indeed seen through it.

"Yes, and it is good for her to get away from the hotel. Although we like to think of it as a resort for all ages of people, I have to admit that our clientele is fortyish at best, and generally older than that. I had discouraged her from associating with the young help, too, until I realized just this week that I was being unrealistic. There is only so much she can do there—"

Jacqui smiled up at him, but in her mind she was thinking how luxurious it would be to have nothing to do but amuse oneself in a resort hotel.

Christopher continued, seeming just a little uneasy about what to do with his hands, as there was really no place to lean or brace himself. "I—I must apologize for getting the wrong impression of your brother," he said. "Since I have been checking more deeply, I've found that your family does enjoy a spotless reputation in your trade."

"I'm sorry that you felt you had to check up on us," Jacqui said, not completely mollified. "Oh, there's a spot—"

"Jacqui, please look at me," Christopher demanded.

"Yes?" she said, turning suddenly and looking up at him.

"Hold very still," he said, putting his hand to the side of her face. "You have a bit of plaster or something very close to your eye." With his thumb, he gently rubbed the particle away. It was no ruse; she actually had felt a bit of grit under the pressure.

His hand lingered, warmly, for a moment longer than Jacqui had thought would be necessary. Gone was the arrogance she had seen in his eyes before, and in its place there seemed a genuine attempt at camaraderie. But her hurt feelings of their previous meeting made her wary of him.

"Thank you, Mr. Warden," she said, flustered.

"Chris," he corrected.

He was trying to be ingratiating, she decided, for some reason that she could not yet fathom. Perhaps he had his own purposes in mind. At this close range, he was incredibly handsome, and in the last of the sunset's direct rays, she saw his features soften.

The gentle pressure of his fingers on her cheek drew her closer to him. "A truce," he said, softly, just before he bowed his head and his lips closed innocently on hers.

Surprised, Jacqui almost put her hands on him to steady herself, but was painfully aware that her hands were sticky with paint. Suddenly all the innocence evaporated and Christopher's arms were crushing her to the fine white material of his shirt until she felt the crisp hair of his chest tickling her skin. For an instant, she thought the room tilted and then righted itself. Her fingers were pressing into the rippling biceps of his upper arms, contributing not a steadying influence, but only confusing her senses more. At the same moment, she heard the Beast rumble and growl to life in the driveway, and the metallic squeal as Kyle oversteered as he backed out into the deserted street.

She took a step backward and swallowed. "We're—ah—ah! I have to wash out the brushes and rollers," she said, almost stumbling from the bedroom.

Christopher's laughter, deep and spontaneous, echoed through the bare and empty house, no less mocking in its effect on her because there was no one else to hear. "Business, always business!" he said, following her to the garage.

Jacqui was sickeningly aware of being alone in the house with him. Rubbing her chin on the upper portion of the sleeve of her cotton shirt, she wiped his kiss away, then began clattering all the painting paraphernalia under the running water in the utility sink. *Oh, Kyle,* she thought, *do something about that mess on the breakfast table. Should I take my time,* she wondered, *to give Kyle a chance to move the table-sized model of Egret Island a la Osprey Builders, or hurry through this chore as fast as possible to spend only a minimum of time with Christopher?*

Christopher had excused himself to look at the rest of the house while there was still some daylight. "Is there anything I can do for you?" he asked, returning to find her still at work.

"Could you hand me that batch of brushes in the can of water there?" she asked, putting a cleaned roller aside to drip dry, then scratching the tip of her nose with the back of her wrist.

Cheerfully, Christopher complied, pouring the water out of the can into the sink when she had taken the brushes out, then rinsing the can and putting it down on the floor. "Here, give me a couple of these," he suggested.

"Don't get your shirt messed up," Jacqui warned, and he made a face at her.

"I have done things like this before," he assured her.

Jacqui squirted liquid detergent on the bristles of all the brushes, but Christopher complained that he did not think there was enough on one of his, and reached around her to retrieve the detergent bottle from her side of the sink, not bothering to make any complicated maneuver but simply surrounding her from behind while he squirted more detergent onto his brushes.

"Christopher!" Jacqui reacted, nearly scandalized, looking sideways at him.

Without haste, he returned the bottle to where Jacqui had put it. "After working all day, you still smell like—roses," he observed, sniffing near her ear.

"That's my soap," Jacqui informed him.

He nuzzled her neck, and she stiffened with surprise.

"Hey! Watch what you are doing!" she begged.

"Oh, but I am," he said, working up a lather on the brushes, then rinsing them and making certain that Jacqui's hands were clean by washing them himself. "I'm always very thorough," he said, at last turning off the water and reaching for the paper towels. "Do you need any more help?"

Jacqui took a deep breath and looked away from him. "You've done more than enough," she said shakily.

Even when she was at last in Christopher's town car, she could still smell paint. "I hope I don't get your car all messy," she said, sitting uneasily in the plush seat, feeling drained, sweaty, and tired. "This is certainly a far cry from 'the Beast.'"

"Oh, yes, 'the Beast,'" Christopher laughed. "Not quite the vehicle I would pick for a lady."

"Simply another tool of the trade," Jacqui told him. "You'd be surprised at some places I have to get to when a new subdivision is being opened. There was a time when that short-cut I took you on was our only access to Shelter Cove."

"I hope there aren't any short-cuts to your home that you want to show me," he said, switching on his headlights.

"I'm afraid there aren't any," she answered, "even if I wanted to."

"I had the kitchen make us a picnic," he told her, a touch of pride in his voice. "I thought you might enjoy deviled crab and a sampling of our salads. I would have brought wine, but I didn't know if you would approve."

"Dinner is more than enough," she told him, reflecting that at the moment, if she had to face fixing something for herself, she would be hard-pressed to put together a peanut butter sandwich.

She was infinitely relieved to find nothing but the aluminum trays of fancifully arranged food on the breakfast table when they arrived at her home. The girls had already helped themselves to the deviled crab, potato salad, bean salad, and other dishes Jacqui did not readily identify, and were sitting on the floor in the living room.

When Jacqui looked at Janice disapprovingly, Christopher merely laughed. "I told you it was a picnic," he said, and when he had filled his own plate, he joined them on the floor, leaning his back against the couch.

Jacqui wondered if it was an attempt to show a certain acceptance of her family that prompted Christopher to follow their lead, and if it took a great amount of self-discipline to relax his posture to this point.

She found Kyle in the kitchen pouring glasses of iced tea. "Where is the scale model?" she asked him with quiet urgency.

"Under my bed," he hissed.

"Did Alaine see it?"

"No," he assured her. "Janice took her directly to your room to freshen up while I hid the incriminating evidence." His eyes teased her for being so serious.

Jacqui sighed with relief. "Did you know Janice was so set against the business?"

"No," he confessed. "But it is better to know now than to find out when you are trying to get her a builder's certificate."

She looked at Kyle for a long moment. "Are you trying to tell me something?"

"Only that Janice might not want to get into the trade."

"How about you?" she asked, picking up a glass of tea.

"Come on, Jac. Would I be doing what I'm doing if I didn't want to be in the business?"

"Frankly, out of the goodness of your heart I think you might."

"Well, I'm not," he told her. "And, if you want my opinion, I don't think you should do anything about Janice for now. If she doesn't like working for Dorothea, maybe she needs to learn more about it. I think she should stick with it for a few months and then decide. And that's what I told her."

Jacqui wiped her hand on a towel and then threw it down onto the counter. "Did you ever have a day when you thought everything had gone real well, only to find that the whole thing suddenly ended up a loss?" she asked him.

"There have been times," Kyle agreed. "Look, we have guests who were kind enough to bring the food. I think we ought to try to do justice to it." He grinned and carried a tray of glasses into the living room.

"Can I help next week when you move in?" Alaine asked Kyle before he had a chance to sit down.

"Of course, so long as your brother brings some leftovers from the Magellan Room," Kyle teased.

"Kyle!" Jacqui scolded.

Christopher Warden smiled. "It's really nothing, Jacqueline, compared to the favor you do us by getting us away from the hotel for a few hours."

Jacqui tried to smile graciously, even though she could not think of a proper rejoinder, and since the girls started talking at their usual level of gaiety, she supposed nothing was necessary anyway.

Time and again, Jacqui looked across the room toward Christopher and found him looking back at her with veiled intensity that reminded her of the stolen moments in the model, and although she was able to keep herself from blushing under his gaze, she was not able to completely erase the moments from her mind.

Even in her fatigue after the long day's work, Jacqui tensed. It was entirely possible that Christopher Warden was looking around the living room, thinking how out-of-date and drab it was. He certainly made it look shabby merely by his presence. Jacqui and Janice did their best to keep it clean, occasionally assisted by Kyle when it was necessary to sweep cobwebs out of the corners—a job not uncommon in Florida. But still, being frank with herself, she saw the room as though with a stranger's eye and was not pleased.

The thought killed her appetite. Wearily, she got to her feet and carried her plate to the kitchen and rinsed it in the sink. She had begun putting dirty dishes into the dishwasher when Christopher came slowly into the kitchen and handed her his plate.

"Your house is very nice," he said. "It looks very comfortable."

Jacqui smiled up at him, thinking to herself that he was only being polite. "Father built this from—oh, about his third set of plans," she told him. "Later plans eliminated some of the problems."

"Problems?" Christopher said, looking around at the kitchen and the adjoining breakfast area. "What problems?"

"Dead spots in the cupboards and closets, for one thing—two things," Jacqui said, flustered. "Places that are hard to reach, hard to clean."

His eyes told her that he was paying only minimal attention to what she was telling him, so she told herself to stop being the fool and shut her mouth before he decided she was a total idiot. Then she wondered why she cared.

Janice led Alaine into the kitchen, asking, "Are you sure you don't want some ice cream?"

"Oh, I couldn't eat another bite!" Alaine protested.

"Don't you think we should be getting home, Alaine?" Christopher asked. "Do you have homework to finish?"

"No homework," Alaine told him, "but I have a

book to read for a report in English. Jacqui, thank you for inviting me along today. It was really great.''

Janice laughed sardonically. ''You'll feel how great it was tomorrow when you are all stiffened up. You'd be surprised how many muscles you used that you didn't know you had.''

''Yes, you really put in a day's work,'' Jacqui told Alaine. ''I know of a painter who might give you a summer job.'' Somehow it did not come out as playful as Jacqui had intended it, and Christopher gave her a cautioning look.

In the confusion of their leave-taking, Christopher's eyes held Jacqui's for a moment, conveying a message that Jacqui did not understand, an expression that recalled the stolen moment while she was inspecting the paint in the master bedroom of the model house. She turned away from them, not bothering to walk out to the car as Janice and Kyle did.

Scarcely knowing what she was doing, she went to her bedroom and prepared to take a shower, taking fresh underthings from her drawer and a light robe from her closet.

''Isn't he something else!'' Janice asked, bounding into the room. ''Oh, Jacqui, he would be a perfect match for you.''

''Hush your mouth!'' Jacqui scolded. ''Don't be ridiculous.''

''He is so handsome—''

''He is also an arrogant snob,'' Jacqui told her. ''Looking down his nose at us the whole time, probably thinking that we are not good enough to associate with his precious sister Alaine.''

''Oh, Jacqui! I don't think he's that way at all,'' Janice said, following her toward her bathroom.

''Do you have any shampoo?'' she asked Janice.

''Sure. Just a minute,'' Janice said, then carried on the conversation as she went to the other bathroom. ''I think Alaine is great. I wish she could meet Lisa. I think Lisa would like her too. We all have a lot in common, but Alaine—she's had some unusual experiences. Don't you love to listen to them talk?''

She was back, handing Jacqui a bottle of shampoo. Jacqui studied Janice's lively blue eyes for an instant, then took the bottle and placed it on the side of the tub.

"Look, I'm going to pull rank and take a nice long shower," she said, "Now, for heaven's sake, don't turn on the dishwasher."

"Would I do that?" Janice asked, teasingly. "That's work, and you say I never do any."

Jacqui looked at her with tired exasperation, then gently pushed her out of the bathroom, closed the door and locked it.

As she soaped herself in the shower, she heard again in her mind the question Janice had asked. *Don't you love to listen to them talk?*

Ha! That would be something, to hear Christopher make love in that sophisticated speech pattern, softly, with intense passion, plumbing the depths of feeling which would no doubt be almost alien to a man as cool and artificial as he seemed.

Annoyed with herself for letting her mind wander down a forbidden path, Jacqui concentrated on scrubbing the middle of her back. Tomorrow she had a lot of work to do, seeing that the carpet was put down in the model—

His touch had been very soft on her cheek, as though he did not remember what it was like to touch a woman.

—and she would have to check with Yvonne to see that the telephones were being transferred. It would be a disaster if they lost any calls when they moved into the model.

What did he mean, kissing her like that? She should have been angry, at least. But it was such a surprise. It had taken every ounce of control she had not to throw all her caution and distrust to the winds.

Well, she would hardly ever see Christopher Warden again. Alaine would tire of Kyle, they would never get the bid for Egret Island, and the kiss in the master bedroom of the model would be forgotten in the million chores she had to do tomorrow.

Someday, someone would be living in that house, probably leaving the master bedroom intact as she had decorated it. She hoped it would be someone, if not still young, with at least some *joie de vivre* left to make proper use of the romantic setting.

Two people barely covered with the elegantly quilted spread, enjoying the touch of warm flesh, encircling each other gently, fondly, whispering intimate, outrageous things to each other.

"*Jacqueline—*"

"*Christopher—*"

"What!" she demanded of herself, her eyes opening wide.

Suddenly the force of the hot water diminished to a thin trickle of cold, striking her between her shoulderblades. She gulped in a breath of air, quivering as she fumbled to turn off the shower and reach for her towel. *Christopher? Don't be silly!*

Chapter Four

The meetings of the Builders Association were always held in a private club, where the lighting was generally gloomy, and the cigarette smoke thick. A "happy hour" collected people before the meal and the meeting, and although Jacqui did not always enjoy the monthly gatherings, they at least gave her a chance to hear, and overhear, what was happening in the diversified areas of the building trade.

Dorothea, in a chic little beige dress, looked her usual businesslike elegance as she sat down at a table with Jacqui, placing her Bloody Mary near Jacqui's ginger ale.

They looked at each other and passed the first, most obvious, topic of conversation, Janice's reluctance to take her job cheerfully.

"Well," Dorothea asked, "who was that charming man I saw you with at your Signal Drive model?"

"Christopher Warden of Leisure Discovery," Jacqui said, hoping that that would be the end of the discussion on the topic, also.

"Very handsome, don't you think?" Dorothea said, drawling as only a transplanted Atlantan can.

"My grandmother used to say that handsome is as handsome does," Jacqui said, vaguely uneasy as she conjured up the memory of Christopher's face.

"Now, now, now, Jacqui dear!" Dorothea scolded playfully. "One must always like one's clients, even when you can't stand them."

"He's not a client," Jacqui told her. "He was merely with me to—to discuss a matter concerning his sister and my brother Kyle, and we are not exactly cordial. Things are a little better than they were, but I think he's an insufferable snob."

Cletus Garwood, the cement mason who was teaching Kyle that trade, sidled up to Jacqui and propped his foot on the brace of the chair beside hers. He was a muscular man of about medium height, whose tanned and lined face proclaimed that he spent most of his life outside, summer and winter. He was normally an affable man, but it was standard knowledge that he was a dangerous man to cross.

"Kyle tells me that you're putting together a bid on the Egret Island project for Leisure Discovery," Garwood said, from behind irregular teeth.

"No one is supposed to know," Jacqui hissed, glancing quickly around.

"Come now," Cletus laughed. "I'm his father-confessor. We spend so much time together, he can't keep anything from me. He tells me that your plans for Egret Island are outstanding."

"He'll break his arm patting himself on the back, won't he?" Jacqui said, taking a sip of her ginger ale.

"So, Mr. Warden is a client of yours after all," Dorothea said, slyly.

"No, he's not," Jacqui corrected. "We don't have the slightest chance of getting that contract. We've totally reworked the specs, and that alone will take us out of the running. I wouldn't know what to do with a big job like that if I got it."

"Well, Jacqui, if you ask me," Garwood said, bending down to speak confidentially over the buzz of the crowded room, "you would be well out of it. Leisure Discovery's slow payments put a real bind on the guys who built the original complex."

Dorothea quickly pushed her drink aside and leaned

forward. "That's what I heard from the decorators too. If you take the job, you are going to have to settle that issue right up front. Make them agree in writing that if they are late with a payment, you can close down until payment is made, and then stick with your schedule. You owe it to yourself."

"And to your subcontractors," Garwood reinforced. "You don't run into hassles like that, building houses when people get their financing from a bank, or have the money in hand. But when you get into a commercial project, you have to be right on top of everything. If those last contractors they used had been tough with them, Leisure Discovery and a lot of the other guys who think they can hold off on payments would have learned a lesson, and the subcontractors would be in better shape."

"Yes," Jacqui said, thoughtfully making a mental note. "I see your point, and I'll look into it."

"But I don't want to discourage you," Garwood went on. "I think I'd like to see you start getting some of these medium-sized jobs, because if Osprey Builders is going to be big enough for both you and Kyle, you are going to have to expand your horizons."

Again Jacqui nodded.

"Of course, we all know that Kyle has an ulterior motive," Garwood said, with a wink. "Excuse me, Jacqui, Dorothea, I have to go talk with one of the other builders."

Garwood had not moved away more than a few feet when Dorothea turned to Jacqui and clacked her tongue. "Now, what are you keeping from me, dear? What is Kyle's motive in all this?"

"He has been dating Warden's sister, and Warden doesn't entirely approve," Jacqui said. "Kyle wants to show Warden that Osprey Builders has a few brains in the company."

"I should have known that there was a woman involved," Dorothea laughed.

"She's not really involved," Jacqui said. "Kyle isn't interested in her other than as a friend, at the moment. It's a point of honor."

Dorothea stirred the ice in her drink. "And what about you? It is exhausting work to write up a bid, Jacqui. You don't do it on a whim. From what you say, you will be getting only attention from Warden, and you don't really want the contract? Do you want—Christopher Warden?"

"I don't have the slightest interest in Christopher Warden," Jacqui said, about to pick up her ginger ale. But a sharp twinge in her shoulder, besides almost making her spill her drink, told her that might have been the biggest lie she had ever told in her entire life.

As THEY NEARED the stately palms and wide-leafed magnolia trees of Leisure Discovery, Jacqui mumbled something under her breath. They were passing a billboard, about as big as was allowed, touting the golf course, swimming pools, spas and other attractions, including a big-name star who was currently performing in the Magellan Room.

At the wheel, Kyle looked over at her and grinned. "Did you say something?" he asked. Cletus Garwood had given him the morning off to help Jacqui deliver the bid to Christopher Warden. They knew full well that Jacqui would never be able to handle the scale model Kyle had built.

Without prompting, Kyle had donned his beige three-piece suit, polished his shoes, and selected a respectable necktie—dark brown with a small white stripe. Aside from the fact that he would probably feel better in his usual jeans and T-shirt or chambray, he looked handsomely impressive.

"Too bad Alaine will be at school," Jacqui had teased him, dusting off his shoulders with her hand before they left the house.

"I wouldn't want to break the poor girl's heart," he

tilted to be carried through the door into the board room, Kyle admonishing the man who was helping him to handle it carefully, that many hours of work had gone into it. Jacqui had the presence of mind to take two dollar bills from her purse to tip the man as he left the room.

With notable and deserved pride, Kyle placed the model in the middle of the burnished mahogany board table, carefully checking several of the details before backing away from it. Taking a deep breath, Jacqui lay the tube of plans beside it and turned around to appreciate the cream-colored walls and draperies of the room, which formed an unobtrusive backdrop for the heavy wood table and the upholstered chairs of coffee brown. It was simple, yet effective, she thought. Dorothea might have added something unexpected, perhaps a touch of yellow or teal.

"That's about it," Kyle said, in the voice he used on solemn occasions. The room seemed unbearably quiet.

Jacqui nodded. She had never bid on a job like this, and did not know anything about proper procedure. She suspected that she should have some sort of receipt for her plans, to prove they were rendered on time, but she was not seriously hoping to win the project, so it really did not matter.

As she turned toward the door it opened, and Christopher Warden entered, tugging at the knot of his beige tie. His black hair was still curled and damp, obviously from a shower, and his eyes were slightly glazed. Seeing him, Jacqui felt a twinge in her shoulder, and was bewildered by it, because she was not even thinking, let alone telling, a lie. All she knew was that there was an endearing quality to his appearance, seeing him momentarily off his guard like this.

"Jacqui! Kyle!" he said, now settling the shoulders of his white blazer with a nervous gesture. "When Audrey told me that someone from Osprey Builders was delivering a bid and was in the board room, I—"

His eyes went to the scale model and his jaw dropped.

"We are bringing this to you only because we don't have any room for it at home," Kyle said, casually leaning on the back of a leather chair.

"Kyle!" Jacqui scolded. "Excuse us both, Chris," she continued. "I really ought to explain. When we saw what your firm intended to do with Egret Island, we began exploring ideas to preserve some of the natural atmosphere of the island. We originally had no intention of bidding at all, but we thought you might like to see an alternative to your plans, and get an idea of the cost differential. Where we could, we included active and passive solar capabilities, and we tried to maintain the natural integrity of the island. We just brought it for you to see.... It's a bonded bid; we certify that we have the capital and the expertise to execute the contract."

Christopher Warden took a breath and moved closer to the model, seeming spellbound. He rocked back on his heels, crossed his right arm on his chest to support his left elbow while he stroked his chin with this left hand. His eyes took on a very speculative look. "If all the bids we get are going to be this elaborate, we may not have room left here for all of them," he said at last. "I—ah—will have to make up a receipt for you—"

Kyle straightened up and tugged the hem of his vest. "How many other bids have you gotten?" he asked.

"Well—um—this is the first," Christopher said, "unless some have been delivered in the mail today. The timing, I have been told, was bad. The project is too small to interest some companies, too big for others, and most of the companies we hoped would bid are heavily committed to other projects. There may be a decision to re-advertise."

Christopher pulled himself away from the model and looked briefly but intently at Jacqui. Jacqui raised her chin and looked back at him levelly.

He waved a hand toward the door and waited for Jacqui to move in that direction. "The chairman of the board and the president of Leisure Development will be coming in tomorrow night to study the bids over the weekend, and some decision will be made within the early part of next week. You will be hearing from us then." His voice was cool, his words almost automatic.

The impersonality of his manner rankled some nerve in Jacqui, and she wondered why. After all, this was just another businessman, doing his job, perhaps starting his day a little earlier than he wanted to.

Kyle was enjoying the escapade to its fullest, seeming to absorb every nuance of Christopher Warden's discomfort and uncertainty. Jacqui saw some humor in this turnabout, but not as much as Kyle obviously did.

Gallantly, Kyle took Jacqui's arm as they started down the sweeping staircase to the resplendent lobby. Christopher Warden followed them, then ushered them toward the door of his office.

"Would you have time for coffee, while I have my secretary draw up your receipt?" he asked, pushing the door open.

"No, I'm sorry," Jacqui told him, though she did sit down on the couch in his small but well-appointed office. "We both have to get to work."

"I thought you might like to walk out to Egret Island," Christopher said, now obviously stalling.

"Another time, perhaps, when we are dressed for safari," Jacqui said, assuming an elegant posture which called attention to her long, stockinged legs and her white sandals.

Christopher chuckled, in spite of himself, and opened the connecting door to his secretary's office. "I'll be right back."

Kyle waited for the door to be securely closed, then made a fist and shook it triumphantly in the air.

"What if," Jacqui said, not joining in his little celebration, "our worst fears are actualized and we win this bid?"

"Oh, we won't get it," Kyle reassured her, sitting awkwardly on the arm of a chair. "Even if no one has sent a bid in yet, the big boys probably do wait until the last minute, don't you think?"

"I haven't the slightest idea," Jacqui told him. No, it was not as amusing as she had hoped it would be. It was not a joke. "Dad would never have done something like this."

"Only because he never thought of it!" Kyle laughed, and she knew he was right.

"What would we do for a performance bond?" she asked, suddenly horrified. "What can we use as collateral to insure that we won't default on the contract?"

"The house, of course," Kyle said. "Relax! We won't even come close."

The door opened and Christopher returned, handing a slip of paper to Jacqui. "If that is satisfactory—"

Jacqui looked at it, her eyes scanning the paper, but her brain not registering the words. She blinked and read it again, this time nodding. "Fine."

"Look, Jacqueline, Kyle, are you sure you have to run off right now?" Christopher said, "I really would like to have you join me for breakfast in the coffee shop."

Christopher's breath caught in his throat when Jacqueline looked up at him with those wondrously blue eyes. He dared to think that she was considering his suggestion seriously and for a fleeting instant he wondered if there was some way he could get rid of Kyle, just for a few moments alone with her, this absolute vision in blue.

But Kyle interrupted. "Jacqui has to go yell at some roofers, and I have a house to build," he said, extending his broad, roughened hand toward Christopher. "Some other time?"

"Of course," Christopher said, with genuine regret.

Jacqueline got to her feet with a fluid motion that he could not help noticing. When she extended her hand to him, it was soft, slightly warm, and firm. He did not let it go quickly, but linked it through his arm while he escorted them from his office and out to "the Beast" as it stood outside the front door.

As Christopher watched them drive away, he tried to think what it would be like to be involved with a woman like Jacqueline. He knew that he had to see her again and the thought of her presence excited him.

MOVING into the new model home was a complicated and wearying job, and by Sunday evening, Jacqui was not only tired, but a bit short-tempered also. When Christopher Warden appeared with his picnic hamper, she tried not to notice him. He wandered slowly around the house, now complete except for the top of one kitchen cabinet and the sink that fit into it. Jacqui looked up as she was sorting tubes of plans into their slots in the bedroom that would be her office.

"I have something for you," he said, reaching into the pocket of his shirt. "I thought perhaps you would like to give anyone who contracts for a house between now and the end of the Parade of Homes a coupon for two free dinners in the Magellan Room."

"Very nice," Jacqui said, taking the coupons and looking at them, then putting them into her desk drawer. "Thank you."

"If you need more, just let me know," Christopher said, smiling. "Everything looks very nice, very nice indeed. Could we talk a little business?"

"Certainly," Jacqui said, giving up on her chore.

"We—the board of directors—would like to have lunch with you Tuesday," he said. "Actually, we wanted to have lunch with you tomorrow, but I told them you would probably not be available tomorrow, since you are moving into your new office."

"How right you are!" Jacqui sighed, sitting down on the corner of her desk, the only place available.

"So we can expect you Tuesday?" he asked.

"Yes, of course," she told him. She tried to ignore the satisfaction that was on his face. It was only business, she told herself.

Christopher handed her the picnic hamper. "I was tired of the hotel cuisine, so I brought sandwiches from the barbecue place—"

"You didn't have to," Jacqui said, taking the hamper. "But I love it. Look, have the girls put this out in the kitchen while I finish up here."

When she went out to the dining room, Christopher had fixed two plates and was looking for a place to put them, since the girls, Kyle, and Yvonne had appropriated the seats around the table.

"Let's go out on the patio," Jacqui suggested, opening the door for him.

"Wonderful," Christopher said, and put the plates on the round glass table.

She was surprised and flattered that he held her chair for her as she sat down. "I thought you threw formality away for picnics," she teased.

"My dear," he drawled, moving his chair closer to hers, "there are picnics and there are picnics."

"And how do you mean that?" Jacqui asked.

"Last week, there were people around."

"There are people on the other side of a glass door, Chris," she reminded him, then opened her bun to see that the pile of thin slices of beef held the right amount of hot barbecue sauce.

"Let's hope they stay there," Christopher murmured.

Jacqui glanced at him, then closed her sandwich and took a healthy bite of it. *So that is the kind of mood he is in,* she thought to herself. She could not avoid the gentle touch of his hand on her arm when he draped his arm across the back of her chair, nor the way his thigh occasionally brushed against hers. His proximity was beginning to alarm her, and she began to wonder if she was going to have to find a diplomatic way to handle him.

There were only scraps left when Christopher crumpled his paper napkin and dropped it unceremoniously in the center of his paper plate. Slowly, he turned toward her, his gray eyes smoldering with a message Jacqui had only dared to imagine. As his hand gently brushed her blond hair back away from her ear, she took a deep breath to calm her sudden nervousness.

"Christopher—" she said.

"Chris!" Alaine called from the patio door as she stepped out onto the green carpet. "I hate to drag you away, but I just remembered that I have a page of really difficult calculus problems I wanted you to help me with—"

Christopher looked out into the distance as though he was trying to control his emotions, then he quickly got to his feet. "All right," he mumbled.

Jacqui started to pick up the plates from the table. "I'm sorry you have to leave so soon," she said. "But I'll see you Tuesday for lunch."

Christopher looked back at her as he started to leave the patio. "Yes," he said, his eyes conveying the message that there was unfinished business between them. "I'll see you then."

MONDAY, just when the day seemed to her twice as long as Jacqui could endure, she looked up from the file cabinet she was reorganizing to see Dorothea Grace smiling down at her. "Well, young lady, do I get a guided tour of your new model, or do I have to get myself lost?"

Jacqui slammed the drawer closed and ran her hand through her disheveled hair. "Dorothea! Of course I'll show you through."

"It amazes me," Dorothea said, nonchalantly sitting down on the corner of Jacqui's cluttered desk, "when I see a house with nothing but bare dry-wall and then two weeks later there it is with paint and carpet and all."

"We still have a few rough edges," Jacqui told her.

"I didn't have time yesterday to get my office set up. Would you like some coffee?"

"I'd love it," Dorothea exclaimed.

"Yvonne! Is there any fresh coffee?"

"Coming up!" Yvonne called back from her desk.

"And how did you come out with your Egret Island bid?" Dorothea asked.

"Well, I had to do some fast talking to get the bid bonded," Jacqui said, sighing and dusting off her hands. "Yesterday Christopher Warden asked me to have lunch with the board of directors of Leisure Development tomorrow. If I weren't so busy and tired, I'd be scared to death. Oh, Yvonne, thanks. Dorothea, the sugar and the cream are there on the credenza."

"Oh, you are so organized already," Dorothea commended. "So far this house is much more impressive than your last model."

"I learned some lessons on the last one," Jacqui said, "about decorating and arranging doors and windows to maximize wall space."

"Frankly, I'm dying to see that master bedroom you were slaving over," Dorothea confessed as she stirred sugar into her coffee, her bracelets jangling together.

"Well, then," Jacqui said, pausing in taking a sip of her coffee, "let's not keep you on tenterhooks any longer." She started from the back bedroom she was using as an office.

"Everything turned out beautifully in the living room and dining room," Dorothea complimented.

"My kitchen will be finished tomorrow," Jacqui told her. "I had to work around someone else's schedule."

"The madness is nearly over," Dorothea laughed. "The family room turned out well too."

"Are you really ready to see this bedroom?" Jacqui asked, with a mixture of pride and apprehension. "Now, be honest."

"It's absolutely glorious in a low-keyed way," Dorothea pronounced. "You know, the good thing about this room is that someone could live with it."

"You were right about the shade of the walls too," Jacqui told her.

"Magnificent," Dorothea complimented. "Now, what is this about the lunch tomorrow that has you all in a dither?"

Jacqui sat down on one of the small velvet chairs which flanked a round lamp table. "I don't know the men, nor what they want to discuss about the bid."

"It sounds to me as though they are fairly serious, if they are willing to spring for lunch," Dorothea said, sitting down carefully so that she did not spill her coffee on the chair or her green pantsuit.

"That's what Kyle said," Jacqui told her. "And at first I said I didn't want to even bid on the project. But the more I think about it—"

"And the more you think about Christopher Warden—" Dorothea smiled. "Oh, yes. I see the signs. It is not the chairman of the board, or the president whom you are afraid of, is it?"

Jacqui blushed in agreement.

"It's times like this a girl needs her mother," Dorothea said, leaning back in her chair and shaking her head sadly. "So—do you want some advice? You'll get it anyway."

"That's what I thought," Jacqui said with a smile.

"Go dressed ever so perfectly," Dorothea started.

"But he has seen my blue dress, the only one I have," Jacqui protested.

Dorothea laughed. "Have you ever thought of going to the store and buying something new?"

Jacqui stared at her for a long moment. "Yes, I guess I'll have to."

"Charge it off to promotion," Dorothea teased. "Whether you get the bid or not, you should try to impress Christopher Warden oh-so-subtly."

"But do I really want to?" Jacqui asked. "He is so snobbish, arrogant and—and—"

"Very handsome, very suave," Dorothea interrupted. "Yes, you want to impress him, just for the practice. Jacqui, there aren't many single men around here who are worthy of you."

"Come on, Dorothea!" Jacqui exclaimed, embarrassed.

"And while we're on the subject of your personal life," Dorothea said, standing up carefully, "where is the old Jacqui who drove that poor Chevy until there was nothing left but the exhaust? When do you have any fun? Where's that old zest you used to have?"

Jacqui shrugged. "That was a long time ago," she said around a lump in her throat.

"Let's see if you can get some of it back," Dorothea suggested, patting her cheek affectionately. "I've said enough, I see. I have to check on a few houses before I get back to the office, so I'd better get moving."

"How's Janice working out?" Jacqui asked, following her from the master bedroom.

"Janice is a smart girl," Dorothea said, noncommittally. "She can do well in anything she sets her mind to."

"Except—"

"She does not think the sun rises and sets on the home-building industry."

Jacqui bit her lower lip. "What do you think she should do?"

"First, I think you should have her help you pick out something for this lunch tomorrow," Dorothea said, winking. "Don't worry about her, dear. She's a survivor. She'll find her own way."

Jacqui watched after Dorothea for a long time, then went back to her office. Leave it to Dorothea to make sense out of chaos.

Chapter Five

The breeze from the Gulf of Mexico alternately billowed the skirt of Jacqui's new buttercup-yellow dress, and plastered it to her long legs. She looked down at her feet as the heels of her white sandals threatened to dig into the soft asphalt paving, then looked toward the entrance of the Leisure Discovery Hotel. Fixing a smile across her face, she clutched her small white purse and black leather portfolio in one sweaty palm as the wind tore at her long honey-blond hair.

She felt at ease with the way she looked. Janice had almost insisted she buy this dress, the fifth one Jacqui had tried on. She had to admit that the shiny knit terry material was comfortable, the wrapped front bodice flattering to her figure. The dress had the merest cap of sleeves over her tanned shoulders.

The doorman smiled and nodded at her as he opened the heavy glass door that led to the sumptuous lobby. It took her eyes a moment to adjust to the dimmer lighting of the interior, and Jacqui had just begun to look for a sign to lead to a restroom to repair her makeup and hair when a smiling Christopher Warden materialized in front of her.

"I admire punctuality," he said. "I get so aggravated when a woman is consistently late."

Jacqui had not anticipated a confrontation with Christopher quite so soon, nor was his compliment terribly flattering. But she smiled and tossed her hair back over her shoulder. "I'm sorry to disappoint you, then, to ask directions to a place where I can comb my hair," she said.

"There is a mirror in my office," he said, taking her arm, "if you really insist."

It was not quite what Jacqui had had in mind, but it seemed that it would have to do. She would have to steel her nerves without benefit of giving herself a pep talk in private.

Christopher led her to his office and opened the door. "Make yourself at home," he invited, genially. "I have a few things to take care of."

Jacqui breathed a sigh of relief, for, even though he had left the door open and she heard him talking to the desk clerk, she had at least a moment to run a brush through her hair. Again she vowed she would have it cut, as she promised herself at least once a week, but there never seemed to be time to indulge herself for even an hour to visit a hairdresser.

The mirror was on a wall over a credenza which held a tall arrangement of dried seed pods and ornamental grasses. Jacqui was momentarily distracted by the arrangement, and when she looked into the mirror again, she saw the reflection of Christopher, leaning against the doorjamb, his arms crossed casually in front of his chest. He wore a light gray suit with a pale blue shirt and slightly darker tie. She was not quite sure whether the implications of his half-smile were flattering or dangerous. Being by habit cautious, she assumed they were the latter.

"You may as well stop right there," Christopher said, the low, unhurried tone of his voice making her jump defensively.

"I beg your pardon?" she said, turning slowly to face him.

"You can not improve on perfection, Jacqueline, so why waste the effort?"

Jacqui smiled briefly, self-consciously, and turned back toward the mirror to hide her nervousness in a few strokes of the brush that were, as Christopher observed, unnecessary.

"How is everything going with your new model?" he asked, obviously making small talk.

"When I left, the plumber and the cabinet man were trying to see who could be in the other's way the most," she said, embellishing for his entertainment a minor flare-up that had occurred minutes before she had had to leave poor Yvonne Halpern in command. It was nowhere near as bad as she made it sound, and the men had long ago established a friendship which allowed for a few heated words here and there. She quickly put her brush back into her purse and turned to face Christopher again. "Will I need my drawings and cost breakdowns?" she asked.

"May as well bring them along," Christopher said.

Quickly looking at Christopher's gray eyes, she felt a chill. Something was wrong here. She was probably going to be lectured on the impropriety of submitting a bid that she had known would be totally unacceptable in the first place. Why anyone would invite her to lunch to humiliate her was a point that she did not want to contemplate, but she had already stepped into the trap and there was no backing out.

"Well," Jacqui said, straightening her shoulders and raising her chin in the hope of at least looking confident, "lead on."

"I feel as though I must tell you that the men you are meeting are my father and uncle," Christopher said, as he led her toward the stairway to the second floor and the boardroom. "Uncle Charles is the chairman of the board, and Father is the president of Leisure Development. I hope you understand that sometimes, particularly in family businesses, arguments tend to turn very hot."

"I understand that very well," Jacqui said, trying to smile, and wondering why he was telling her this.

"My father's name is Merrill," Christopher continued. "Aunt Alexis is here, too. She is a member of the board and votes my mother's shares. It was a whim that backfired when they were given voting shares."

"That's very interesting," Jacqui observed, then skipped over the revelation of the attitude of the members of the board. "Now, let's see if I have the names right. Charles, Merrill, Alexis—"

"Very good!" Christopher said, a wry smile crossing his face. "You pick up names very quickly."

"I wish I could keep pittsoporum, ligustrum, and viburnum straight!" she sighed, and was rewarded by the sound of his unexpected hearty laughter.

"I hope you feel that people are more important than shrubbery," Christopher said, pausing before opening the door to the boardroom. His left hand straightened his necktie and brushed the front of his jacket too, in a nervous gesture that somehow struck a chord in Jacqui.

She looked deliberately up at his gray eyes, amused and slightly sympathetic, and when he looked down at her, there was an instant of questioning vulnerability that he immediately hid again.

His long, strong fingers gripped the knob and the door of the boardroom swung open, inexorably leading them both to a meeting they may have rather avoided— each for a different reason.

"Miss Belpre," Christopher started introductions almost before Jacqui's feet were planted on the cream-colored carpet of the boardroom, "my aunt, Alexis Warden, my uncle Charles, and my father."

Alexis stood almost the height of Jacqui, her pale blond hair combed back from her forehead with sweeping waves elegantly arranged over a face incredibly beautiful for a woman in her sixties. Her eyes sparkled a clear, playful blue, set off by the same shade of blue in her jacket over a white linen dress. Such perfection at her age was the product of directed effort.

Charles Warden exhibited the family gray eyes and refined features atop an unexpectedly thickened body. The hand he extended toward Jacqui was graced by a heavy signet ring on one strong finger. He seemed genuinely pleased to see Jacqui, while beside him, a slightly taller, younger and slimmer version of the family pattern was disapprovingly grim as he took her hand.

Merrill Warden had a shock of gray white hair, which in his elder brother had been reduced to a fringe. He was an opposite to Charles, and Jacqui was reminded of her slight knowledge of the polarity of electricity, Charles being the positive and Merrill being the negative.

In the center of the mahogany table was the scale model that Kyle had spent so many hours constructing. Jacqui looked at it fleetingly, then turned to Charles Warden.

"Miss Belpre," he said, pulling a chair from the table and beginning to sit down, as Christopher held a chair for Jacqui, and Alexis lowered herself to the chair she had been occupying before they had entered the room. "We wanted to discuss a few details with you before going to lunch. Your presentation for Egret Island is a most interesting and innovative concept, but—"

Here it comes, Jacqui thought. *A lecture.*

Charles reached out to touch the roofline of the topmost unit of the scale model, the smile on his face fading a little. "—We must question you about compliance with codes and the ability of your company to handle such an extensive undertaking. Are you personally certified to handle this project?"

"Yes, sir," Jacqui responded, with a little more pride than she had intended. "I haven't built any commercial buildings because I haven't been asked before. But I do have the proper credentials, and many of my subcontractors do commercial work as well as residential.''

Charles looked quickly to his brother, who stood hovering like a dark cloud at the other end of the table. Then he looked at Jacqui. "So your design meets all the current specifications."

"Absolutely," Jacqui assured him. "Where we had questions, Kyle checked with the county office, in several instances, in fact."

"It is a prodigious undertaking for you both, isn't it?" Charles asked, admiration in his voice. Then he sighed. "I'll be honest, Miss Belpre," he said, flicking a glance toward Merrill, then back at Jacqui, "this was not only the most impressive bid we received, but it was the only bid. When I saw it, I was immediately overwhelmed by it. Merrill, however, has his reservations."

Jacqui looked at Merrill Warden's face, defensiveness stiffening her spine.

"I find it hard to believe that a woman your age, assisted by a boy not even old enough to be certified, can competently carry off a project as ambitious as this," Merrill stated, his voice cutting to the heart of Jacqui, just as his logic cut to the heart of the issue.

"Osprey Builders built forty-seven houses last year, sir," Jacqui heard her voice reciting. "I hired only competent subcontractors to build those houses, and if something is not done to my satisfaction, it is redone until I approve. I don't cut corners, and I don't inflate my prices. I admit that this bid started out merely as a learning experience for Kyle and me, but it is accurate and our best work. I'm prepared to follow through on it."

Merrill Warden shrugged his shoulders and looked from Jacqui to Charles, and then out the window. Charles got to his feet and motioned for Merrill to follow him to the far end of the room, where they stood, obviously arguing in hushed but animated discussion.

Alexis rested an elbow on the table and fingered the perfect string of pearls at her throat. "Miss Belpre," she said, "you have done such a beautiful presentation here."

"The model is Kyle's work," she said, not wanting to take credit for something that was not strictly her own doing.

"Not many people have the courage to go against the grain," the woman said, a smile lighting her face. "Fewer have the skill to do it successfully."

Jacqui could not think of anything to say, so she smiled uncertainly and leaned back against the coffee-colored leather of the chair, only to feel the bulk and warmth of Christopher's hand on the back of her chair, digging into her spine. Slowly, she sat forward enough for him to remove his hand, and when he did not, she turned her head to look up at him. He had obviously been engrossed in the argument at the other end of the room, and when he looked down at her, his eyes had a distant expression.

"Oh, excuse me," he said, and pulled his hand away from her chair.

While she was still trying to figure out what was going through Christopher's thoughts, Jacqui's attention was drawn to the rising voices of the two men at the other end of the room.

"—but if we re-advertise," Charles was saying, "it will be more expensive, not only in the cost of materials and debt service, but we may miss a good portion of the fall tourist season. Merrill, just because she is a woman—"

Merrill stiffened, his outline against the light streaming through the window becoming more compact.

"Merrill," Charles sighed, heavily, "I have made up my mind. To me, Osprey Builders can not only handle the project as they redesigned it, but make a great success of it."

"Are you overruling me then?" Merrill asked defiantly.

"Yes, I am," Charles said, with understated dignity, his hand touching his brother's shoulder gently in a gesture of conciliation.

"I hope, for all our sakes, that you are right," Merrill sighed, lowering his proud head in defeat.

Charles turned toward Jacqui, rubbing his hands together with apparent satisfaction over his victory. "So, Miss Belpre, we are awarding the bid to your company. Shall we go down to lunch and discuss the details of the agreement which need further amplification?"

Blinking her eyes, Jacqui got to her feet. "Thank you, Mr. Warden," she said, wondering if she could sit at a table with these three men with their divergent attitudes toward her and actually eat anything. Charles seemed willing, if not eager, to allow her to build the Egret Island project, seeming to view it as an adventure and a challenge. Merrill, for some reason she did not even want to guess at, had seemed to take an instant disliking toward her.

"First of all, the clause you have in the contract asking for payments to be made strictly on schedule or you reserve the right to cease work—" Charles was saying, and Jacqui had to quickly catch up to his line of thought.

"My subcontractors wanted that," she told him, "based on the payment record of your company during the original construction of the complex."

"Agreed," Charles said. "But we have reorganized our management since that happened. The man who was in charge of seeing that this place was built is no longer with the firm." The look in his eye as he spoke told her that he felt the less that was said about the matter, the better. "I doubt that payments will present you with any problems on this project."

"I prefer not to delete that clause," Jacqui said,

standing her ground firmly, although she noticed with
the corner of her eye that Merrill Warden wheeled
abruptly from the window and glared at her. It was as
though he was daring her to be as tough a business-
person as he could have been.

"Very well," Charles said, unaware of Merrill's reaction, "if you do insist. I do understand that you have to
keep peace with the men who do the work." His arm
swept toward the door and Christopher hurriedly moved
to open it.

Jacqui noticed that Merrill held back as they began
their little procession down the wide flight of stairs,
through the lobby, and into the posh restaurant. She
wondered if his mood was colored by considerations
other than the contract for the Egret Island project, and
if it was, she had little respect for him as a businessman. One of the few things her father had taught her,
and Dorothea Grace had reinforced, was that personal
considerations should always be put aside when it came
to business.

The Magellan Room seemed an incongruous place
to discuss contracts and construction. Square tables
were dressed in pale blue linen cloths, with lanternlike
candle lamps centering them, lining up precisely, carrying the eye to the Gulf shore on the other side of plate-
glass windows, where the surf and sky echoed the same
shades of blue. The hostess, in her slightly artificial-
looking hair and heavy makeup, came forward eagerly
as she recognized the importance of the men in the
party.

"Five?" she said. "Would you like a table by the
windows over there"— she pointed out with the
menus in her hand —"or one in the other corner?"

Charles Warden glanced down at Jacqui. "Miss
Belpre, what would you prefer?"

Jacqui looked at Alexis for help. "By the window,
Mrs. Warden?" she asked.

"Of course," Alexis said, smiling as Jacqui moved aside for the older woman to enter the dining room ahead of her.

Jacqui breathed more easily, reassured that she had not made any glaring mistakes of etiquette before these wealthy, powerful people who all shared the intimidating Bostonian accent. She did not know why she felt it so important to impress them, only that she needed to watch each word and gesture carefully. Her mother had always stressed proper respect and deference, but Jacqui had never felt that she measured up to her mother's yardstick in manners. Her mother had been a hat-and-gloves lady, discarding the Sunday-best rituals only reluctantly when Southern society finally let them go.

When they were seated around the table and a waitress had taken their orders, Charles told Jacqui, "Christopher will be in charge of this project, from our standpoint. Will you be handling all the responsibility, or will Kyle be helping you?"

"We will have to work that out," Jacqui said, catching a cautious look from Christopher's deadly gray eyes.

Merrill Warden suddenly glared at her. "You would not assign your brother to be here full-time, would you?" he demanded, and Jacqui wondered whether it was Kyle's age and supposed inexperience he was objecting to, or his friendship with Alaine.

"We will do what is best for the project," Jacqui told him, trying to speak calmly and not allow her words to be colored by her growing dislike for him. "Kyle has more hands-on construction experience than I do. His expertise in the more down-to-earth aspects of building may be needed."

"I'd prefer you to be here full-time," Merrill stated.

Jacqui saw the corner of Christopher's mouth curl up in a secret smile, then concentrated on Merrill's hard, gray eyes. "I'm afraid that would be impossible. There are too many things I must do in the office that Kyle is not yet qualified, either by experience or certification, to do."

She had to smile. Merrill was as afraid of throwing Kyle and Alaine together as Jacqui was afraid of working closely with Christopher. No matter which combination came up, there was going to be fireworks.

Alexis touched her silverware ever so slightly to realign the spoon and knife to her satisfaction. "Alaine has told me quite a lot about you and your business, Miss Belpre. She seems fascinated by architecture and interior design suddenly, whereas she never seemed to have any real direction before. With all this talk about houses and building, I'm very anxious to see this new model I have heard so much about."

"I'd love to have you come see it," Jacqui said. "Will you be here long enough to see our Parade of Homes?"

"No. I'm afraid I'm returning to Boston later this week," Alexis said.

"My house is not the only one ready to be shown," Jacqui said, conscious she was becoming a salesman again. "If you do find time to come over, I'll show you our house and the other ones that are open for inspection."

Alexis looked thoughtfully toward her husband, then back at Jacqui. "Yes, I think I will make a point of it then. We're coming down here in October, permanently. Now would be a good time to start looking at models to see what we want built on our property."

Jacqui was relieved that Charles and Alexis handled the small talk during the lunch. While Merrill turned more attention to a glass of Scotch than to his food, Christopher was called away time and again to settle small crises. Jacqui tried to listen to stories of the resorts the Warden family owned, wanting to keep the information filed away in case she ever needed it. Paying strict attention helped her avoid looking too closely at Christopher when he was seated across the table from her.

When at last they had all finished, Jacqui glanced at her watch and was shocked to see how much time had elapsed since she had arrived. "Do you mind if I call my office?" she asked Christopher. "I thought I would have been back there half an hour ago."

"My office is yours," he said graciously, moving her chair for her.

"Thank you," Jacqui said. When she reached Yvonne Halpern on the phone and related the news to her, a stunned silence hung on the line.

Replacing the receiver, Jacqui had the feeling that something was missing, and realized that she had left her portfolio somewhere. The dining room? No. It must still be up in the boardroom, where she had placed it on the floor, leaning against a leg of the table. She hurried from the office, noticing as she passed the desk that Christopher was involved in a conversation with a clerk and a guest. Running up the stairs, she returned to the boardroom, pushing the heavy door open cautiously, feeling almost like an intruder. For a moment, she was again arrested by the impressiveness of Kyle's model, so familiar, yet in a strange setting, its minute details and innovative design so lifelike.

She would have to run over to Sierra Drive, where he and Cletus Garwood were working today, and tell him the news. They were going to have to do some reordering of their priorities to bring this contract off.

Jacqui stooped to retrieve her portfolio which had slipped to lie flat on the floor, and when she started to stand up, she found Christopher standing beside her, blocking her way, as the chair she had used confined her on the other side.

"I wondered why you came running back here," he said lazily.

"I—ah—wouldn't get far without this," she told him, tapping the portfolio with her fingertips.

"I could have brought it to you," he said. His hand dropped to the back of the chair, effectively closing the trap around her. "I'm glad you got the contract, Jacqueline. Working with you should be very interesting. We'll have to get together almost immediately for a discussion of the exact process of getting Egret Island built. Perhaps tomorrow you will come dressed for safari, as you say."

"I hardly think you want me running around here in my chambray—"

Christopher chuckled and placed his free hand at her waist. "You only tease me that you forget blue is my favorite color, although you seem to make the simplest clothing exciting."

Before she could stop him, he was holding her tightly to him, his mouth hard and warm on hers, overwhelming her with a burst of fiery passion for which she was totally unprepared. She blinked her eyes furiously, trying to resist the unexpected treachery of a part of her which was rising to the occasion with something resembling anticipation. She forced her conscious mind to deal with the provocation of the lips pressed demandingly against hers.

Her hands were full with her purse and her portfolio, or she would have been more effective in pushing him away. She was only successful in withdrawing from his kiss.

"Chris!" she managed to gasp, her breathlessness sure to be interpreted more as desire than rebuke.

He caught her hair in his hand, tangling the honey-blond tresses around his fingers, making even retreat from his plundering kisses impossible.

In desperation, Jacqui dropped her purse and portfolio to push herself away from him, kicking the chair backward until it crashed into another. "How dare you!" she spouted at him, enraged.

"You didn't react that way the other time I kissed you," Christopher reminded her, confident in himself and very amused.

"That was different!" she said.

"A kiss is a kiss," he countered in a lazy, philosophical drawl.

"There is a vast difference between a spontaneous tenderness and this flagrant intrusion on my person, Christopher Warden," she told him. "I do not tolerate such treatment."

"Maybe that is why you are on your way to being an old maid," he said, his voice taking on a mocking edge.

"I have no time for this," she said. "I have a business to run."

"Oh, yes," he said, insolently. "Your rigidly detailed timetable. Is there any chance that sometime in about five years you will have time to realize that you are a woman?"

Jacqui did not hesitate to retrieve her purse and portfolio and bolt from the room; by the time the cream-colored carpet under her feet had turned to the red of the hallway and stairs she had accelerated to almost a dead run.

The doorman was surprised that she scurried past him without so much as turning her head toward him on her way to the rough solitude and familiarity of the Beast. Her face burning with shame and confusion, she quickly started up the car and threw it into gear. She was halfway to Sierra Drive before she was finally in control of herself.

"You knew that was going to happen," she told herself aloud, suddenly aware she was in real pain, pain from the throbbing twinges in her shoulder, the ones that usually reminded her that she was telling a lie. Why was her shoulder acting up now, she wondered, rubbing her left shoulder with her right hand.

If she knew that it was going to happen, why had she

not known how to stop it, she demanded of herself, and knew that there was no answer.

Turning onto the block of Sierra where the house was going up, Jacqui pressed the button of the Beast's special horn, not knowing which of its seventeen songs it would play, and not really hearing it.

Kyle hailed her from the half-completed cement shell of an Osprey Builders' house as she drove up. "How'd it go?" he asked, wiping his face with a red bandana as he stood, the sun glistening on his sweat-drenched chest and shoulders.

"We won the bid," she yelled back, picking her way across the expanse of sand and debris that was treacherously going into her sandals. "We were the only bid they had. They almost had to accept it to be ready for the fall season."

"We got the bid?" Kyle asked, staring in disbelief. "We—got the bid?"

Jacqui steadied herself against the edge of the doorway and shook sand out of her shoes. She calmly repeated herself. "We got the bid."

Cletus Garwood tapped the corner of a cement block he was setting with the handle of his trowel. "Congratulations, Jacqui," he sang out, putting his level across the block.

"Do you think you can handle the job, Cletus?" she asked him. "To get it done with any speed, I'm going to have to have all your men, and maybe someone else's, too."

"I can handle it," Cletus told her confidently.

"Yeah, I'll just bet you can," Jacqui agreed.

"You look right pretty, Jacqui,' Cletus observed, backing down off his platform. "Ol' Jack sure had handsome kids. I'll give him that."

"Mind if I talk with Kyle for a few minutes?" she asked him.

"Whatever the boss-lady says," Cletus agreed. He

wiped his face and ambled away, toward a stand of thin-trunked oak trees that had been left in the front corner of the lot.

"What's up?" Kyle asked, reaching for his thermos jug of iced tea.

"We've got problems. Christopher and his father want me to supervise the job," she told him. "I'd rather you do it."

Kyle paused in his raising of the thermos to his mouth. "You finally figured out what was happening, eh?"

"What do you mean?" Jacqui asked.

"Alaine said she thought Chris was developing some feelings for you," he said, his blue eyes narrowing in the strong sunlight.

Jacqui turned her face away from him, ostensibly to keep the wind from blowing her hair into her eyes. "You could say that...."

"He made a pass at you, didn't he?" Kyle demanded, suddenly angry. "Am I right?"

Jacqui swallowed, then jerked her head upward and nodded.

Kyle made an enraged gesture with his arm, then immediately controlled himself. "Want me to do something about it?" he offered. "I'd be more than glad to settle two accounts at the same time—"

"That's what I would be afraid of," Jacqui said, assessing her brother's blue eyes, usually so cheerful, now dangerously piercing. "I don't want to work with him, not with the attitude he has. He's schooled to say the right things, do the right things to get a person's confidence, and then turn everything to his own advantage. I just don't want to have to play silly games with him while I'm trying to get that project built, and built right."

Kyle exhaled forcefully, causing the muscles under his bronzed skin to move almost convulsively. "You know I can't do everything."

"I don't expect you to."

"Do you really think we have to handle this to-gether?" he asked. "Truthfully, are you that afraid of Christopher?"

"Truthfully? I'm deathly afraid of that man."

Kyle's jaw set. "Hey, Cletus! Come back here a min-ute. I want to ask you something."

"What is it?" Cletus asked, coming back from the small copse of oak trees.

"How much do you need me?" Kyle asked. "This Egret Island job is going to take more than Jacqui can put into it and still ride herd on the houses."

"Want to split time?" Cletus asked, scratching the stubble on his chin. "Joe's got about half a man more than he needs. We could work it out between crews."

"Sounds fine," Jacqui said. "I'm going to need him tomorrow, then we'll get back to you and work out a schedule." She felt her composure seeping back into her mind and body. "Well, guys, I have to get back to the office. See you later."

On the way back to the office, just for good measure she took the time to drive out to the end of one of the roads in the Shelter Cove development, where there were still three unsold lots, bearing Ted Marks's for-sale signs. They overlooked what might be the last of the undeveloped beach, and she wished, if she could not buy one of them—they had premium pricetags—she would at least get the contract to build one of the houses. She really did not think that was too much of a dream to have.

At last able to smile to herself, she headed back to the office.

Chapter Six

Christopher Warden's smile suddenly died when he entered the boardroom the next morning and saw that Jacqui had been accompanied for their ten o'clock appointment by Kyle. Since they had intended to go out to take a close look at Egret Island, they were both wearing their jeans and work shirts. Before Jacqui had left her bedroom that morning, though, she had taken a critical appraisal of herself in the mirror, and now she knew what Christopher had been talking about when he said he did not mind seeing her in her working clothes. Consequently, she had buttoned her shirt one more button than usual and searched her dresser for a pair of jeans which did not fit her derriere quite so snugly. She had not realized that she had, out of necessity, adopted a uniform which could be interpreted as alluring.

She had vowed then and there that she was going to have to be defensive. The twinge in her shoulder gripped at her once, but she ignored it, no longer understanding its reason for striking at her, and vowing not to let it annoy her.

"Well, now, where shall we begin?" Christopher asked, regaining some of his composure as he closed the door behind him.

"Are there any legal matters or adjustments in the specifications that have to be dealt with?" Jacqui asked, sitting down near the model and taking her copies of the contract and reduced floorplans from her portfolio.

"Not that I know of," Christopher Warden said, after some thought.

"Changes are hard to make once the work begins," Jacqui warned him. "They get harder and more expensive by the day. Now, we can have the surveyors here Friday and start clearing Monday morning. I had to make some calls around to my subcontractors to schedule everything between their commitments. There is going to be considerable hurry-up-and-wait until the trades slow down for the hot weather. But I want to get as much done as I can before the summer rains begin."

Christopher nodded and opened a file folder. Then he looked at Kyle suspiciously. "Are you going to be in charge of this job?" he asked.

"We are doing it together," Kyle said, taking a seat between Christopher and Jacqui. "In effect, we have decided to chaperone each other. It is absolutely ridiculous that such a thing should be necessary in a business transaction, but your actions yesterday made it imperative."

"You discussed—" Christopher asked Jacqui, suddenly reddening with anger.

"She didn't have to discuss it with me," Kyle said. "You upset her so much that I knew exactly what had happened without her having to put it into words. Now, I think we could come to an understanding, couldn't we, Christopher? My sister is as precious to me as yours is to you. I would hate to have anything unpleasant happen to either one of them."

Christopher Warden's head nodded in agreement, ever so slightly. But his eyes burned a defiant message to Jacqui, chilling her, causing a twinge in her shoulder that made her hand clutch into a fist.

LATER, back in the office on Signal Drive, Jacqui could almost feel Kyle taking charge of the project, plotting the rough construction that would begin almost immediately. He was seizing control, not waiting to be deferred to, but he so clearly knew what he was doing that even Jacqui was surprised. Her initial feelings were of hurt and crushed ego, but these she forced herself to put aside without delay, knowing that eventually Kyle was destined to take over Osprey Builders and her own pride would only stand in the way of the progress that would benefit them both.

Kyle sprawled in Jacqui's chair as though it were his own, talking on the phone with the men who were to make the main bridge over the channel to the island. Jacqui was searching for her plans for the house on Sierra to check the specifications of the kitchen cabinets when she heard a familiar Bostonian accent behind her.

Alexis Warden stood in the doorway. "Ah! I've found you!" she said. "Mrs. Halpern—is it?—showed me through your house. She thought you and Kyle were busy—"

"Only Kyle is," Jacqui told her. "Did you get one of our brochures?"

"Oh, yes! Very impressive." Alexis did not enter the room where Kyle was talking on the phone but glanced into the other bedroom and then studied the bathroom thoroughly. "Chris told me about this," she said, pointing to the sliding partition.

"I'd be glad to answer any questions you have," Jacqui said, trying not to sound too much like a salesman, then wondering why she should care how she sounded. After all, if Alexis Warden was moving to Florida, why should Jacqui be bashful about trying to get her business.

Alexis smiled and walked slowly out to the dining room area and turned toward the screened patio. "Seriously, dear, would you answer me truthfully if I asked you a question about something other than your house?"

"I'll try," Jacqui said, opening the sliding glass door to the patio and standing aside so that Alexis could move past her. They sat down at the round, glass-topped table, on metal chairs that were wrought to look like they were formed of grape clusters and leaves.

"About Christopher," Alexis said. "Oh, you don't know how much Alaine has been confiding in me, things that I don't think she has the nerve to tell anyone, except that beautiful brother of yours. And I use that word not in a physical sense, though he is very handsome, but in regard to his wonderful sensitivity. But even I can see a difference in Christopher between yesterday afternoon when you left the hotel and this noon when he came back from Egret Island looking like he had lost his last friend."

"The situation, Mrs. Warden, is this," Jacqui said, leaning back in her chair. "Since Kyle and Alaine have become friends, Christopher has been trying to interfere with their relationship. Yesterday, Christopher made a pass at me, so Kyle told him frankly that it is going to be a *quid pro quo* situation. If Christopher does anything to me, he puts Alaine in jeopardy of a reprisal, and he is not prepared to handle that kind of threat."

Alexis studied Jacqui's face for a long moment, then laughed, looking gloriously impish. "I'm surprised that Christopher would take Kyle seriously, but then, he has his own perspective. I admire the move, though, more than you could possibly appreciate. Christopher has had his own way all his life, and I am pleased as I can be that he had finally gotten his comeuppance."

Jacqui smiled and looked away toward the tortuously bent oak tree. "He's very handsome, though," she said. "Intelligent, well-educated—"

"And hopelessly spoiled," Alexis said. "I'm glad that Merrill did not have as much to do with Alaine's upbringing. Some advice, Jacqueline."

"Yes, ma'am?" Jacqui asked, thinking, *here comes the lecture. Alexis has been sent to give me the word to leave the precious scion of the Warden family alone, proba-*

bly for someone who had been picked out as a more suit-
able mate for him.

"Let him suffer," Alexis said, with mock-evil emphasis, her head making a little quiver at the last word, causing
her elegantly waved hair to glisten in the filtered sunlight.
"Make him wait until it is convenient for you."

Jacqui was suddenly giggling at the sheer absurdity of
the situation. "Mrs. Warden, I thought you had been
sent to warn me away from Christopher, just as he
came to coerce me to warn Kyle away from Alaine,"
she confessed.

"I would do that only with the added statement that
you are too good for Christopher," Alexis said. "Unless he mends his ways."

"What ways?" Jacqui asked, enjoying Alexis's forth-
right approach.

"Christopher is thirty-two," Alexis told her. "Past
the age for a man to be married, if you ask me. He was
engaged to a perfectly lovely girl a few years ago. She
broke off the engagement because he would not or could
not give any affection or emotional support when she
needed it. He wanted her to do all the giving, and returned nothing to her. She was drained emotionally, and
no amount of promised material wealth can make up for
that. One must have one's dignity and self-respect. Merrill's problem with Dianna is just the very same, except
Dianna put up with it much longer. I admire the women
of today. They don't have the stupid, useless pride my
generation did. They are more willing to tell a man when
he hurts them."

Jacqui could not understand why she was surprised
to hear that Christopher had been engaged, not that his
fiancée had left him and allowed his shortcomings become family knowledge. Alexis was doing her a great
favor by telling her all this before she got emotionally
entwined with him.

Not realizing what she was doing, Jacqui began to

massage her left shoulder through the lightweight chambray of her work shirt. The shoulder was becoming an aggravation, especially when she thought about Christopher Warden. The obvious cure, therefore, was to stop thinking about him and get back to work.

"Thank you for telling me all this," Jacqui said, slowly. "I really don't know what use I'll make of the information—" She was hedging her words, conscious that someone was coming through the house.

At that moment, Kyle came and opened the sliding door. "Jacqui, Joe Quinn is on the phone," he said. "He says it's important."

"I'll just run along and look at the other houses," Alexis said, getting to her feet.

"But we haven't finished our conversation," Jacqui protested.

"Business before pleasure," Alexis said, with a broad smile.

Jacqui returned to her office, cursing the intrusion of the telephone, the feeling that when it rings one is duty-bound to answer it. "Yes, Joe," she said into the phone, wondering why the president of the Builders Association would be calling her and saying that it was important.

"Jacqui," he said, his drawl slow and jovial, "I heard that you got the Egret Island project, and that you'll need Kyle to help you with it."

"News really travels fast, doesn't it?" Jacqui asked, marveling.

"I've been talking to Hathaway at the county office, and he says that if Kyle can take all the tests and pass them, he'll waive the age requirement, so you can have him certified in about eight weeks," Joe told her.

"That would be wonderful," Jacqui said, enthusiastically, "but I hoped to have all the rough construction out of the way by then."

"Then he could take over the houses you'll be building by then," Joe suggested, "while you put the finish-

ing touches on Egret Island. The way your business is
growing, you'll need him anyway, Jacqui."

"You're absolutely right," Jacqui said, doing some
quick calculating. "Thanks for going out on a limb like
this for us, Joe. What does Kyle have to do?"

"Send him over to talk with Hathaway as soon as
possible," Joe said. "He may have to do some studying, but you have all the code books. If you need any
help, let me know."

"Thanks, Joe," Jacqui said. "I'll tell him right now,
and we'll get right to work."

When she hung up, Kyle was standing in the doorway, watching her. "What was that about?" he asked.

"Joe has arranged for you to take all the tests for your
certificate, and Inspector Hathaway will waive the age requirement," Jacqui told him, suddenly becoming excited
about the prospect. "If you're working for Garwood tomorrow, you better go see Hathaway right now."

Kyle nodded. "One thing, Jacqui," he said, pausing
before leaving her office. "Can we do without my income from Garwood?"

"We're going to have to, aren't we?" Jacqui replied,
sobered by the realization.

She sagged back in her chair and closed her eyes, listening to the sounds of Kyle leaving, starting the Beast,
and driving away. She had never contemplated how
much they had depended on Kyle's income, even
though there were times when it seemed like a matter of
taking money out of one pocket and putting it into
another. Nor had she ever thought of Kyle as a protector,
as he had become that morning. She had always thought
of herself as the protector of the family, as having to
cope with every situation as it came along by herself.

It was unfair to lean on Kyle now, when he would be
working so hard on his certificate. The threat he had
made to Christopher Warden was surely not serious,
and how Christopher would take it would be a matter

of some debate. She would not be amused if Kyle and
Christopher came to blows, nor would she get any satisfaction from Kyle taking vengeance out on Alaine.
How could he have threatened such a thing? Had she
not tried to instill in him a respect for women, based on
the groundwork her parents had already laid? She
would have to discuss the matter with him when he got
back, or at least after dinner.

SHE HAD NOT COUNTED ON Kyle's disappearing into his
room with code books as soon as he got up from the
dinner table that evening, and nearly every evening
thereafter. She admired his diligence, but missed his
company, conveniently discounting the nights that she
had closed herself away in her own room to work out
some problems with her model or a special custom
adaptation for a client.

The days were busy, even with Kyle now and then
running the project at Egret Island. The service road
had been cleared and the modular bridge put across the
channel to the island, then the island had been carefully surveyed, cleared of only the vegetation which
would be in the way of construction, and the ground
leveled and excavated with great care.

Late one afternoon, Kyle called Jacqui to come inspect the work and see if she approved of it as far as it
had progressed. She was initially relieved that Christopher was nowhere to be seen. She parked the Beast
and got out to join Kyle on the Island.

"Looks good," she told him, comparing the stakes
in the ground to the blueprint in her hand.

"I just wanted you to take a look before we start putting the foundation forms in," Kyle said. "The sterile
sand will be here tomorrow, and I hope to have the
whole thing ready for the reinforcing iron and the
plumbers by the end of the week."

Jacqui nodded and rolled the blueprint carefully in

her hands. "The weather ought to hold that long," she agreed. "Look, Joe was telling me that his plaza over on Heathcliff is being stolen clean. Cement blocks, drywall, anything that isn't locked up. Do you think we ought to hire a guard?"

"What kind of security does the hotel have?" Kyle asked, adjusting his hard hat. "We should have thought of that before. I suppose it would be best to discuss it with Christopher—"

"Discuss what with me?" Christopher asked, approaching them from his golf cart, which he had driven across the bridge without them noticing him.

"A security guard," Kyle said. "Some of the projects around here are being looted of their building materials. What kind of security do you have?"

"We have two shifts at night, with two men on each shift," Christopher told them. "I'll put this on their schedule, no problem. We can be very reasonable."

"Good," Kyle said, flatly.

The atmosphere had changed, soured in some way that Jacqui sensed in Kyle's attitude as he stood, proprietary and defensive of the project.

"Alaine has been wondering if you could all come for dinner Saturday night," Christopher continued, his mission now obvious.

"I'm sorry," Jacqui said. "The Parade of Homes starts Friday, and Saturday will be one of the busiest days."

"Besides," Kyle contributed, "I'll be studying for my tests."

Christopher seemed to take any disappointment in stride. "Well, it was a thought," he said. His eyes turned from Jacqui to the roughly laid out plan of the construction. "It's hard for me to visualize what this is going to look like," he said.

"Would you like to look at the plans?" Jacqui asked him, extending the rolled-up blueprint toward him.

Christopher grinned and shook his head, waving her

offer away. "No, thank you. I'm sure everything will be fine. I'd better go see to rescheduling the security men."

Jacqui watched as Christopher strode over to his golf cart and turned it back toward the hotel. When she glanced up at Kyle's face again, he was smiling enigmatically with his warm blue eyes. "Too bad you had to turn down that dinner," he said, trying hard not to let her know he was teasing.

"It's no great loss," Jacqui said, tapping the plans absently with the fingers of one hand. "Tell me. Would you ever hurt Alaine?"

He frowned and shook his head. "Not even if I was provoked, Jac. I couldn't hurt any woman. But he doesn't know that. He sees me as a mirror of himself, and that is the only power I have over him."

"How do you know that?" Jacqui asked, surprised.

Kyle shrugged. "I've given it a lot of thought. That's one good part about construction jobs. You have plenty of time to think. Let's call it a day. I'll see you at home."

When Jacqui drove past the hotel, she saw Christopher talking earnestly with a man in a green uniform, gesturing toward the island. Quickly snapping her head forward, she made certain that if he should look toward her, he would see that she was intent on driving her car. Then she felt a twinge in her shoulder.

Maybe it was time to have that twinge looked into. On second thought, it was frivolous to go to a doctor about a silly muscle spasm. It was doing no harm. Besides, with the Parade of Homes, the Egret Island project and everything else going on, when would she have time to see a doctor?

"I DON'T KNOW what the problem is," Jacqui mused to Yvonne Halpern as another day passed in the model home. "So far, we've had only three orders, and usually we sign four or five, considering the traffic we have had through here."

Yvonne plumped a cushion on the couch and replaced it thoughtfully. "I don't think you should be so disappointed, Jacqui," she said, her optimism well-considered. "The comments I have heard have been the type that indicate people might be coming back for another look later on. If you go talk to Chesterfield, and some of the others, I think you'll find the same thing is true up and down the street."

Jacqui closed the drapes and looked them over carefully. "Still, only three orders...." She sighed. "Did I do something wrong this year? I thought that we looked a lot better."

"Don't forget that you have Egret Island to finish at the same time," Yvonne reminded her.

"I'm not forgetting that. I still think that I have to get at least five contracts out of this show to make it worth the investment."

"You worry too much," Yvonne laughed. "Just like your mother. Sandy was always worrying about the number of contracts, when they came in, when we would get paid. Stop worrying. You're doing all that is humanly possible."

"Sometimes I think that I'm letting everyone down by not increasing the number of contracts each year. We're only holding steady," Jacqui complained, checking the patio door to be sure it was locked.

"You're doing very well in a business where big companies and established firms get most of the business."

"But this is supposed to be an established firm," Jacqui said.

Picking up her purse from the coffee table, Yvonne looked at Jacqui seriously. "You need some rest, Jacqui. Why don't you take off until noon tomorrow? Sleep in late or something."

"No, I have to go down to Egret Island in the morning," Jacqui said. "They are starting to pour the foundation, and I want to be close by."

THE CEMENT TRUCK made too much noise to allow for decent conversation, let alone coherent thought. Jacqui squinted through the early sun, enjoying the moment to herself as she leaned against the rough trunk of a palm tree.

Kyle, already having discarded his shirt for the morning, was actively supervising the first pour of the foundation, while Cletus Garwood stood by, eagle-eyed and not in the least bashful about offering his advice. Cletus had almost adopted the Egret Island project as his own. Jacqui had never seen him take so much care. It was a matter of pride to him, and he had brought in his best men.

A rhythm was emerging in the tempo of the work and the movement of the men. It was something that was hard to explain, and anyone not acquainted with the trade in an intimate degree could not appreciate the performance of men who knew exactly what they were doing and did it without wasted motion.

"Well, things are getting serious, eh?" Christopher asked her, almost at her elbow before she noticed him. He wore a red zippered sweatshirt over red running shorts and a white tank top. It was obvious from the slight sweat that gleamed on his tanned throat that he had been out for a morning run.

"Good morning," Jacqui said, politely, glancing toward Kyle, who was intent on the project and was of no use at the moment as a chaperone.

"It's a little noisy here!" Christopher shouted over the sudden roar of the motor of the cement mixer.

"Don't worry. It'll get worse!" Jacqui assured him, crossing her arms in front of her to enclose the clip-board that she held.

"Any problems?" he asked.

"None!" she replied, a bit loudly as, almost predictably, the whine and roar of the cement mixer growled and died.

"Ah-h-h," Christopher sighed, the noise reduced to men's voices as they yelled instructions to each other, and the sound of cement being raked into the foundation forms. "Are you really needed here, or could we take a walk along the beach?"

"I should hang around..." Jacqui said, reluctant to be alone with him.

"How would it be if I promise to behave myself?" he asked. "I have a message for you from Alaine, and we can't talk above all this noise. You might be more comfortable walking along the beach than going back to my office."

"I can't argue with logic," she chuckled. "Just let me tell Kyle where I'll be."

"He won't even know that you're gone," Christopher told her, and she had to agree.

"Let me leave my hard hat in the car," she said, jumping to her next best stalling tactic.

"I don't see why you have to wear that thing," Christopher said, falling into step beside her.

"Maybe it is a symbol of authority," she laughed, removing it and turning it upside down to hold the chin strap that dangled from it. "Besides, at this stage of a job, you never know what is going to come loose."

She left the clipboard in her car, too, and started out across the access bridge with Christopher. They walked along the cart path that skirted the golf course on their way to the beach beyond, Christopher's bared and hairy legs shortening his stride slightly to accommodate Jacqui.

"Now, what did Alaine want you to talk to me about?" Jacqui asked, drawing her hand through her long blond hair as the sea breeze ruffled it.

"She told me that Janice is upset because you canceled your plans to go down to Sarasota weekend after next, and she thought—" Christopher started.

"Oh, no! Janice has really gone too far this time!"

Jacqui exploded. "She is forever trying to get me to do things for her by embarrassing me. She had no business bringing Alaine into this. It is simply a problem of Kyle having to take one of his examinations for his certificate that Saturday. He can't go with us, and I refuse to take the Beast so far without him along."

"I know it's a family problem —" Christopher started to interrupt.

"But she will not allow me room to just wait until Kyle can go with us," Jacqui went on. "Then she has to go and worry other people about it."

"But you don't understand," Christopher said, raising his voice. "Listen to me. Alaine had wanted you to come to dinner last Saturday night. Well, we got our heads together, and we thought it might be fun if, instead of you and Janice going down to Sarasota that weekend, you come and stay at the hotel in the suite we reserve for the family. You can use the pool and anything else you want, and Alaine will have some company her own age for a change. Then, in the evening, Kyle can come for dinner with us. Yves de Croiux is going to be singing here that week."

Jacqui laughed. "That is not quite an incentive," she told him. "He appeals to an older group than us."

"Oh, I don't know," Christopher said. "He's been here before and brought in quite a nice crowd."

"I hardly think Janice would be impressed," Jacqui said, digging her hands into the pockets of her jeans. "She is so headstrong!"

"I can see where she gets it," Christopher said, laughing.

Jacqui stopped walking and glared up at him, and he grinned back at her. "I am not headstrong," she told him. "She is stubborn and unruly. I may be stubborn, but I live strictly by the rules, either professionally or personally. I try to set a good example with my life, but she despises the very things I stand for."

"Aren't you being a little hard on her?" he asked.

"I try not to be too strict in what I say, try to be modern and loving but still make my expectations clear," Jacqui went on, "but I know I am losing the battle."

"Perhaps you have taken on too much for a woman your age," Christopher suggested.

"Ha!" Jacqui said flatly, allowing her feet to sink into the sand of the deserted beach. "It's a package deal. When I took over running the family and the business, I knew what I was getting into. I knew there would be long hours of work, lean times, busy times. I knew that Kyle and Janice would resent me for denying them what they wanted because it was not wise for them to have it. I've accepted all that—"

"But now it is wearing on you, isn't it?" Christopher asked, his gray eyes strangely sympathetic as he tilted his head to look down at her.

Jacqui turned away from him, watching a fishing boat making its way up the coast a few hundred yards off the beach, while she took a deep breath and let her mind come to rest on the one bright spot in all her problems. "At least, now Kyle is going to be able to take over some of my responsibilities."

Shaking her hair out of her eyes, she looked further out into the Gulf. "You know, sometimes I look out there, and wonder if there is anything on the other side. I've seen maps, but it's hard to believe when you can't see anything. I know, for instance, that time is moving, and that eventually everything will work out, but in the meantime—"

"You have everything all planned, don't you?" Christopher asked. "Things that you cannot control are difficult for you to handle."

"Since when do hotel keepers dabble in psychology?" Jacqui asked, and felt her shoulder twinge.

Christopher laughed. "Since I met you," he said.

"I'm trying to find out what makes you tick, and you baffle me."

Jacqui searched the pockets of her jeans for a rubber band to put around her honey-colored hair to hold it in a pony tail at the back of her neck, and finally found it. "Don't waste your time on what makes me tick," she advised him, working her hair into the rubber band. "All I do is what I have to do."

Christopher tilted his head to one side and brushed a strand of her hair away from her cheek, his hand lingering in a caress. The gentle pressure of his lips met hers before she was braced for it, before she was prepared to be engulfed in his warm embrace. Surprised and breathless, she twined her arms around his waist, meeting his strength with her own, realizing that this moment was what she had feared all along. Her own passion for Christopher could not hide itself any longer.

When his lips parted slightly, she resisted, not ready to trust herself. *I'm being silly,* she thought. *This will pass. It's merely physical.*

She had to break away from him, to take a breath and settle this trembling in her knees. It embarrassed her to acknowledge the attraction between them.

"You said—you wouldn't do anything," she managed to say.

"I guess I forgot," he apologized, not without a roguish glimmer in his eye. "Do you blame me?"

When she raised her chin to confront him, the rubber band broke suddenly, and a gust of wind sent her hair swirling. "Story of my life!" she spat out, annoyed, then started laughing so hard that she abandoned the search for another rubber band, which she knew she would not have.

"What's so funny?" he asked.

She looked up at him sheepishly. "I was too proud to admit you were right. But you are. If I don't laugh about it, I'll cry. Laughing is better, right?"

A wisp of her hair blew across her face, and Christopher moved it aside with gentle fingertips brushing her cheek and smoothing the lock behind her ear. His eyes seemed amused, but without the condescension she expected. For a moment she thought he might kiss her, the gentle unassuming way he had that first time, then she scolded herself for allowing herself the delicious anticipation.

Christopher dug his hands into the pockets of his jacket. "How about the weekend here at the hotel?" he asked.

"It sounds tempting," she said. "I'll talk it over with Janice."

"You know that she will jump at the chance," Christopher said, his gray eyes smiling. "You may as well say you have a reservation...."

"All right," Jacqui agreed, grinning up at him. "I know when I'm licked."

"You'd better go back and see that the foundation is up to your standards," he said, nodding toward the roar coming from Egret Island. "And I had better go run my hotel."

He backed away from her a few steps, watching her as though he thought she would say something, and when she could not think of anything, she felt awkward. Overhead a few gulls keened and swooped on the wind on no particular mission.

Jacqui watched as Christopher walked up the steps to the promenade led back to the hotel, assessing the graceful way he moved. He was so self-assured, so self-possessed. There was no way of understanding him, running hot one time she saw him and cold the next, yet still being the same fascinating, exasperating man.

Sighing, she turned and kicked her feet into the sand, then began loping along the beach, feeling strangely warmed and happy just for being with Chris for a while.

Chapter Seven

"I really don't know how to read this situation," Jacqui confided in Kyle that evening, after Janice had gone into a fit of ecstasy over the prospect of two days at Leisure Discovery. "Christopher was so—human today."

"Accept it at face value," Kyle advised. "He just wants to be nice, and it's not costing him anything, is it? He can write it off. After all, it is a business expense for the hotel, if you want to look at it that way. If they had a company come in from any great distance, they would probably make a suite available for their brass."

"You always get right to the heart of the matter, don't you?" Jacqui said. "How are you coming with your studying?"

"I constantly have the feeling that I'm missing something somewhere," Kyle confessed. "It seems too easy. I already knew most of this material. But this county has a reputation for giving extremely hard tests. I don't know what to think."

"Did it ever occur to you that you might be smart?" Jacqui asked.

Janice came into the room with a scratchpad and a pencil in hand, writing something. "And we're both going to need two suits," she said. "There is nothing as bad as getting into a wet, clammy swimsuit."

"Two suits?" Jacqui demanded. "You'll get one new one and make do with the one you already have."

"And what about you?" Janice asked. "You're going to need two suits. And something nice to wear to dinner. And you can't traipse around in one of those shabby housecoats of yours."

"Jan, this is a weekend five miles away, not a cruise to the Bahamas," Jacqui laughed, dismissing her sister's plans.

"I wouldn't be surprised if we have a chance to meet Yves de Croiux, and I want to look really nice," Janice was going on. "Of course, I can borrow Lisa's long dress because we're the same size."

"Where are you getting these wild ideas?" Jacqui asked, breathless.

"Well, Alaine was telling me that she always meets whoever is coming in to entertain. Sometimes she even has dinner with them in the private dining room," Janice was rattling on.

"I hardly think we'll be included in anything like that," Jacqui said, looking to Kyle for help in controlling Janice's grand plans. But he was already back to his code books and notes. "Look, Jan, I'll get you a new swimsuit, but that is going to have to be the extent of new wardrobe."

Janice turned to Kyle. "Don't you think that Jacqui ought to get a few things for herself?" she asked him, although he did not look up from his studying. "A swimsuit, and a dinner dress, and maybe a sports outfit—"

"Anything you say," Kyle said, without looking up from something he was underlining.

"Kyle!" Jacqui exclaimed, trying to stop Janice from manipulating him.

Kyle put down his book and looked up at her. "Jacqui, be reasonable! You always spend your money on us and never on yourself. If you don't get a few new clothes for yourself, Jan and I will."

Jacqui laughed at the thought of Kyle trying to pick

out clothes for her. "All right, but I just got a new dress, and—"

"Don't pull this on us, Jac," Kyle said, acting as though it was a matter that should have been settled the moment he spoke. "If you don't get what we think you need, then we will take care of it. I do have a little money put back, and I think you should try to make a good impression on Christopher Warden. Now, will you both be quiet while I study?"

I guess he is taking over, Jacqui thought to herself, sitting back in her chair and picking up a book of house designs. Maybe by next year, she would not have to struggle through the Parade of Homes madness by herself.

She heard Janice calling Alaine on the phone again, and glanced back at Kyle. So far as he was concerned, everything was working out perfectly. Alaine seemed to ask for Janice when she called three times to every one she asked for Kyle. Kyle had taken on a new stature almost before her eyes, but with it, there was a distance between them that had not been there before.

She put it out of her mind, as she studied again a house plan that intrigued her. It was a beautiful house with a space in it she had always thought of as a studio. If she could only build it on that piece of land out on Red Key that her parents had always envisioned as their future home-away-from-home! But it would cost about three times as much as she could think of spending on a house, and they really did not need another home. This house would do as long as they needed it. Janice would go off sometime, and either she or Kyle would possess it by default. Eventually, maybe Kyle would build himself his own house. He talked of it sometimes.

Still she pictured the dream house, with a skylighted studio looking out on the dunes of Red Key. *How would you afford the insurance,* she chided herself, *even if you could build it?*

"But I'm going to need the Beast if I'm going to Leisure Discovery for dinner," Kyle was saying. "I cannot possibly use the motorcycle if I am wearing a suit. Imagine what that would do to my suit."

"Leave it to Christopher Warden to throw a monkey-wrench into our plans," Jacqui spouted, baffled by Kyle's sudden Janice-like display of clothes-consciousness. "All right. Drop us off at Leisure Discovery on your way to the county office. Does that solve that problem?"

"Yes, Ollie, I think it does," Kyle teased. "Look, the weather is going to be great, you don't have a thing to worry about."

"Except sewing this button onto your jacket," Jacqui said, bending over Kyle's good suit. "Kyle, why did you let this go until the very last minute like this? I'm so nervous I can hardly see what I'm doing."

"Nervous? Whatever for?" Kyle said, folding his lanky frame onto the stool beside her at the counter of the kitchen, where the light was best in the whole house.

"I haven't even had time to pack."

"Jan is packing for you."

"That is what I am afraid of," Jacqui told him, smiling lopsidedly as she fought with a knot that tried to form as she pulled the thread through the hole in the button. "Besides, two whole days with Christopher Warden! I don't know if I can survive it."

"He'll be so busy running the place, he will scarcely know you are there," Kyle said, fidgeting with the good shirt that he wore. It was a shiny knit fabric and was printed in a geometric pattern of bronze and beiges. Jacqui always marveled that he had the nerve to wear it, though it looked very attractive on him. She was more used to seeing him in working clothes, she knew, and seeing him dressed neatly was always strange. All in all, he was a stunningly attractive young man, and she thanked whatever powers that watched over them that he had not become vain or conceited.

"Jacqui! What makeup do you need?" Janice called from somewhere in the bedroom wing of the house.

"I have everything I need in my purse," Jacqui called back. "Will you just finish packing? Kyle wants to get started here, or he'll be late getting over to the office, and with Mr. Hathaway going out of his way—"

"I've heard it before, Jac!" Janice called back, suddenly her harsh, demanding self. "Besides, I've finished packing your bag, and I'm just cleaning out your purse. A quarter ton of used tissues, quarter ton of receipts from stores—"

"Save me the recital and get out of here," Jacqui said, finally making a deliberate knot in the thread and snipping it with her scissors.

"Green stamps and keys—"

"Leave those keys alone!" Jacqui ordered, handing the jacket to Kyle, who inspected her work, and then hung the jacket on its hanger with his trousers. "I still think that you should dress down there."

"No," Kyle refused. "I want to be able to come back here and say a few heated words in private if it doesn't go well. I can't do that with a lot of people around."

"I suppose that does make sense," Jacqui said, sympathetically. She took her purse and bag from Janice as she brought them into the kitchen.

"Let's see how you look," Janice said, surveying Jacqui's new white slacks and pink blouse. "I really think you should have gotten that skirt and jacket."

"Janice!" Jacqui exclaimed in exasperation. "I'm not being presented at court, or being awarded a Nobel Prize, not even going to the Builders Association Christmas dance. I am just going off for a weekend five miles away! And may I add that this little excursion is for your benefit almost exclusively."

"If you know you look good, you'll have a good time," Kyle said, smiling playfully. "That is what you have always said to get me to shape up!" He took her suitcase and started out the door, saying, "We don't have time to stand around here and talk. Jan, get the door."

FIFTEEN MINUTES LATER, Alaine was greeting them in the lobby of the hotel where Kyle had dropped them off. "Isn't Kyle coming in?" Alaine asked. "I wanted to give him a kiss for good luck on his exam."

"He'll do just fine," Jacqui assured her, smiling. "Besides, it's the thought that counts."

"And he has blueprints for brains," Janice said snidely between looking at the high beamed ceiling of the lobby and studying the elegantly casual people around them.

"Our rooms are up on the second floor," Alaine said. "The two family suites are connected, and we have a balcony overlooking the swimming pool. Come on, Janice, let's get into our suits and hit the water. Wait till you see the lifeguards on duty today...."

When they reached the room, at the end of a long corridor across the hall from a door marked MANAGER'S RESIDENCE—PRIVATE, Alaine unlocked the door and handed the key to Jacqui. "See, we're right across the hall," she said, and the undeniable proximity of Christopher's quarters to their own troubled Jacqui. "And there is a parlor in between. It's like the celebrity suite above—parlor with two bedrooms on either side. You know, I was telling Kyle that he should plan to stay the night, but I couldn't talk him into it."

Jacqui had to smile at the way Alaine had begun to run on when they were together. Looking around the room with its floor-to-ceiling glass windows opening out onto the swimming pool and part of the golf course and the ever-present Gulf of Mexico, Alaine explained, "This is half the parlor—the wall folds into itself."

"Very nice," Jacqui said, lowering her suitcase

to the floor and examining the wall very closely.

"Next thing we know, she'll be making a sketch," Janice sighed.

Alaine's eyes sparkled, even though she glanced tolerantly toward Janice and then turned her attention back to Jacqui. "See, this is why Chris and I were so fascinated with what you did to the bathroom in your model," she explained. "We thought this was clever, but you had taken it one step further in what you did."

"Don't tell me *you* are going to talk shop, too?" Janice wailed, collapsing onto the couch, doing her Sarah Bernhardt imitation, eyes rolled heavenward and the back of her hand to her forehead.

"Just two things," Alaine bubbled on, ignoring Janice. "First of all, I've decided to go back home to college and study either architecture or interior design. Second, Aunt Alexis sent down a plan for a house she wants you to look over. They have ten acres not far from here that they plan to build on, and she wants you to look over the plans and the land survey to see what you think of it. But she told me that you are not to look at it once while you are here for your weekend."

"She'll look at it twice," Janice groaned. "All day today and all day tomorrow."

"Well, she won't if I don't give the plans to her until she leaves tomorrow night," Alaine laughed.

Janice bounded to her feet and grabbed up her suitcase. "Come on, there is no sense standing here looking at that pool," she said, "when we could be swimming in it."

"Absolutely right!" Alaine agreed.

Janice was already scampering off to decide which of the two rooms she was going to appropriate while Jacqui stood staring at the pool below, beyond the balcony which held several padded chaise longues, an umbrella table, and four chairs. "This is really nice," she mused to herself.

She sat down on a modern-looking couch and listened to the girls chattering and laughing. It was good to hear Janice happy and excited, after weeks of hearing nothing but complaining and wheedling about one thing and another, and good to forget about Osprey Builders for a while.

The telephone at her elbow rang, and Janice called out, "Want me to get that?"

"No, I have it," Jacqui said, thinking that surely it was for someone else. "Hello."

"Oh, good, you're here. This is Christopher," he said. She could not have mistaken his accent if she had tried. "I wanted to meet you when you got here, but we're always shorthanded on Saturday mornings."

"Alaine met us, thank you," Jacqui said.

"Is everything all right?" he asked solicitously.

"Well, I haven't taken the grand tour yet," she told him, trying to put him at ease, "but I'm certain everything must be fine. The girls are getting ready to go swimming."

"If you need anything, just tell Alaine," Christopher suggested. "I'm going to try to be free to have lunch with you."

"You don't have to," Jacqui said. "We'll get along just fine."

"I didn't mean you, plural," he said with emphasis. "You, singular."

"Oh!" Inwardly, an alarm went off.

"If I'm not there by one, come down to my office and drag me away, please?"

"Christopher—" Jacqui said, knowing that protest was futile.

"Promise?" he pleaded.

"All right," she agreed, chuckling. "If you're not here by one o'clock."

When Jacqui hung up the telephone, Janice and Alaine were standing in the middle of the floor, Janice in a new bias-cut bathing suit she had gotten a few days before.

"Chris wants to have lunch with you?" Alaine asked, catching her dark hair behind her neck, shaking it, and letting it go.

"Yes," Jacqui said, standing up slowly.

"He said he did," Alaine said, then turned to the folding wall. "Look, there is no sense in having to go through the hall. Chris doesn't like people running back and forth in swimsuits. He says that it isn't dignified. Jacqui, are you coming down to the pool?"

"You go on," Jacqui told her. "I'll be out in a few minutes. I really should unpack and hang up my dress."

"I already did that," Alaine said breezily, skittering off beyond the wall into the other suite.

"Talk about service!" Jacqui called after her, then laughed and went to see which room Janice had left for her and what state of disaster she had been able to put her own room into during this short time.

Her suitcase was sitting open on the bed in the second bedroom. Laid out on the bed was an exotically printed one-piece swimsuit she had never seen before, and hanging from the closet rack was a long white silk jersey dress with a low-cut neckline and a lower backline. "What on earth!" she exclaimed, then shook her head.

Suddenly the last-minute repairs to Kyle's jacket and Janice's largess in packing for her made sense. Kyle had made good on his threat to buy her what she would not get for herself, and Janice did her part to make certain that the new wardrobe was brought along, not left hanging in her closet at home. And with Kyle having to use the Beast, their plans had worked perfectly. In a way, she had to be proud of them.

Jacqui shook her head again and fingered the silkiness of the fabric of the dress. Even so, she thought she could keep Christopher at bay. Quickly, she set about changing into the new swimsuit and pulled her hair into a braid above her right ear. If there was one thing she did not like, it was wet hair that went everywhere in the water, and was nearly impossible to drag a comb through later.

"I SEE YOU FOUND OUR PRESENTS," Janice called out to Jacqui from the center of the pool. "Turn around and let me see the back."

Jacqui complied, pirouetting once before starting down the tiled steps into the shallow end of the pool.

"It was a committee decision," Janice told her. "Kyle has no taste in swimsuits, though. Color, yes, style, no. Isn't this water great?"

"It's wet," Jacqui agreed. Swimming bored Jacqui, but the girls were playing a game of tag they insisted on drawing her into. She paddled around for a while, then to finish their game decisively, she dunked them both at the same time and scrambled up the steps of the pool before Alaine and Janice could enact their revenge.

Enjoying her meaningless victory, she swaggered up the steps to the balcony, ignoring their taunts and dares, and stretched out on one of the chaises to get some sun.

A few minutes, she thought, *then I will go in and dry my hair and dress for lunch.* She knew she should get her watch so that she would be sure she did not lie in the sun too long.

But the warmth of the sun, the clear blue Florida sky, and the quietness were very seductive. Jacqui sat for a longer time than she intended, watching the girls swimming, almost alone in the pool, its blue water echoing the color of the sky.

When she finally got up to go inside, Christopher was just stepping out onto the balcony, having discarded his jacket across one of the chairs in the parlor, and now unbuttoning his shirt cuffs and folding up his sleeves.

"Well..." he said slowly, appraising her in the swimsuit and gradually grinning in approval.

"Excuse me," she said, blinking, feeling slightly embarrassed. "I—I must have lost track of the time. I'll go get dressed."

"Don't run off so quickly," he said. "I'm early. By a couple of hours, actually. How could I concentrate, knowing you were here?"

His gray eyes were teasing her, knowing that she was uncomfortable, caught unawares, before she had had time to steel herself for his presence.

"Then you are just taking a break?" she asked hopefully.

"No. As I said, I'm of absolutely no use to anyone at the moment."

"I—I should go get dressed," Jacqui stammered, preparing to move past him.

"You look beautiful," he said, trying to detain her.

"I'm afraid I'll get too much sun," Jacqui said, rubbing her left shoulder with her right hand, and in the process shielding herself from Christopher's embarrassing scrutiny.

"Go, then," he said, yielding to her argument. He followed her back into the parlor and she felt his eyes watching her almost until she closed her bedroom door.

In trying to undo the straps of her swimsuit, Jacqui found that he had succeeded in knotting them hopelessly. They resisted any attempt at loosening them she made with her blunt fingernails. Sighing, she resigned herself to the only recourse she had—asking Christopher for help.

Retracing her steps to the parlor, she turned her back toward Christopher and pointed to the snarled straps.

"Only too glad to be of assistance," he assured her,

his fingertips making much more contact with the sensitive flesh of the nape of her neck than she thought was necessary.

Modestly, she held the top of the suit to her bosom. Without a word, he turned Jacqui toward him, raising her chin so that his mouth touched hers.

"Thank you," she managed to say.

"This is all the thanks I want," Christopher whispered, his arms binding her to him powerfully as his mouth trailed kisses to her bared shoulder.

Not thinking of the consequences of her actions, Jacqui turned her hands to lay on the fine fabric of his shirt. She held her breath, trying not to feel the excitement that threatened to undermine her resolve not to enjoy his kisses.

"Christopher, you're expecting too much gratitude," she playfully warned him.

Christopher raised his chin and looked down at her, a smile spread to his lips. "The lady has her limits?" he asked.

"Yes," Jacqui agreed. "And your mind seems to have taken a quantum leap beyond them."

"Is there any chance of wiggling my toes on the edges?" he asked lightly.

His humor was so unexpected, Jacqui leaned away from him. While she tried to think of a clever rejoinder, she clutched at the skimpy material which threatened to fall away from her breasts.

Suddenly the telephone rang, causing Christopher to release her with a muttered oath. For a moment, Jacqui did not move, watching him cross the room to grab up his special phone as though it was an object of hate. When he glowered back at her, she could not avoid starting to giggle. She decided to let him win that point, knowing instinctively that he was not angry with her but with the call that had interrupted them.

When she saw a muscle twitch at the corner of his

jaw, she knew it was time to retreat. Hurrying back to her room on her bare feet, she was certain that the door was closed behind her before she started to laugh.

When she returned to the balcony wearing her pink blouse and white slacks, Christopher looked up from a book he was reading. "It was worth the wait," he said, marking his place in the book and sliding it across the umbrella table out of his way.

Jacqui cocked her head to read the title of the paperback novel, somehow surprised that it was a much-ballyhooed piece of escapism. When she looked back at Christopher, he seemed embarrassed to have been caught reading it.

"Well, I have to read something," he said, shrugging.

Jacqui sat down across from him. "I wish I had time to read," she said.

"You can not imagine how boring this job is at times," he said. "When we are organizing a golf tournament or building something, it is interesting, but just as day-to-day work..." He shook his head.

"Where are the girls?" Jacqui asked, noticing that they were not in the pool.

"They decided to take a walk around the golf course," Christopher said.

"In this heat?" Jacqui asked.

Christopher shrugged. "I decided that since I'm not chained to this place, I'd take you somewhere else for lunch."

"To spy on the opposition?" she asked, conscious of teasing him.

"Exactly," he laughed, pleased that she seemed to have read his mind and would tell him so openly.

"Am I dressed suitably for the place you have in mind?" she asked him apprehensively.

He got to his feet and reached to take her hand. "Jacqueline, any man who would not be proud to escort you as you are would have to be sick."

Jacqui was surprised by his directness and by the strong pressure of his hand around hers. She averted her eyes from him as she stood up, trying to get her emotional as well as physical bearings. Maybe coping with Christopher for the weekend was going to be more of a challenge than she had counted on.

They strolled down the steps to the grounds and to the place where Christopher's car was parked under a protective overhang.

"I hope you haven't had any complaints about the noise from Egret Island," Jacqui said, trying to shift his attention away from herself in an attempt to fill the silence as they left the resort complex.

"I doubt that I would tell you, even if we have," Christopher told her, his voice deep and untroubled. "Besides, we are not going to talk about business, understand?"

"Then what are we going to talk about?" Jacqui asked, and the moment the words left her mouth, she knew that she had blundered.

"We'll think of something," Christopher said, turning his attention to the traffic as they drove out onto the highway.

"Alaine told me that she has decided to go back up north to college," Jacqui said, in another attempt to fill the silence and yet keep the conversation impersonal.

"You realize what that will do to the threat Kyle made, don't you?" Christopher said, without taking his eyes off the road.

Jacqui swallowed hard. Her thoughts on the matter had not gone that far. "Did you talk her into the decision?" she asked.

Christopher snorted. "Alaine has, in a short time, gone from being the child who would do exactly what she was told," he said, with some feeling, "to a woman with a mind of her own. I don't think anyone is going to be able to order her around ever again. I don't know if it is a good thing or not. I suspect, down deep inside, that it is, but it is a fact that her family is going to have to accept.''

Jacqui was surprised that in the way he chose to speak, he seemed to be putting some distance between himself and the situation. ''I hope you don't think that she has caught this from us,'' Jacqui said.

Unexpectedly, Christopher laughed. ''An independence virus? I don't think it would have been all that bad if that is where she picked it up. I think we failed her, at home. I never thought of her as a sister, as someone I had any responsibility for, and I resented her coming down here and interfering in my life. But in a couple of conversations we have had—which could have been confused with being fights, by the way—she made me understand that she loves our parents both too much to go through all the pain their divorce is generating. They were going from being painfully polite to painfully brutal, and she thought she was in the way at best and a hindrance to their getting everything out in the open at worst. You were right, this is the best place for her for now.''

''Whoa! Don't involve me in this—'' Jacqui interrupted.

''You are whether you want to be or not,'' Christopher said, glancing over at her, then back at the road. ''Until I met you and Janice, I viewed Alaine as some alien thing. But you have tried so hard to guide Janice through the troubled waters, that I realized that it was a mistake to avoid my duties to Alaine. Did you ever make any mistakes?'' Christopher asked her, playfully challenging her.

''No, I didn't have the opportunity,'' she said. ''I didn't have much of an adolescence, what with taking care of Kyle and Janice, studying hard, and then working for Dorothea.''

''I almost made a mistake once,'' he confessed. ''Right out of college, I almost got married. Now that

I've met you, I understand why that would have been a wrong move."

"Christopher, I suddenly don't like the direction this conversation is heading," Jacqui cautioned. Her shoulder had twinged, more at the deep note of persuasion that was creeping into his voice than at what he was saying.

He smiled blithely as he steered the car into the parking lot of a Greek restaurant. "All right, I'm not going to tell you how much I am in awe of you for being so totally in control of your life and yet so totally a fascinating woman."

"I am not totally in control of my life," she protested.

"But you do not deny being—"

"Chris!"

"See, that is what makes you so fascinating," he laughed, switching off the ignition. "You do not have the slightest idea of what you are."

Jacqui let out a puff of breath in resignation. "And I don't have the slightest idea of what you are talking about, either."

"You're like Alexis," he explained. "Talented, intelligent, shrewd, goal-oriented. I respect my mother, you understand, but I idolize Alexis. She and Uncle Charles must love each other fiercely, because he used to be a scoundrel when it came to women. I rather imagine she put her foot down and told him she wouldn't tolerate faithlessness."

"And you admire that?" Jacqui asked, surprised, intrigued, and not completely convinced.

"I'd like to marry a woman who would stay with me only out of love," he said, "not because of responsibility or economics or legality."

"That's very—profound," Jacqui managed to say, her mind reeling, unable to grasp all the implications of what he said.

"Look, since I am playing hooky this afternoon,"
Christopher said, turning toward her with a boyish grin,
"let's go for a drive after lunch. I've only been here a
few months myself, and I don't know my way around
too well. I'm going to eventually have to find a house,
so if you don't mind—could you give me a guided tour
of the best neighborhoods?"

"Come on, I can't believe you want me to show you
around," she laughed. "On my own turf? All the disas-
trous short-cuts?"

"If we get stuck, we get stuck!" he said, opening the
car door.

"There are some nice lots out in Shelter Cove, on
the beach—"

"Sounds great!"

"Expensive, though."

"I'm just looking!"

Jacqui let him open the door of the car for her.
Maybe it wouldn't be so painful, after all, she thought,
smiling up at him.

Chapter Eight

Jacqui was dressed for dinner, although self-conscious, in the long white dress which clung to her curves and showed off her perpetual tan. Frankly, she wondered if perhaps too much of her tan was showing. She turned one way and then another before the full-length mirror in her room, which also reflected Janice surveying her critically while she absently fluffed the flowery ruffle of a peasant dress she had borrowed from her friend Lisa.

"Is that how you're going to wear your hair?" Janice demanded, reaching for the styling brush which lay on the dresser.

"I thought so," Jacqui said, turning away from the mirror.

"Brush it back over one ear," Janice instructed, handing the brush to her firmly.

"Okay?" Jacqui asked, skeptically complying to maintain peace.

Alaine strolled into the room, wearing a severely plain blue gown which seemed oddly perfect for the occasion. "Love it," she said, appraising Jacqui's dress. "Oh, I have just the thing for your hair. A magenta comb."

"Magenta?" Jacqui asked, incredulously.

"How many chances do you get to wear magenta?" Janice shrugged. "Oh, come on, Jac! Make it really daring."

"Exactly why?" Jacqui asked, brushing her hair smooth far back behind her ear, and grimacing into the mirror.

"Why do you think Chris asked us here?" Janice hissed. "Certainly not so Alaine would have my company and Kyle's. I'm almost embarrassed to look at him when he is around you."

"That's certainly not my fault," Jacqui said. A sharp twinge in her shoulder sent the brush flying through the air. "Oh," she groaned, disgustedly flexing her fist. "I'm sorry."

Alaine came running back into the room with a handful of hair ornaments. "Here. Pick one," she offered, breathless and flushed from hurrying.

"The silk lily, Jac! Isn't it perfect?" Janice asked.

"Perfectly gaudy," Jacqui countered, passing it by.

"Don't be a dunce!" Janice ordered. "The dress is plain, the hair is plain. You can afford it."

"In the interest of getting to dinner," Jacqui sighed, and let Janice slip the flower into her hair. "I wonder why Kyle isn't here yet."

"Want me to call him?" Alaine asked, reaching toward the phone beside the bed.

"Maybe you should," Jacqui said, looking at herself in the mirror again.

"Oh, forget it! He'll be here," Janice said, firmly, her hands on her hips as she gave Jacqup a lastchecking over.

"Is everybody decent?" Christopher called from the parlor.

Janice and Alaine giggled, and he appeared in the doorway in a dinner jacket and trousers, a pleated shirt and black tie.

"A little formal, aren't you?" Jacqui asked him as he stepped into the room.

Christopher shrugged. "Part of my working wardrobe, like your hard hat."

Jacqui had to laugh at the simile.

Alaine and Janice left the room, passing him on the way to the parlor and the corridor beyond. He watched after them, then turned to Jacqui, his gaze flickering over her so thoroughly that she was vaguely embarrassed.

"You're absolutely stunning," he said, the tone of his voice subdued.

"You're not so bad yourself," she said, surprising herself with her flippancy. "But, then, you don't have so far to go as I do."

"Maybe that is what makes you all the more spectacular," Christopher said. "Are you ready to go downstairs?"

"Kyle's not here yet," she told him. "Should I turn out the lights or leave one on for him? He should have been here already."

"He'll make it," Christopher assured her. "Stop worrying about Kyle." He repeated the essence of these words while they were dancing and Jacqui kept one eye on the door of the dining room.

When she did not relax, but merely glowered at him, his condescending attitude changed. "Would you like me to go call the house and see if he's left?" Christopher asked.

"No," Jacqui said, shaking her head. "I'm being silly. Of course he'll be here soon." She vowed she would give her full attention to Christopher, even if it gave him ideas she did not intend for him to have. After all, he was holding her, using everything he must have learned in dancing classes. She might as well enjoy it, she thought, smiling up at him.

A few minutes later, Alaine came sailing to the edge of the dance floor and motioned furiously for Christopher to come to her. "The headwaiter won't let Kyle in because he isn't wearing a tie," she said.

"That's ridiculous!" Jacqui said. "I picked out his tie myself."

"I'll take care of this," Christopher said. "Jacqui, why don't you wait at our table?"

When he returned without Kyle or the girls, Jacqui looked up at him questioningly. He pulled out a chair and sat down before leaning toward her with his explanation. "Kyle had a flat tire on the way and forgot to take off his tie. It got ruined, so I sent him upstairs with the girls to get one of mine, and by the way, calm down a little. It didn't do his temper any good when Johan became officious. I was afraid that Kyle would take him apart right there!"

"A flat tire!" Jacqui sighed. "After taking that test—"

"I'm just as glad you didn't go down to Sarasota and have a flat tire all by yourself," Christopher said, then grinned. "You *can* change a flat..."

"Not on the Beast," she admitted, sheepishly.

Christopher raised an eyebrow. "You disappoint me! I thought you could do anything. You do need a man—for something."

Jacqui laughed, slightly ashamed of herself. "I'm sorry I dampened your evening by fretting about Kyle."

"The evening has barely begun," Christopher said. "There is plenty of time for you to make it up to me."

YVES DE CROIUX'S LAST ENCORE was a love song he had made famous ten years before, his rich baritone voice sounding poignant and wistful. Jacqui felt Christopher's hand tighten on her shoulder as they sat in the darkened dining room. No one spoke, even in a whisper. It seemed, in the silence, as though no one even breathed until he had finished. Then there was a stunned void before the audience began to applaud.

"Would you like to meet him?" Christopher asked. Although she was tempted, Jacqui shook her head, as did Kyle, but Janice and Alaine followed him as he moved swiftly through the room and out of sight.

As the room emptied, Jacqui turned to Kyle and asked, "Why are you in such a bad mood? A simple flat tire doesn't usually put you in the deep blues like this."

Kyle sighed. "I did too well on that test. Hathaway

accused me of cheating, but I didn't take a thing into that room with me but my pencils."

"So—"

"Finally, grudgingly, he accepted my score," Kyle sighed, drawing squares on the tablecloth with the blunt tip of his finger. "But it really burns me."

"I'm sorry," Jacqui said, sympathetically. "Sometimes it's difficult to establish credibility."

Kyle nodded and leaned both elbows on the table. "It means I'm going to have to do just as well on the other tests."

"You will," Jacqui said, trying to bolster his confidence.

"It means four more weeks of hard work," Kyle sighed, "and cheating you out of my duty to the firm."

"Don't worry about that," Jacqui said, lightly.

"But I do worry. I'm supposed to be helping you with Egret Island, and most of my energy is going into my certificate."

This was not the place for telling him he was copying her weakness of being too devoted to work. Maybe she had set too good an example!

"Is something wrong with your shoulder? You've been rubbing it every five minutes since I got here," Kyle observed.

"Muscle spasm or something," she acknowledged. "It's really nothing."

"Has Christopher been behaving himself?" Kyle asked, his eyes intensely searching hers. "Because if he's not, I'll—"

"He's been a lamb," Jacqui said quickly, almost defensively.

Kyle tried to look skeptical, but succeeded only in yawning. But the skepticism quickly won out. "Come on, Jac! I haven't seen so much chemistry since I tried to blow up the lab in high school!"

"It may be obvious to you and Jan, but I'm not—repeat, not—attracted to Christopher Warden," she said and immediately gripped her left shoulder. At the same moment, another hand came to rest on her shoulder, and she looked up into Christopher's smiling face.

"The girls are back in the green room with Yves and his wife Josetta, eating hamburgers and talking in French," Christopher informed her, amused. "We may never get them out of there. Kyle, I think it's a foregone conclusion that they will want to have a slumber party in Alaine's room, so why don't you use Janice's?"

"Please, Kyle?" Jacqui pressured him. "I'd worry about you driving even the five miles home in the mood you're in."

Kyle studied her for a long moment, then nodded. "Now that you mention it, I am having a hard time keeping my eyes open."

Slowly, Kyle got to his feet, bent down to kiss Jacqui on the cheek, and left the dining room, followed by Christopher as far as the doorway. Jacqui was surprised to see that Christopher actually patted Kyle on the back as they parted.

Almost at the same time, a waiter placed an exotic-looking drink on the table in front of her. Jacqui looked up at him questioningly. "What's this?" she asked him.

"A rum screwdriver," the waiter told her. "Mr. Warden ordered it." Then he took a short glass of liquor on the rocks from his round tray and set it at Christopher's place.

When Jacqui eyed the tall drink's yellow color, topped with a tiny blue parasol, with some wonderment, the waiter leaned down and whispered to her: "It's mostly orange juice, miss."

Jacqui smiled up at him uncertainly, then glanced across the floor at Christopher. Now he was initialing a bill for another waiter. Again he picked his way across the floor and sat down beside her.

"I'm sorry I have to work so much while you're here," he said, apologetically.

"Think nothing of it," Jacqui said, taking the parasol

from her drink and sipping the rum mixture warily. "Let us consider the score settled for the ride on the short-cut to Signal Drive. It is interesting to watch you."

"It can't be that interesting," he laughed, then looked at his watch. "Usually the crowd thins out about now. The band plays until about one o'clock, and the bar closes, so..." He tasted his drink, then looked at hers. "Is something wrong with that?"

"No, I don't suppose there is," Jacqui said. "I'm just not used to—drinking."

"Do you think I'd lead a maiden astray?" he laughed.

"Frankly, yes," Jacqui giggled, feeling a knot of apprehension unravel.

"Would you object if I led you to the dance floor?" he asked, pushing his whiskey aside and reaching for her hand.

She nodded, almost mesmerized by his polished manner.

"I've been waiting all evening to get my arms around you," Christopher growled playfully into her hair, then grinned down at her.

"Well, that's progress, I suppose," Jacqui said, "since it seemed for a time you wanted your hands at my throat."

"I'm going to pretend you didn't say that," Christopher countered, but she could see that he had taken the remark in the bantering spirit that she had intended it. There was a new level of understanding between them and she wanted it to last forever.

When the tables were empty and the waiters were upending chairs and taking brooms from the closet, Jacqui looked at her watch and then at the band, which began to play another song.

"I thought you said the band plays until one o'clock," she said. "It's almost ten after."

"They play a little longer if someone slips them a few extra bills," Christopher told her. He looked so serious and then grinned.

Jacqui giggled and was instantly ashamed of herself, because she considered herself above silliness. It was a shock to know how far Christopher would go to impress her, and more of a shock to realize that she was loving every moment of it.

Unexpectedly, Christopher curled her hand inward until her knuckles were crushing the tiny pleats of his dress shirt. Involuntarily, Jacqui looked up at him and found his dark eyes looking down at her with electrifying intensity.

"Don't do this to me, Christopher," Jacqui gasped in a strangled voice.

"What?" he asked, his sensuous mouth teasing her.

"Make me feel something—"

"Why shouldn't you be as miserable as I am?" he laughed, softly, then kissed her forehead.

"Oh, Christopher," Jacqui sighed, forgetting the weeping clarinet and the tinkling piano of the band. "You are a very attractive man, and I'm flattered by your attention more than you can know, but the time just isn't right."

"When will it be?" Christopher demanded, exasperation in his voice.

"When—when Egret Island is finished," she told him, off the top of her head.

"All right," he agreed in a tone that told her that he was going to hold her to those words as though they were a contract. His eyes flicked from hers to another point in the room, conveying some signal, and then fixing on hers again. "We'll get Egret Island out of the way first. By then I'll have had plenty of time to think up ways to persuade you."

As the last note of music died in the darkened room, Jacqui sighed, unable to take her attention from Christopher's face. "The party's over," she said.

"Never!" Christopher said. He turned her toward a door which led to the broad, palm-lined patio which led to the pool.

"Don't you have to close up?" Jacqui asked.

"It's all taken care of," he said, as the last of the lights went out behind them. "That's why I'm the boss."

They walked slowly toward the open stairway which led toward the double suite, Christopher's arm draped carelessly around her shoulders. With his free hand, he pointed to a lighted window on the second floor.

"The girls are still up, huh?" Jacqui asked.

"Probably waiting to share all sorts of gory details with you," he said, then chuckled.

"Gory details?" Jacqui asked. "I don't think there are any, are there? Besides, I could never tell Janice—or Alaine—anything that took place between us."

Christopher paused at the foot of the flight of stairs, while Jacqui lifted the front hem of her gown so that she would not trip over it, then he put his hand under her elbow to help her negotiate the steps in her high-heeled sandals. "You don't look like the type who would kiss and tell," he said with a note of humor oddly coloring his words.

Jacqui nearly choked trying to control laughter that would carry in the stillness of the night. "I wouldn't know how?"

"How to tell, my dear? Or how to kiss?" Christopher asked. When they reached the top of the stairs, he took her into his arms. "Maybe I can give you something to open the discussion with."

"Christopher," she muttered before his lips crushed hers. Flustered, she tried to pull away from him. "Really, Christopher."

"Really, Christopher?" he mimicked.

"I try to set a good example for Jan—"

"You set an admirable example," he commended, running his hand through her hair, silvered in the moonlight.

"Look, Kyle is behaving himself," Jacqui said. "Why don't you?"

"Obviously Kyle isn't as excited by Alaine as I am by you," Christopher said. His warm fingertips traced a line along her shoulder. "I think that's all the excuses you're entitled to have. Business, Janice, Kyle. Three's the limit."

Jacqui wrenched herself away from him, and in turning toward the door of the suite, noticed the two drinks on the umbrella table. "What's this?" she asked him.

"Waste not, want not," he said. With a graceful movement, he pulled out the chair for her to sit down. "Let's talk for a few minutes," he suggested.

Jacqui looked up at him warily, as he moved to sit down beside her. "It's late, Chris—"

"Oh, stop being so sensible for once in your life, Jacqui!" he scolded, keeping his voice low. Even so, Jacqui heard a certain note of anger, well concealed. "If people were always completely sensible, there would never be any humor or adventure or romance in the world."

He jerked the end of his tie until the bow fell apart, the sound of the fabric scraping against itself distinct in the quiet of the night. He folded the tie and put it into the pocket of his jacket, then leaned back casually in his chair.

"Sometimes," he said slowly, "I think you've let go a little, but then you turn right around and..."

"I'll confess," Jacqui said, "it has almost nothing to do with my responsibilities to my family or my business. I just can not be comfortable with a casual relationship. I'm afraid it would cause me more pain than a serious love affair that would go wrong. Not that I know much about either."

"I find that hard to believe," Christopher said, covering her hands with his. "You are a very attractive woman."

"Would you believe that I haven't always been attractive?"

"No, I wouldn't."

"I used to be fat. I lost thirty pounds when my parents died, and with Janice's watching almost everything I eat, I've kept it off. Does that shock you?''

"If you hoped to cause me to lose interest in you by your telling me this," Christopher said, "you've failed. Miserably."

"What I wanted to say was that I'm never going to allow myself to get hurt by being fooled into thinking a man is committed to me when all he wants is a fling."

Christopher's chin stiffened, and his mouth became a stern line.

"I—I didn't say that very well," Jacqui stammered.

"You made your meaning quite clear," Christopher said.

"I don't have the hide of a walrus, Chris, and I know it."

He let go of her hands, squared his shoulders, and took a deep breath. She wanted him to say something, but nothing came from the stony mask he presented her.

There seemed to be nothing more to say, nothing more to do, so Jacqui got up from the chair, scraping it on the cement floor of the balcony as little as possible, and went into the darkened suite.

She had just paused in front of the door of Kyle's room when she heard Christopher enter the suite and lock the door behind him. Then she heard the grating noise of the sliding partition closing behind him, and the distant rumbling of Christopher's voice that made the girls' giggling come to an abrupt stop. She had not intended to make him angry, but it was best that they understood each other.

Sighing, she slipped out of her gown and carefully hung it in the closet, deciding to put on her robe while she brushed her hair. Leave it to Janice to bring along the blue satin wrapper that had been tucked away in tissue in the bottom of her dresser for two years. Janice had at times asked her what she was saving it for, and had apparently thought this must be the appropriate time for it to surface.

She had only taken a few swipes of her brush through her long blond hair when she lost interest in the project, sitting on a bench before a mirror at a combination dressing table and desk. For a long moment, she stared at her reflection, wondering what Christopher saw in her that he said she did not recognize in herself. Their association had taken some turns in uncharted directions at a breathless speed.

Unbidden, memories of his embrace as they danced came flooding into her mind. There had been a moment when she almost wished that the music would not stop, that the evening would not end, and she wondered now if it was Christopher's dynamic presence or just her own loneliness that prompted these feelings. If only she could recapture . . .

The brush, unheeded in her left hand, clattered to the glossy top of the dressing table. Gritting her teeth, Jacqui picked it up, wondering if the noise had disturbed Kyle, then deciding that Kyle slept much too soundly to be roused by such an insignificant sound.

She was about to look for her nightgown when she heard a soft rustling noise in the hallway and went to the door, thinking that it must be Janice coming to get some silly item that she had forgotten when she had gone to the other side of the suite. Hoping to keep any noise to a minimum for Kyle's sake, she reached to open the door.

Christopher stood in the hallway, his hand poised to knock on her door, a dark and distracted expression on his face.

"I came to apologize," he said slowly. "I hope you'll forgive me for not understanding the—the importance you place on emotional commitment. It's a little rare, given the temper of the times, but—"

Touched by the humanity in his face in the dim light coming from her room, Jacqui smiled at him. "I was pretty hard on you, too," she said. "I'm sorry."

"Would you mind if I—ah—said good night to you

in a more appropriate way than the way we just left each other?'' he asked, his occasional sighs as he spoke opening the half-buttoned evening shirt he still wore and showing the dark mass of hair on his chest.

"I—ah—" Jacqui said, weakly, not knowing exactly what to expect.

Christopher took her into his arms, holding her gently to the length of his body, then burying his hand in the flaxen fall of her hair. The kiss he insinuated on her lips held nothing of the pride or arrogance or domination he had expressed before.

Almost with a will of their own, Jacqui's arms went around his waist, her hands moving over the fine fabric of his shirt, assessing the smooth, strong muscles beneath. Christopher's hand moved up and down her spine, causing her heart to race and her skin to tingle.

"You're not wearing anything under your robe," Christopher observed.

"No," Jacqui affirmed, unconcerned, her eyes closed, willing herself to prolong the moment, to absorb each new sensation of his closeness.

The tightening embrace lifted Jacqui to her tiptoes and Christopher blazed kisses down her throat to the cleavage between her swelling breasts. Jacqui was shocked by her own wanton desire for him not to stop when he reached the edge of her robe. But as she felt him fumbling with the sash at her waist, a shred of her resistance surfaced.

"Chris," she whispered.

"What?" he asked, straightening his head to return to the hollow of her throat.

"Not just yet," she said softly, settling back on her feet.

"Does that imply—sometime?" Christopher asked. But before Jacqui could answer, he was working his powerful persuasion on her lips.

Sometime. Jacqui considered the word. *Oh, yes, definitely sometime.* As his kisses blurred the sharp edges of her reasoning, she was only vaguely aware that there were problems that stood in the way of her abandoning all her principles and allowing him to carry her into her bedroom and make wild, impassioned love.

"Jacqui, you are so beautiful," Christopher mumbled, shattering her fantasy before she had fully explored it.

All Jacqui could be certain of was that she had never been as exquisitely happy as she was at this moment, clinging to Christopher, wanting him more than she had ever imagined she could desire any man.

The opening of a door seemed far away, as did the sound of someone clearing his throat.

"And what is going on here?" Kyle demanded.

Christopher drew his mouth away from hers, but did not slacken his arms to allow Jacqui from his embrace. "I am saying a proper good night to your sister," he said, with more composure than Jacqui could have thought possible at that moment.

"Just how proper?" Kyle asked. "So that I will know how I can treat *your* sister?"

"I'm just leaving," Christopher said, allowing Jacqui finally from his arms.

There was no humor either in Christopher's face, nor in Kyle's. Frozen in her tracks, Jacqui watched as Christopher retreated through the hallway. She should be angry at Kyle, but somehow she did not have the energy or the inclination. He returned to his room, closing the door with neither a slam nor an attempt at noiselessness.

When Jacqui finally slept that night, she had exhausted every memory of the evening in a fruitless attempt to understand her innermost feelings.

"How are you going to top this celebration when you get through your other tests and are certified?" Alaine asked, as they sat around the umbrella table after a morning dip the next day.

"If and when I pass my test," Kyle said, then waggled his thumb toward his bronzed chest, "I'll throw the party."

Jacqui shifted uneasily in her chair and draped a damp towel over her shoulders, conscious of Christopher's attention boring into her from across the table. "You'll throw the party?" she asked Kyle. "Exactly what do you have in mind, and how much of it do you plan on me doing?"

Kyle laughed and stretched out in his chair. "I thought we'd take everybody up to Red Key and have a cookout."

"We haven't been there since—" Jacqui said, then bit her lower lip.

"Since Dad and Mom drowned," Janice said, her eyes suddenly skittering away to the horizon of palms and sea.

Kyle's smile died on his lips. "You don't like the idea?" he asked.

"It stinks!" Janice countered.

Jacqui swallowed hard. "It's about time we went to look at our property up there," she said, directing her remark to Janice.

"You have property at Red Key?" Christopher asked, suddenly interested in more than staring at her.

"Ten acres," Jacqui said. "More or less, depending on the tides and currents. Dad bought it very cheaply and expected to develop it one day."

"It's beautiful up there," Kyle said, his wistfulness taking the edge off his enthusiasm.

"Personally, I don't want to go," Janice said, a pout beginning on her lower lip.

"Well, sis, you don't have to go," Kyle told her firmly. "The rest of us will go up there, catch some crabs, and have a feast."

Janice got to her feet, almost tipping the chair over behind her. Without a word, she ran down the steps and dove into the pool.

"Is she upset?" Alaine asked.

"She'll be all right!" Kyle said with a wave of his hand. "There are little things each of us has to face and this is hers."

"Maybe we shouldn't go to Red Key," Jacqui said, not wanting to cause Janice any pain. "Maybe Bayport or—someplace else."

Kyle took a deep breath and looked up at the azure sky above them. "We can't just avoid Red Key. We own a big chunk of land, and we should check on it every year, but we've been avoiding it like a toothache. We have to deal with that. If on one hand we go there just to take a look, we'll have problems with our memories. But if we go to celebrate my certificate and take someone with us—"

"He's got a very sound idea there," Christopher ventured gently.

Alaine looked from Kyle to Janice, who was slicing through the blue waters of the pool. "I think I'll go back into the pool," she said.

"Good idea," Kyle agreed, following her, his long legs quickly catching up to her.

Christopher watched after them, then slipped into the chair beside Jacqui, acting as though he had moved so that he could watch the activity in the pool. Almost predictably, he leaned his muscular shoulders back in the chair and stretched an arm across the back of Jacqui's chair, calculatedly allowing his hand to graze the back of her neck.

"You're not sold on going up to Red Key, are you?" he asked.

"It's something we have to do," Jacqui told him.

"That doesn't answer my question," he said. "You aren't going to answer it either, are you? See, I'm beginning to understand how you think. You just do what you have to do, whether you feel like it or not, huh?"

"Pretty much." She looked from him out into the Gulf. "There's a house plan I look at, and think how nice it would be to build it up there. But when it comes down to—"

"Your folks drowned up there?" Christopher asked.

The breath that Jacqui took stung the back of her throat. "The boat was found about three miles out," she said. "The Gulf can get choppy without a lot of warning, and Dad wasn't a very good seaman."

"I'm so sorry," Christopher said, his quiet sympathy cutting through the discomfort of the grief she had never really allowed herself to feel.

"I really don't want to discuss it," Jacqui sighed.

Christopher shrugged. "This house you'd like to build," he said. "Tell me about it."

Jacqui cleared her throat and looked back at him. "You really want to talk houses?"

"It's a safe topic, isn't it," he asked, "compared to, say, what Kyle might have said about that episode last night?" His eyebrow turned upward briefly.

"He never said a word this morning," she told him.

He smiled, then encouraged her, "What's this dream house like?"

"It's designed around a skylighted studio—"

"That sounds different."

"Oh, not so different. I want a stone fireplace with a raised hearth, flanked by floor-to-ceiling bookcases with space for seashell collections and my mother's paperweights." Jacqui was suddenly aware that she could not talk about houses without using her hands to express space and contour, and became self-conscious. "I get carried away," she said, apologetically.

"Go on," Christopher urged. "What else?"

"Lots of windows, overlooking water—"

"Of course!"

As they talked, Jacqui could almost believe in her plans, just as she could almost believe Christopher was as enraptured by her dream as his attentive gray eyes suggested.

Chapter Nine

"Miss Belpre," the gentleman said, waving his hand toward the brochures she had spread out on the model house's dining table for him and his wife, "this is all very impressive and very attractive, but we do have an appointment with another builder to compare figures."

Jacqui could not ignore the feeling of disappointment in the pit of her stomach. But she fought against allowing any sign of her feelings to reach her face. "Why, of course," she forced herself to say as evenly as though she had twenty other contracts pending and this one meant nothing to the survival of the firm. "After all, this involves a considerable sum of money, and you must be satisfied with your investment. I like working with people who are careful with their money."

"May we take all these brochures with us?" his wife asked.

"By all means," Jacqui said. "I'll get you a folder to keep them in so you will have all the figures right in front of you."

When she watched them leave, she chewed on her lower lip. The couple got into their car, looking one last time at some particular detail of the outside of the house, then backed out of the parking area.

Jacqui's attention was drawn to Chesterfield's model, where a sheriff's car sat in the driveway, its red and blue lights flashing on top. As she watched, Dorothea Grace drove into Chesterfield's parking area and hurried into the model, her portfolio clutched under her arm.

"Yvonne!" Jacqui called. "Something is going on over at Chesterfield's." She tried in vain to get a better view.

"I suppose we'll just have to wait until it's all sorted out," Jacqui said, then went back to straightening up the brochures on the dining table.

"I take it that Mr. and Mrs. Bush have not decided on signing a contract yet," Yvonne said, pausing before going back to her office and her account books.

"They want to check with another builder," Jacqui said, her statement dangerously near sounding like a complaint.

"Did they say who?" Yvonne asked.

"Obviously no one here on Signal Drive," Jacqui said.

Yvonne made a face and shrugged. "They are definitely not casual traffic, but I don't know who they would go to besides the builders here on Signal."

"I can't worry about that," Jacqui said, looking at her watch. "I'm going to have to leave for Egret Island in a few minutes, and I'm dying of curiosity about Chesterfield's."

She had just given up the wait and reached for her tube of plans when the front door of the model opened and, breathlessly, Dorothea came in, her face pale and her hair uncharacteristically disheveled.

"Jacqui, darling, you will never guess," she started, then sank to the nearest chair.

"Well, I saw the sheriff's car and yours," Jacqui said. "Yvonne, could you get Dorothea a cup of coffee? She looks like she needs it."

"Everything was taken, stolen—stolen!" Dorothea was saying, between shuddering deep breaths. "Except for the drapes and carpet. The silk flower centerpieces, the plastic ferns in the hanging baskets in the baths, for heaven's sakes! That lemon-yellow velvet couch that I practically based the whole scheme on! Gone! All the work I did. I tell you, Jacqui, this has never been just a job to me, but a fulfilled fantasy of having house after house perfect and beautiful, so people could move right in and live comfortably, with an uplifted heart, because they can see beauty all around them...."

Dorothea accepted the coffee from Yvonne with a heavy sigh.

"Chesterfield's insurance will cover the loss, won't it?" Jacqui asked. "I know ours would."

Dorothea sipped her coffee, then put it on the end table and leaned back in the chair. "Of course," she said, stroking her forehead with a surprisingly frail hand. "But they want me to redo the house by the end of the week. Can you guess how much business they will lose in a week without furniture in that house?"

"I can only sympathize so much," Jacqui said, making an attempt to squelch her smile. "They get about five contracts a week, and I'm lucky if I get that many in a month. They can just send a few people over here."

Dorothea looked at her for a moment, then smiled. "You're right, of course. It's an ill wind that blows no one any good."

"But, then, it could have been this model that was burglarized," Jacqui reminded herself, aloud. "No, no! The thieves would rather have seen your work than mine in some fancy house."

"There is talk of it being—an inside job," Dorothea almost whispered.

"Nonsense," Jacqui scoffed. "All their people are fine, upstanding—"

"Of course they are," Dorothea said. "But think about this. Whoever did this must know something about the business."

Jacqui stared at Dorothea for a long moment, then shook her head. "I just can't take it all in," she said.

Dorothea took another swallow of her coffee. "Also the sheriff said that he wants to see all the guest books from the Parade of Homes until yesterday."

Yvonne, who was still lounging in the doorway, straightened up. "I may as well run off a photocopy of our book so it's ready for him," she said.

"I thought it was bad that the sites were being stripped clean," Jacqui sighed, "now the model homes."

"I was in Hawkins' Appliances Saturday, and Mr. Hawkins told me that he had a whole house installed, everything, including a trash compactor, and someone took it all. I tell you, Jacqui, it is really frightening," Dorothea said.

"It certainly is! It sounds as though someone is trying to put a whole house together—furniture, appliances…"

Dorothea seemed to recover her composure, then smiled. "How are you doing, Jacqui?" she asked. "How was your weekend at Leisure Discovery?"

"Very nice," Jacqui answered, wondering how much Janice had told her.

"And how was Christopher Warden?" she asked, pointedly.

"He was a perfect gentleman," Jacqui said.

"Well, that's no fun!" Dorothea laughed.

"Should I say 'nearly perfect'?" Jacqui amended, remembering his good night kiss.

Dorothea raised an eyebrow and a satisfied smile moved across her mouth. "It's too bad you don't have a mother like I did, who kept track of half the eligible men in Atlanta in her mind, pairing them off with the girls she thought they would be best suited to. My! She would have the two of you married and on a honeymoon in the Bahamas before you knew what had happened to you."

Jacqui smiled at the thought before she could mask her reaction.

The phone had rung, and now Yvonne interrupted them by calling Jacqui back to her office.

"I'll run along," Dorothea said, getting to her feet, but she was clearly reluctant to end the conversation. "Thanks for the shoulder."

"Call me later in the day," Jacqui advised, moving toward the phone. "I want to know that you are all right."

"Oh, I'll be sure to," Dorothea said, leaving with a pleased expression.

"This is Jacqui," she said into the phone, as Dorothea closed the front door behind her.

"This is Hathaway in the county office," the gruff voice came back. "I wanted to get in touch with Kyle to tell him that I'll have to move his next test up two weeks. I'll be out of town for an extended period after that."

Jacqui groaned and reached for a pencil and a pink message slip. Poor Kyle, she thought.

KYLE RAN A HAND through his sweat-tangled curls when she gave him the message from Hathaway. "Well," he sighed, smiling uncertainly, "I'll get the test out of the way that much sooner, and you'll be getting a full day's work out of me every day."

"That's not my major consideration," Jacqui told him, leaning back against the ragged trunk of a palm tree on Egret Island. "I just want to see you get that certificate."

"You don't think that he is trying to wash me out by making the tests closer together, do you?" Kyle asked. "He didn't mention anything to you about accusing me of cheating, did he?"

"I think he would know better than to say anything like that," Jacqui laughed. "How is the inside framing going?"

"Fine. Dowling's keeping a tight hand on his men. He has a very different attitude than Cletus Garwood has, but he gets good work out of them."

"Oh! By the way, Chesterfield's model was burglarized last night," Jacqui told him. "All Dorothea's lovely decorating, except the drapes and carpets."

"No!" Kyle gasped. Then he grinned. "It couldn't happen to a nicer guy."

"Kyle!" Jacqui scolded.

"All right. I know. It could have been us," Kyle said, shrugging apologetically. "But can you just imagine? I'll bet that yellow couch glowed in the dark!"

In spite of her exasperation with Kyle, she had to laugh. Kyle could always seem to cut through the gloom to some bright spot.

"What's the joke?" Christopher Warden asked, coming from his golf cart.

"It's not really funny," Jacqui told him, but was not able to hide part of her amusement. "You know, I told you some weeks ago that some of the sites have had, oh, lumber, blocks, roofing paper and so on stolen? Well, one of the model houses was picked clean of its furniture last night. And Dorothea, my friend the decorator was telling me that someone had taken all the appliances from a house recently."

Christopher stroked his chin, then looked toward the structure of the cottages. "I was going to slack off the patrols of the project because one of my security men is leaving," he said, concerned, "but now I think I'll try to leave this schedule the way it stands. What do you think someone would take next?"

"How should I know!" Jacqui exclaimed. "It would seem that, if they are going after the silk-flower centerpieces, they must have the place pretty well finished."

"They just may," Christopher laughed. "Nonetheless—"

"It has to be more than one person," Kyle said. "I wouldn't be surprised if they got greedy and started all over again."

Someone in the structure of the cottages called to

Kyle to come inspect some work, so he excused himself to be on about his business.

Jacqui and Christopher eyed each other warily for a moment, then his mouth curled in a hesitant smile. "How about lunch today?" he asked.

"I'd love to, Chris," she told him. "But you fed me too well this weekend. Besides, I do have to get back to the office."

"I'd settle for a short walk on the beach."

Jacqui looked at him sympathetically, not unaffected by his presence, his crisp white shirt covering solid, tanned flesh, light blue trousers accentuating the long muscular legs developed by jogging and sets of tennis. "I wish I could," she sighed. "But, look, I do have some good news. Kyle is going to take his test in two weeks instead of four, so you're that much closer to being our guest up at Red Key."

"I'm looking forward to it," Christopher said, his grin wide and friendly, making Jacqui's heart thump oddly in her chest.

"So am I," she admitted.

"But I hope that is not going to be the next time I see you," he went on.

"Oh, no," Jacqui laughed. "You'll have to put up with me flitting around here a lot between now and then. Oh, there is something I have to discuss with you. With the housing construction taking a slide, I'm not having to schedule around other projects as much as I had planned into the schedule. We are already one day ahead of schedule, and we could be as much as four days ahead when your next payment is due. Now, if you can arrange to make the payments by the completion of the actual work stages, rather then the dates that we have set up, it would be a big help, because the good prices I am giving you are based on cash discounts for supplies, and I don't have the funds from houses to back up as much of my budget as I thought I would have."

"I don't understand a thing that you are saying, but you are so pretty when you say it that I have to believe you," Christopher grinned.

"Don't make me explain it all to you again," she pleaded.

"Darling, I understood every word, and I agree with you," Christopher laughed. "Why don't you just cut through all the rhetoric and say you have a cash-flow problem."

"I have a cash-flow problem," Jacqui said, then laughed.

"So do I," he confessed without a shadow of concern in his eyes. "But I'm sure I can work out my problem very easily, and I promise not to make you wait a day more than you have to."

"Good to hear that!" Jacqui said, taking off her hard hat as she started toward her car. "You're a joy to do business with!"

"Hey! You're forgetting something!" Christopher said, jogging a few steps to catch up to her.

Rattled, Jacqui checked the tube of plans in her hand and glanced toward the ground where she had been standing. "What?" she asked, baffled.

Putting one hand on her shoulder, Christopher bent to kiss her cheek, an uncomplicated, feather-soft, almost brotherly kiss. "That," he said, pleased with himself.

Then he looked back over his shoulder to see if anyone was watching them. Apparently satisfied, he pulled her energetically into his arms and pressed his lips on hers. Before she could steel herself against the unexpected expression of his affection, Jacqui realized that she was kissing him back. It was Christopher who broke off. Almost as abruptly as the kiss began, it was over, leaving Jacqui off balance, wanting more.

The suntanned hand that had been resting possessively on her shoulder moved along her throat to caress her cheek. Christopher's expression implied an understanding, thrilling her to some secret place inside her.

With a touch of nervousness, Jacqui laughed, remembering how upset she had been with him when he had kissed her in the boardroom. It would take her half the distance back to the office of Osprey Builders to figure out why she was not so angry with him this time. If Yvonne noticed the slightly distracted look in her eyes when she returned to the model, nothing was said.

Smiling, Yvonne looked up from her desk and said, "Mr. and Mrs. Bush called to say that they will be coming back around one o'clock to sign a contract."

Jacqui extended one hand with a carrying tube in it, and the other with her hard hat clutched tightly, toward the ceiling. "Hallelujah! We may be able to make the payroll after all!"

IT WAS THE FIRST TIME Jacqui had taken the time to look at the house plans Alexis Warden had sent to her, and as she spread the floorplan out on the drawing board in the bedroom, she immediately spotted some problems. The house was designed for the northern climates, with two stories and an extensive heating system.

"Oh, this won't do," she said to herself, reaching for a scratchpad on which to figure square footage to find a cost estimate.

Janice stuck her head in the open door. "What are you doing?" she asked, coming into the room and looking over Jacqui's shoulder.

"I'm looking over plans for the house Alexis Warden wants to build."

Janice studied the floorplans for a long moment. "I like the kitchen, with the island sink and rangetop in the middle of the room like that," she said at last. "She must like to entertain."

Jacqui looked at her sister, and back at the plans. "Then I'm afraid she'll be disappointed moving down here, to a place where there aren't many neighbors. I hate to see things like that happen, you know—"

"It's their money, not yours," Janice said with a shrug.

"It still reflects on the builder if he builds more house than is advisable," Jacqui said.

Janice turned away from the drawing board. "Have you a minute to talk?"

"Of course," Jacqui said, leaning back in her chair.

"Well, Lisa's a little put out of joint because she says I talk about Alaine all the time."

"Well," Jacqui asked, "don't you?"

"Maybe. But Alaine goes to another school, and— Jacqui, has something like this ever happened to you? I mean, Lisa usually talks about herself constantly, and now I have something to talk about, she's jealous."

"That may be," Jacqui said, "but you have to be civil, Jan. You and Lisa have been friends for several years and have another year to go before you both graduate. Alaine will be graduating in a matter of weeks, and she's planning on going back north to college. I'd advise you to make peace with Lisa, because she'll probably be around here a lot longer than Alaine will be."

"But I don't want to have to choose," Janice wailed. "Why can't Lisa just accept the fact that she is not my one and only friend? She's got other friends and boyfriends, but she expects me to spend all my time listening to her problems and her bragging, and she doesn't want to listen to me."

Jacqui looked at Janice sympathetically. "I've never had a problem like yours," she confessed. "I never had any close friends because I had to take care of you after school. But there ought to be something.... Yes, you know, Dorothea was telling me today—like she always seems to—that we need a mother to talk to. Why don't you talk to her about this? I'll bet she could help you out, because her family was very social when she was a girl. I'll bet she has just the right solution."

"Dorothea?" Janice moaned, drawing the word out with each syllable.

"Believe it or not, she can give you a lot of good advice."

"But she's so old. . . ."

Jacqui laughed. "I'm young, and I don't have any magic ideas for you."

"Besides, she's in quite a state over that model being ransacked."

"Yes, I know."

"But if you think she could help me, I'll see her after school tomorrow." Janice took another look at the house plans. "Are you going to build that just as it is?"

"I doubt it," Jacqui said, then laughed. "When did I ever build a house the way the plans came out of the tube?"

"I don't know," Janice said. "Have you ever?"

"I can't say that I remember," Jacqui laughed.

KYLE'S PATIENCE had gotten extremely thin while he crammed for his final construction tests, putting Jacqui on edge just to talk with him or see him across the dinner table. It did not help her to know that there was no new contract for a house after the Bushes signed theirs, and the cash-flow problem verged on the critical.

"One more day!" she told herself as she eased the Beast into its place on Signal Drive. Kyle would take his test tomorrow, and with any luck they would be spending Sunday at Red Key, lying in the sun and eating freshly caught crabs. The picture brightened further when she thought of Christopher.

Yvonne Halpern was already hard at work on her books, pointing to figures with a sharp-pointed pencil and shaking her graying head. "Jacqui, I think we are in danger of being overdrawn here," she said, her dejection as real as if she was looking over her personal account.

"By how much?" Jacqui asked, leaning over the books.

"A lot!" Yvonne told her.

"What do we have outstanding that we could call in?" Jacqui asked.

"You don't want to know!" Yvonne said with a twisted grin.

"Egret Island? Is Chris Warden behind?"

"The date of his next payment, according to the schedule, is Tuesday," Yvonne pointed out, in another ledger. "But according to Kyle, the work covered by that payment was finished yesterday, so—"

"And his payment would cover a large part of what we are short?" Jacqui asked.

"I think that we can juggle things around," Yvonne said, "to make the payroll and everything but the insurance on the vehicles, which isn't due until next Friday, but I like to send everything that has to go through the mail at least a week early. We could wait until... maybe Tuesday for that."

Jacqui studied the figures once more as Yvonne put them all in order on her scratchpad, marveling that Yvonne had the ability to add large numbers in her head, without the use of a calculator.

"So," she sighed at last, when the inevitable became clear, "I have to go crawling to Christopher Warden today and beg for our money, or we're in deep trouble. Look, Yvonne, take only twenty out for my pay this week. We have plenty of groceries and all my bills are paid up. I think we can get by."

"I could get by with a little less this week," Yvonne offered.

"No! No, Yvonne, you earn every penny of your salary, and I'm not going to touch it, or Kyle's, for that matter."

"Really, Jacqui, it wouldn't matter this once."

"Not another word," Jacqui said forcefully. "And I want to see your check when you write it out.

You're not going to pull any fast ones on me."

"That doesn't mean that I can't wait until next week to cash it!" Yvonne countered triumphantly.

"You're impossible!" Jacqui said, with a wave of her hand. "And I love you for it."

"You have to help lay out the lot for Bushes' house this morning," Yvonne reminded her. "The guys were over there yesterday afternoon, and said that there has to be a choice made as to which trees are cut."

"Oh, that's right! Well, that gives me some time to get up my courage to talk to Christopher Warden," Jacqui said.

She went into her office and grabbed up the plans for the house she was about to lay out, dug a fresh bandana from her purse, and headed back out to the Beast. Thoughts of Christopher Warden could be forced aside with the contemplation of how the house the Bushes had chosen was going to look on the wooded lot they had bought in an area of live oaks and tall pines.

Jacqui enjoyed driving through that particular plan even as much as she enjoyed the area where her model was. She only wished that there were more houses going up, because she could be sure, then, of having a constant flow of contracts. Here and there men working on houses turned and waved to her as she passed, and she responded by playing the horn, a special one that Kyle had installed in the car, today set on "Oh, What a Beautiful Morning."

She spotted her men on the lot as they drove stakes where the house would be built. This was a preliminary to deciding which trees had to be cut down and how much of the earth had to be dug up and leveled before the sterile sand would be laid and the outline of the foundation would be re-staked for the pouring of the cement foundation.

Jake Henderson and Mel Price were in charge of this phase of her construction company, and it never ceased to amaze Jacqui at the amount of care Jake took in positioning a house. He seemed to have, through his many years, acquired a precise knowledge of how much root system could be cut away from a tree and yet it would survive.

Now he held the rough plan of the house in one hand and scratched the back of his neck with the other. "Jacqui, we have to either take that big tree out over there, or those little ones there, but I refuse to cut that little sweet gum tree over there. It is the first one I've seen in this block."

Jacqui squinted at the sapling in question, barely six feet tall. "Is that a valuable tree?" she asked, not having run into this problem before.

"If Manuel were around, he'd landscape his whole garden around that tree," Jake told her.

"So, what do you suggest?" Jacqui asked, unrolling her plans and looking again at the terrain.

"I'd sacrifice the little trees," he said, but something in his tone told Jacqui that to uproot anything would be against his principles.

"Let's see what we can come up with," Jacqui said, motioning for Mel and Jake to remeasure the space.

They had started from scratch a second time when Mr. and Mrs. Bush drove up in their sleek little white car. Mr. Bush alighted, wearing white shorts and a printed shirt, typically tourist with a camera swinging from his neck.

"We thought we'd like to take a shot of the lot before you start to clear it," he sang out.

"Perfect!" Jacqui called back to him. "I was just going to go back to the office and call you. We're having a little trouble positioning this house without losing these little trees here."

The buyers of the house listened to Jake's explanation of the problem attentively but without any great concern. Finally, Mrs. Bush pointed her finger at the plan.

"Why can't you just move the garage forward as many feet as you need to save the sweet gum tree and still leave the little trees?'' she asked Jacqui.

"That would be beautiful, if you would approve it,'' Jacqui said. "The only adjustment would be that it would make the house cost a little more to build, for that amount of extra outside wall surface.''

Mr. and Mrs. Bush looked at each other, communicating in some way that only people who have been happily married a great number of years can understand, then nodded to Jacqui in a rhythmic unison. "Go ahead and do it,'' Mr. Bush said, putting his arm around his wife's shoulders. "She's the boss.''

"I wish all my problems were as easy to solve as this one,'' Jacqui told them. "How many feet are we going to have to move the garage?'' she asked Jake.

"Three, maybe three and a half to give that gum tree a really good chance,'' Jake said. "At that, you still may lose one or two of the little oaks. We can leave them in until the construction is finished and see if they survive.''

"Sounds fine to me,'' Jacqui said. "Let me do some quick figuring here and we'll position the stakes.''

Mr. Bush took the lens cover from his camera, and began shooting pictures while Jacqui adjusted the dimensions of the house. Just as she handed the plans back to Jake, Mr. Bush snapped a picture of her.

"Oh, I must look a mess!'' Jacqui laughed.

"Next to my wife, you're one of the prettiest girls I know,'' Mr. Bush said gallantly. "Now, I'd like you to stand next to her over there so I can get a good picture of you where our living room will be.''

"All right,'' Jacqui consented, amused by people who want to take step-by-step pictures of their houses being built. "But I have to get back to my office and redraft this plan before I forget what we're doing.''

Not only that, she thought to herself, as she smiled for Mr. Bush's camera, but somehow she was going to have to shake some money loose from Christopher Warden so that she could pay her bills by the end of the day.

Chapter Ten

"I know that you're not officially on duty yet," Jacqui said into the phone when Christopher was finally located for her, "but I have a big problem, and you are the only one who can help me."

"That sounds promising," Christopher responded, his Bostonian accent tempered with anticipation. "What is it?"

"Money," she said, bluntly.

"Oh," he said, his voice suddenly flat.

"Chris, I have to come over to Egret Island to check out the work with Kyle," she told him, forging ahead into the unpleasant task ahead of her. "How would it be if I met you on the site in half an hour?"

"I'll be looking forward to it," he answered, and she wondered how he could sound genuinely eager when she felt so apprehensive.

You may be, Jacqui thought to herself as she hung up the phone, *but I am not.*

Kyle braced his heavy boot against a tree stump and listened to Jacqui carefully as she told him all the figures she and Yvonne were juggling. "If you're taking only twenty dollars this pay, cut mine back, too," Kyle advised her. "Everything is taken care of, isn't it?"

"Well, I didn't know—" Jacqui stammered. "I don't know your affairs and—"

"I could get by," Kyle told her. "After all, after tomorrow, I'm going to be management, too."

"Well, you aren't just yet!" Jacqui reminded him, trying to treat the matter lightly.

"I could get by with less than a full paycheck this week," Kyle told her, "so long as we can straighten things out by next Friday, when I have a payment due on my motorcycle."

"It really is just a drop in the bucket, though," Jacqui told him.

They both turned quickly to see Christopher standing by, near enough to hear their discussion. Jacqui was momentarily distracted by his composed, confident virility. He was not yet dressed for working, clad in slacks and a knit shirt, both in pale blue.

His expression told her that he knew exactly what the problem was, and he was having problems of his own. "I take it that you want the payment that was scheduled for next week," he said.

Kyle straightened up and wiped his hands on the sides of his jeans. "The framing is complete, Chris," he said, with a wave toward the structure. "The county inspector was just here to confirm this stage is finished, and I have electricians standing by to start the wiring."

"How would it be if you show me yourself that the work is done?" Christopher asked. "You people don't mind showing off your work, do you?"

"Not at all," Kyle said, breaking into a proud grin, leading him into the shell of the building. Jacqui tagged along, occasionally making a mental note of something she did not like or had a question about.

Christopher seemed to be stalling, stopping to talk to the electrical installers as they measured partitions and distributed boxes of coiled wire in the units.

On the balcony of the highest level units, Jacqui paused and looked out at the water beyond the palm trees and scrubby palmetto of the island. Christopher, satisfied by the tour, came out of the unit and stood beside her for a moment, looking off into the distance. The deep breath he took expanded the pale blue shirt across his chest, and then he braced himself against the railing of cement blocks.

"I'm satisfied that the work is done to the point covered in the contract," he said, directing his remark to Kyle, who was wiping sweat from his forehead with his bandana. "Let's go back over to my office and I'll see what I can do to find some money to pay you."

We're in trouble here, Jacqui told herself, looking up into Christopher's veiled gray eyes. He resisted looking directly at her.

"Jacqui, you can handle this, huh?" Kyle said, stuffing his bandana back into his hip pocket. "I want to get the electricians started."

"Yes, you go along," Jacqui said. "I can handle this." Brave words!

"Kyle," Christopher stopped him, as he started down the steps to the lower levels, "if I don't see you again today, good luck on your tests tomorrow."

Kyle grinned and made a wave of his hand. "Thanks. We'll pick you and Alaine up at ten Sunday morning," he promised. "Bring your swimsuits."

Jacqui turned back to view the Gulf, and Christopher took one lingering last look with her. "You really did know what you were doing when you designed this project," he told her.

"You can believe that if it makes you feel better," Jacqui laughed. "Actually, I have nightmares that I'm in over my head. Way over."

Christopher smiled down at her, and she felt a twinge in her shoulder that she had almost forgotten existed.

"I—ah—of course, designed from the outside looking in," she said, forcing her mind to function on business, not on the memory of his strong arms wrapping around her in the still of the night. "But it does impress a person looking from this angle. I can't wait to see how Manuel will landscape the garden."

"This place is beautiful in the moonlight," he told her, "even without being finished."

"Chris, back to business," Jacqui suggested, as much for herself as for him. She turned and started back down the flight of stairs.

Christopher followed close behind her. "Aunt Alexis called and asked me to check with you on those plans she sent you. Have you had time to study them?"

"Yes, I did," Jacqui told him, glad to get onto an impersonal topic. "I've got them on my drawing board at home, actually."

"What do you think?" he asked, eagerly.

"Interesting, but they aren't suitable to Florida without some major redesigning," Jacqui said, cautiously picking her way past a pile of debris.

"Then make the changes," Christopher suggested.

"It's not that easy," Jacqui told him, taking off her hard hat, now that they were clear of the structure. "First of all, I have no real assurances of the contract, and second, I'd have to have a really long face-to-face conference with your aunt to be sure that the plans meet her requirements, and, third, I haven't seen the site she has in mind."

"I'd say that pretty well covers it," Christopher said, then laughed at her thoroughness.

"Yes, it does," Jacqui agreed. For a smart business-man he knew very little about construction and con-tracting, she realized.

"I could take you out to see the property," Christopher offered willingly. "Sometime next week? It's a beautiful piece of land. Uncle Charles bought it years ago when he was down here for a vacation. They both fell in love with the area, and then he started moving the business down here. Discovery is going to be the corporate headquarters in a matter of months."

Jacqui shrugged. "Really, though, Christopher, your aunt wants a two-story house, and the cooling problems are going to be horrendous if there aren't a lot of trees around to shade the place and if there isn't a good breeze pattern."

"There are plenty of trees on the property," Christopher assured her. "It depends on where she wants the house built."

"It would be simpler just to redesign the whole thing on one floor," Jacqui told him.

Christopher led her to his golf cart and they whirred across the golf-course cart path to the hotel. Being so close to him, even with all the problems she had on her mind, was a heady experience for Jacqui. She only hoped that she could keep a level head as the hour wore on; otherwise she was going to be in bigger straits than she was already.

In his office Christopher asked his receptionist to have coffee and pastries sent in while he spread ledgers across his neatly appointed desk and ran off figures on his calculator.

Jacqui eyed the plate of pastries a waitress placed in front of her with some dismay, and resigned herself to drinking her coffee.

"Help yourself," Christopher invited, with a nod toward the pastries, while he worked his calculator with one hand and held a place in a column of figures with the other.

"You are a wicked one, Christopher Warden," she teased. "You know very well my old addiction. If I eat one of those gorgeous things, I'll swell up like a puff-fish."

"One or two couldn't possibly hurt," he said. "I imagine you would burn off the calories in the twinkling of an eye, at the rate you wheel and deal. Besides, I like a woman with a little substance, shall we say?"

"You talked me into it," Jacqui sighed, weakening, "but just one."

Christopher punched the total button and grimaced at the figure. Then he sighed and leaned back in his swivel chair. "Jacqui, I'm afraid I can't pay you the full amount today, and worse luck, I don't know that I can give you the rest for—well, the closest I can figure off the top of my head—a week.''

Jacqui closed her eyes and took a deep breath. *I shouldn't have touched this job,* she told herself, *after what Cletus Garwood told me about this firm. I should have ignored the whole thing. What if I lost Osprey Builders over this?*

"Okay," Jacqui said, around the lump in her throat. "How much can you give me?"

Christopher went back to his calculator, a moment later tearing the tape from it and handing it to Jacqui. "What do you think?" he asked.

Jacqui looked at the figure, then studied Christopher's face for a long moment, to see if he was bluffing. Inwardly she groaned. What if he were counting on her being confused, the edges of her professional toughness being blurred by what he hoped was a personal, romantic attachment growing between them? And in that instant she began to doubt his intentions. Maybe he had known there would be a problem like this and had laid the groundwork so skillfully to coerce her into taking delayed payments without her protesting.

But the figure was enough for today, just barely. "All right," she agreed. "This is acceptable. But if we don't get the rest of the payment soon, I'm going to have to stop construction."

"When do you want the rest?" Christopher asked, picking up a pencil.

"The payment was due next Tuesday morning," she reminded him firmly, "according to the original payment schedule."

"Jacqui, can't you give me a little more time?" he pleaded, drumming the pencil on the edge of his desk calendar.

"We have a lot of work scheduled for next week," she explained to him. "Material will be delivered that has to be paid for on the spot, or I don't have the advantage of cash discounts. That's why there are penalties for late payments. Besides, the rains will be starting in earnest soon, and that means half days if we don't have all the outside work done, and windows and doors in."

"I'll see what I can do," Christopher promised her, writing something on a pad before him, then getting to his feet and moving from around the desk to stand directly in front of her. "One thing, though," he said, placing his hand on her shoulder as she got to her feet.

"What?" Jacqui asked, becoming tense with his touch.

"This Sunday," he said. "We're not even going to think about this problem, are we? We'll not spoil Kyle's celebration by talking business, hm?"

"I wouldn't think of it," she agreed brightly, forcing herself to smile.

"In the meantime I'm going to talk to Uncle Charles and my father and see if there is any way we can expedite this matter. Just wait here a minute while I have my bookkeeper make out a check."

He started to turn away. "Chris."

"Yes?"

"I'm tempted to give you until Friday," Jacqui said, "but I want you to realize that it will put me in a real bind."

"I understand that," he said. "I'll do everything I can to get the money before then."

"All right," Jacqui said, but she was still apprehensive.

JACQUI TOOK THE PICNIC CHEST DOWN from the shelf in the garage and dusted off the cobwebs with a rag, trying not to think of the last time it had been used. She had spent two weeks trying to put her misgivings about returning to Red Key into some nether region of her subconscious, but they surfaced again as she prepared to hose off the chest and the other picnic paraphernalia.

Clad in a swimsuit, Janice wandered into the garage, a beach towel thrown carelessly over her shoulder. She had been distant for days, and Jacqui was surprised that she came seeking company.

"You're still serious about going up to Red Key?" Janice asked.

"It's what Kyle wants," Jacqui said, turning on the hose into a bucket which already held some detergent.

Janice made a sour face. "I never want to see that place again," she said vehemently.

"I understand that," Jacqui said, and wished that her voice had not sounded so harsh over the splashing of the water into the plastic pail. "But we own that land up there, and I had hoped to build a house for myself up there someday."

"That's stupid," Janice said forcefully. "Aren't you afraid of storms and hurricanes?"

"Of course I am," Jacqui told her.

"If you do build up there, I'll never come to visit you," Janice said, defensively crossing her arms in front of her.

"Is that a threat or a promise?" Jacqui asked, not so sure that she meant it as a joke. Janice's brooding was becoming a strain on the entire household.

"Jacqui! How can you be this way?" Janice demanded, whining.

"Jan, we own that land, and it would be in your own interests to—"

"We don't have to own that land," Janice interrupted impatiently. "You could sell it."

"And who would want to buy it?" Jacqui asked, vigorously attacking the inside of the picnic chest with sudsy water and a scrub brush. "I have no idea what the land is worth right now anyway. It's not a good market."

"Dad used to say that a piece of land is worth what someone is willing to pay for it," Janice said. "That's the sum of what I know about real estate, and it's all I want to know."

Jacqui looked up at her quickly, but decided not to

make an issue of her younger sister's attitude. "What are you going to do while we're gone tomorrow?"

"Denny Behersen is having a pool party, and he invited Lisa and me. It's sort of a hurry-up thing. He just decided on it last night," Janice told her.

"Sometimes those are the best parties," Jacqui said, throwing the scrub brush aside and starting to rinse out the picnic chest. She supposed Denny was harmless enough, and so were the kids who would be at the party. "Do you have to take anything?" she asked.

"I thought I'd make up a double batch of brownies, if that's all right with you," Janice said. "I plan to wait until after you and Kyle leave to bake them."

"Good thinking," Jacqui laughed and turned off the hose. "I take it that you and Lisa are back on friendly terms, then?"

"Yeah," Janice said, without much enthusiasm. "But she really hasn't changed. She still is rather overwhelming and possessive."

Jacqui propped the picnic chest on its side to drain while she thought of several things she could have said about the subject, but Janice had been so touchy lately, she decided against any advice.

"Anyway, I'd feel like a fifth wheel going up to Red Key with you tomorrow," Janice went on. "Kyle has Alaine, and you have Christopher, and—"

"Whoa!" Janice said, facing her sister squarely.

"It's the truth!" Janice defended. "You and Christopher. Alaine and I made a bet. I said I thought it would take quite awhile for you two to get together, but Alaine says that she thinks it will be the end of June."

"That is a terrible thing to bet on!" Jacqui nearly yelled, scandalized that the girls would be speculating her affairs. "There is nothing but business between Christopher and me."

"Oh, sure. That's not what Kyle told us."

Jacqui set her teeth and clenched her fists. No, don't

overreact, she ordered herself. "I don't want you kids talking about me behind my back. And you are at a good age to learn that you should not interfere in other people's lives. That shows a lack of feeling for the other person's welfare."

"Is it totally lost on you that he is absolutely gorgeous?" Janice demanded, totally ignoring Jacqui's lecture.

"Janice!"

"He's got a fantastic build and that heartbreaking smile...."

"Don't you know that it all means nothing if there isn't something solid behind the facade?" Jacqui asked.

"It is totally lost on you!" Janice restated. "What does it take to impress you?"

Jacqui looked at her sister for a long moment, then coiled the hose around the faucet. "Something I haven't seen in Christopher Warden yet," she said. "Something I can't define."

Janice stared at her with her blue eyes then turned and walked away. It was just as well. Janice had a lot to learn, but she would never accept Jacqui as her teacher. There were some things which only experience could teach.

RED KEY WAS REACHED by a long, almost rickety bridge over a channel, which in this particular year was shallow. The community of fishing boats and the few people who plied them in the Gulf waters clung to the windward fringe of the island, in houses that stood on stout pilings to keep them above the rough seas when the storms whipped the usually placid Gulf of Mexico into a frenzy.

But this day could not have been more perfect, except if the wind had been a little calmer. The four-wheel drive wagon made its way to the northeastern end of the island, through a rough track that was only visible to someone who knew it was there. The Belpre land was on the leeward side of the channel, facing the mainland, its dunes covered with sparse grass and palms arched by the incessant currents of the winds.

Overhead, gulls fought the strong winds on porcelain wings, canopied with a china-blue sky. The luxuriant fronds of the palm trees rustled restlessly, throwing meager, shifting shade in the sand below.

Jacqui lay on her stomach on a beach towel and tried to envision her dream house built on the highest portion of the ten-acre plot that stretched behind her.

The Gulf was choppier than they had expected, but having heard on the radio that small craft warnings would be up, Jacqui had decided to pack hot dogs and buns in case they could not find any crabs to cook in the enamel cauldron which they also brought along.

Jacqui knew without looking that Christopher was about to lie down on the towel beside her, which Alaine had vacated for a walk along the leeward channel with Kyle.

"Do you need suntan lotion?" Christopher asked, lowering himself to the bright woven towel.

"No," Jacqui told him flatly, knowing that she was ruining his opening gambit.

"You picked a really nice day for this," he tried again.

"It was actually Inspector Hathaway who chose the day," Jacqui said, "by scheduling Kyle's test for yesterday."

"You seem to forget Kyle's accomplishment in passing his tests," Christopher reminded her, commanding her attention with the tone of his voice.

"That," Jacqui laughed with a hint of irony in her tone, "was a foregone conclusion."

"Well, be that way if you want to," Christopher said, the steadiness of his gray eyes and the set of his jaw conveying the message that nothing she said was going to discourage him.

"Besides, it's almost too windy and rough to swim," Jacqui observed, tucking a strand of her honey-blond hair into her bandana.

"If I recall correctly," Christopher went on, "you don't much care for swimming anyway, even in a pool."

Jacqui shrugged and plowed the sand with the rough edge of a broken scallop shell she had found within reach. "Kyle was right," she said. "Getting out here was half the battle. Now that we're here, it is hard to understand why we didn't come before. If I could, I'd build my house here. But—"

"But what?" Christopher asked, leaning on his elbows, his chin resting on his interlaced fingers.

"The insurance. The distance from town," she said. "It would make living out here impractical."

"And we have to be practical," Christopher taunted.

"When it comes to money, of course," Jacqui said, then sighed. "We may just as well get rid of this place. With the taxes on it going up and up, it's more of a liability than an asset."

"But I think your father had the right idea," Christopher said, turning from his stomach to his back, then propping himself up on his elbow. "With the natural marina down the shore, it would be perfect to develop. He just didn't buy enough of the land."

Jacqui laughed at his seriousness. "Mom thought it was more than enough. One of the few arguments they ever had was about buying this land. Mom wanted him to buy some land closer to town for some reasons which were perfectly valid to her, but he insisted on this."

"Legally how does it stand?" Christopher asked, drawing squiggly lines in the sand between their beach towels.

"Since I'm the only one who is over twenty-one, I can sell it, but I have to split the proceeds with Kyle and Janice. I don't know if, since Kyle is being recognized in majority for the purposes of his builder's certificate, it carries over into disposing of our parents' estate, but the point would be moot."

"Hm!" Christopher looked up from his sketches in

the sand. "What do you think land out here would go for?" he asked.

"Who cares!" Jacqui said, hopelessly. "No one has money to buy anything now, do they? And what good would it be? You have to use the bridge or the ferry to get over here. Half the time the electricity in the village is chancy. Every bit of food, clothing, or material has to be brought in—except, of course, for the seafood."

"But don't you see, Jacqueline," Christopher said, "there are people who would spend good money to visit a rather primitive place like this? For the fishing and the sailing, if they could be sure their bed was clean, their food was good, and their Scotch was neat!"

"If you are talking hotel, forget it!" Jacqui said. "Heavens, Chris! Do you want to put a hotel on every piece of land you see?"

"How could I?" he laughed. "You've got your sights on putting a house on it!"

Jacqui threw the shard of seashell as far away as she could, watching it land a few yards away with a little kick of sand rising and being blown on with the wind.

"Janice has been asking me questions about the resort business since you stayed at the hotel," he told her. "Where to go to college, what to study. I swear, she and Alaine have traded family businesses."

"That's this month," Jacqui said. "By the end of the summer, Jan will be exploring the possibilities of something else."

"So what?" Christopher asked, tilting his head to one side. "It is something she can make a living at. If you will notice, my family is not in need of charity."

The look Jacqui gave him was dangerous. "Neither is ours," she hissed.

"I didn't mean that it was," Christopher apologized. "It's just that I can see that times are rough for you now, and if I can do something to help you out, I would be glad to. Picture this. A rather exclusive resort, for sailing and fishing enthusiasts, with separate, rustic cottages, and a main building for dining hall, bar, shops—all very much like the old Spanish Main.''

"You're ridiculous!" Jacqui laughed. "Your clientele would have to be super-rich, first of all, and—"

"Who do you think are lining up for reservations on Egret Island?" Christopher asked, causing her to suddenly feel very naive.

"I know very little about your balance sheets and your registry books," Jacqui admitted, "but I say it isn't worth wasting drawing paper on."

"You may be right," Christopher said, suddenly very conciliatory, "but it is something to think about."

Jacqui wrenched her attention away from the intensity with which he was looking at her, and stared off toward Kyle and Alaine, who were strolling along the beach having a heated discussion made unintelligible by the keening of the breeze through the palms.

"I see Alaine just told Kyle that she's decided to go back home to get ready for college," Christopher observed, turning on his stomach again, and supporting himself on his forearm. "She has to make up two courses in summer school."

The wide, abrupt arm motions Kyle was making bespoke his frustration at the news. Suddenly, he grasped Alaine's hand and made a gesture toward himself. When Alaine broke free and started to back away from him, Kyle pulled her into his arms and kissed her forcefully, picking her up off her feet while she flailed against him briefly, then stopped.

Jacqui groaned and turned onto her back so that she could no longer watch them. "Damn!" she exploded, closing her eyes against the silver-white sun and china-blue sky. "He did fall in love with her!"

"Can you blame him?" Christopher said proudly.

"Whose side are you on anyway?" Jacqui demanded. She opened her eyes and turned to squint at him.

Christopher laughed unconcerned. "Kyle's a good, level-headed young man, and Alaine is a sweet, intelligent girl. Just let them solve their own problems."

"Christopher Warden!" Jacqui spouted angrily, jumping to her feet. "A few months ago you were screaming at me to keep Kyle away from her."

"So I was wrong," he conceded with a shrug. "But my concern wasn't a total loss. I met you, didn't I?"

He stood up, his expression turning unexpectedly penetrating as he stared down at her. It took no great experience on her part, luckily, to read what he was thinking as they gazed at each other.

"I've learned that people should be given the latitude to solve their own problems," he told her, his voice soft and controlled, but with an undercurrent that told her she had been wrong to think him incapable of deep emotion. "Kyle and Alaine will work things out for the best."

He leaned closer to her, his hand caressing her cheek, then drawing her mouth to his. His lips held hers with a passion that took her breath away. His arm tightened around her as his kiss deepened, shocking Jacqui in the knowledge of how she reacted to the sensation of his warm, bare flesh touching hers.

Shuddering, she pulled herself free, gulping for air, forcing herself to remember the misgivings she had about his sincerity, how she was afraid that he was using his virility and her loneliness to his own ends, all of them centered on the bottom line of his ledgers.

With all the concentration she could muster, she walked the few steps across the sand to where the Beast stood with his tailgate open, and grabbed up the chambray shirt she had brought along. Thrusting her arms into the sleeves, she felt as though she was retreating into armor.

"What is wrong with you?" Christopher demanded, following her.

"Nothing is wrong with me," Jacqui told him, then felt a devastating twinge in her shoulder as she tried to button her shirt. She gritted her teeth against the pain and turned away, abandoning her attempt to close her shirt.

"Don't tell me that you didn't want me to kiss you," Christopher said, "or that you didn't enjoy it."

She felt ashamed to admit to herself that he had spoken the truth. She had wanted him to kiss her since the moment she had first seen him today, and for one split second, when she had forgotten everything else in her life, she had enjoyed it. There was something about seeing Kyle kiss Alaine with such unselfconscious passion that told her there was a great gnawing void in her life that cried desperately to be filled, and never more impatiently than when she was with Christopher.

Jacqui rummaged through the picnic chest for a can of grape soda she had hidden at the bottom. With great frustration, she tried to grip the can with her left hand and hold it steady enough to pop the top with her right.

"Let me do that for you," Christopher said softly, taking the cold metal can from her trembling fingers. He returned the opened can to her, then took a can of beer from the cooler and motioned toward a grouping of palms further along the beach in the opposite direction of where Kyle and Alaine were.

Jacqui shrugged, but followed him, protesting that the clump of trees and fan-like palmetto scrub had nothing of value to offer.

"But this is much better, don't you think?" he asked, gesturing toward the patch of shade created by the dense foliage. He took her can of soda from her and placed it on the sand beside his can of beer. "Sit down; we have some unfinished business."

"You said we weren't going to talk about business today," she reminded him as he pulled her down to sit beside him.

"Perhaps I should call it unfinished pleasure then," he said, his lips smiling but his eyes smoldering with a passion she thought he had put aside. Before she could say anything, he put his fingers to her lips and cautioned her not to speak. "It couldn't have been my imagination that you didn't exactly fight me off tooth and nail two weeks ago—"

Jacqui took a deep breath and bit her lower lip.

"If it had not been for Kyle interrupting us," Christopher said, "who knows where that would have led."

"Christopher!" she said, unable to contain her exasperation a moment longer.

He smiled at her as though she had said exactly what he had expected her to say. "My spies tell me that all you ever do is build houses. Don't you do anything just for fun?"

"Not anymore," Jacqui said. "In school I liked sports, particularly the type of volleyball we played—we called it killerball. And there was a certain old Chevy that I drove until it blew a rod straight through the motor. Aside from that—"

"I think I know of something a lot better than either of those recreations," Christopher said, his arms surrounding her, forcing her back against the cool, shaded sand. As his kisses grew more insistent, she lost her will to resist him. Her fingers sought the silken strands of his waving hair, the strong, smooth muscles of his shoulders and back.

When Christopher began to explore the soft, full curves of her breasts, Jacqui shuddered convulsively, as though shocked by electricity. Surprised, Christopher rolled slightly away from her, disengaging a leg which had tangled between hers.

"I'm sorry," she said, when she had caught her breath. Struggling to sit up, she righted the top of her old red bikini and clutched her shirt to her defensively.

With a sigh, Christopher sat up and reached for his beer. Still cold, the several swallows he took stung his throat and helped him focus on reality after wandering at will. "I overstepped your limits again, didn't I?" he asked her, tracing the shoulder seam of her shirt with his fingertips. She looked sideways at him, and when she did not say anything, he handed her the can of grape soda. "Did it ever occur to you that I have my limits too?"

"I have no assurances that this is not just a casual affair on your part," Jacqui said. "We've never discussed love—or marriage…."

"To put the record straight, Miss Belpre, we have discussed marriage," Christopher corrected, then took a long swallow of beer to fortify himself. Her surprised and questioning look amused him. "I told you that I equate you with Aunt Alexis, who is my ideal woman, and that I want to marry an independent woman who will be motivated more out of love than the need for a meal ticket."

"I did not expect a marriage proposal to be presented as a logic problem," she said, exasperated.

"I didn't realize what I'd said until later, myself," he confessed. "Then I was afraid you had understood more than I'd intended. The next time I propose, there aren't going to be any questions about my intentions."

There was a touch of irony in Jacqui's sudden laugh.

"As for our relationship going beyond the bounds you want to set for it," Christopher continued, taking her grape soda from her hand and putting it aside, "I realize that to compromise your principles would destroy the very traits I respect most."

"That's very… understanding of you," Jacqui said slowly, the steely glint that had been in her eyes dissolving slightly.

"Now that we know where the limits are," Christopher said, putting his arm around her shoulders and drawing her closer to him, "there's no reason not to explore the territory they surround."

He put his lips to hers just as Jacqui started to smile, and the kiss they exchanged had a new understanding in it. It was no longer a matter of his initiative and her acquiescence, but of sharing something which was too delicately perfect to bear expression in mere words.

Chapter Eleven

Blinking his eyes blearily, Kyle poured himself a glass of orange juice and yawned noisily. He had not been his usual ebullient self since Alaine had announced her plans to go back to Boston within days of her graduation from high school. He had tried valiantly to keep from showing his feelings and ruining his own celebration, but the strain was written on his face every time he relaxed his guard.

Jacqui had spent a restless night herself, hearing him pacing the floor at odd hours; the plan of force-feeding Alaine on his presence had backfired with a vengeance, and he had become too involved for his own good. Feeling responsible for this turn of events only made Jacqui feel more miserable.

Janice, on the other hand, came bounding into the kitchen and searched through the pantry for a box of cereal. "Do we have any shredded wheat?" she asked. "No? Well, I guess I can survive on corn flakes. Hey! What's got you two so glum?"

Fixing her with a baleful stare, Jacqui poured herself some coffee. She suspected that Janice had known what Alaine had wanted to tell Kyle and had resisted going to Red Key, among other reasons, to avoid the fall-out the news had caused.

"Alaine's going back up north," Kyle said bleakly, sitting down at the breakfast table.

"Oh, I thought you were just upset about not catching enough crabs to cook," Janice said blithely.

"Sure you did," Kyle said, spreading peanut butter on his toast with disgusted strokes of his knife.

"And what makes you so cheerful?" Jacqui asked Janice.

"Well," Janice said, drawing out her answer in her favorite way of making the most of what she had to say, "Denny Behrensen asked Lisa and me to help him clean up after the party yesterday, and afterward he would take us home. Well, he took Lisa home first, and then brought me over. He said that since he's broken up with Brenda, he has been thinking how long we have been friends and how much he thinks it would be nice if we spent a lot of time together this summer."

"So you had to spend half the night on the telephone telling all this to Lisa?" Kyle asked.

"Oh, I wasn't that bad!" Janice exclaimed, pushing his comment aside. "Besides, Lisa thought that he was going to pair off with her when he broke up with Brenda, and I had to do some very fast talking to spare her feelings. I reminded her of how many times I've liked guys she had been going with and just kept my mouth shut about the whole thing and let her jabber on about every little detail till I was sick of it."

"Let me give you some advice," Kyle said, looking from Janice to Jacqui and back again. "Don't ask Jacqui for advice if you want Denny to get lost."

Jacqui sighed. "Come on, Kyle," she pleaded. "Don't be so unfair. I did my best. How was I to know—"

"I know better than to go to Jacqui," Janice crowed, pouring milk on her cereal. "Look how she's messed up things with Christopher Warden. She could have that wonderful man eating out of her hand, and she just sits there."

"Who wants Christopher Warden?" Jacqui demanded. "He's just a client."

"Sure he is," Janice laughed wickedly.

Jacqui looked across the table at Kyle and saw his expression unusually hard and knowing as he stared back at her. She vowed to change the subject to save them both any further pain.

"Kyle, let's go over to Egret Island first this morning and see that the electricians are getting to work, and then go back to the office to go over some ideas I have for advertising," she said. "And then there's the matter of how the company responsibilities are split up. We really should sit down and talk that over. I've wanted to, but you've had to study every minute you've had free for so long."

Kyle looked at her without showing any interest in what she was saying. "I told Alaine that she would have a job with us any time she wanted it, whether she finishes college or not."

That's all I need, Jacqui told herself, *for Kyle not to be able to get his mind off Alaine for the day.*

"I'll bet that impressed her," Janice laughed.

"Ah, Jan!" Jacqui scolded. "The last thing Kyle needs is for you to be teasing him about Alaine. Can't you see he is hurting?"

For a split second, Janice looked almost sympathetic. There was no reaching her, though, as she floated on her good fortune of having Denny Behrensen's attention when she had thought that Lisa would be his next girl friend. Her insensitivity to Kyle's feelings was inexcusable in Jacqui's eyes, yet how could she know how to react to her own situation or anyone else's? This was the first time the family had been invaded so thoroughly by such elemental vibrations.

Kyle got to his feet slowly. "I know that Alaine has to go to college," he said. "Her parents are both adamant about that. I just hope she will come back, even if it is just to visit Christopher. All I can do is hope she will miss me and think about me."

"Kyle, there are other fish in the sea," Jacqui said, knowing as the words left her lips that they would be of no comfort at all to him.

"That's what I'm afraid of," Kyle said. "She'll be meeting guys from Harvard and Boston College and even MIT."

"I mean, there are other girls," Jacqui stressed.

Kyle only glared at her, as though she had suggested some heresy.

Decisively, Jacqui got to her feet and went to rinse her coffee cup in the sink. "Unfortunately, we have a business to run. You no longer have the luxury of letting me make all the decisions, while you just take orders. I need you to take over some of my responsibilities, and I think you had better start today."

"Can't I do it gradually?" Kyle asked.

"No. And it will help you get your mind off Alaine," Jacqui said.

Kyle made a face and disappeared toward his bedroom to get his shirt.

"Now who is being insensitive?" Janice demanded, when he was out of the kitchen.

"He has to snap out of this," Jacqui told her firmly, thinking that it was good advice for her to take too in regard to Christopher. "There is nothing he can do about Alaine's leaving. It is probably the best thing for both of them. I can not go on running Osprey Builders seven days a week forever. I need time to myself and—"

She broke off what she was about to say. She needed time to sort through the feelings that crowded into her calculations and plans. It seemed that just when she had complete control over herself and what was going on around her, Christopher Warden's presence crowded in. He had forced her to think about her destiny, about what would be happening to her life after Kyle took over his share of Osprey Builders, after Egret Island was finished, after there was no longer a business bond between them.

And after yesterday she knew there was no way she could face the future without Christopher Warden in it. She did not trust him one little bit as a businessman, she was deeply in love with him. Even though he lacked some indefinable quality that Jacqui desired so desperately in the man she would commit herself to, she knew that without him she might just as well forget any happiness in her future.

She glanced up at the clock on the wall. "You'd better get moving," she said to Janice, dragging her thoughts back to the mundane matters of stacking dirty dishes and seeing that she had put her car keys back into her purse.

KYLE had been only too glad to get to the office after a quick inspection of the Egret Island project, but once there he dawdled over meaningless chores like straightening up her desk and looking through the filing cabinets, until Jacqui was about out of patience with him. In exasperation, Jacqui slammed her ledger book down on her desk.

"Kyle, we have to go over these books," she exploded. "I want you to see what we are up against in the next few weeks."

"If you have to cut back on wages, Jacqui, go ahead," Kyle said. "I already told you that I'd take a cut."

"What we really need to do is put some pressure on a few people who owe us money," Jacqui said, knowing that only one person—or firm—owed them a substantial amount, "and come up with some advertising scheme to attract more sales."

"If you have all that figured out, what do you need me for?" Kyle sighed, sinking into a chair and propping his right ankle on his left knee, in the process taking up a lot of space in the office.

"Because you should know what is going on in the company," Jacqui told him, uncomfortably conscious that her voice was becoming shrill.

"All right, I guess I have to agree with you," Kyle said, resigning himself. He was able to concentrate on the ledger for a short time, then turned to Jacqui. "If Leisure Development came across with what they owe us, we would be all right for a couple of weeks," he said. "The banks seem to meet their financial commitments on time."

"We need more contracts!" Jacqui stated firmly. "Forget Leisure Development and Christopher Warden. If those payments come through, fine. Without more business, we are going to have to mortgage the house, or something to come up with some cash. It's been done before."

Kyle laughed. "I promise that I won't yell as loud as Mom did when Dad took out that second mortgage."

"At least he paid it off," Jacqui said, looking again at some figures that no amount of wishful thinking was going to change.

"Jac, I think it makes some sense to call up Christopher Warden and see if he is going to make this payment tomorrow—"

"I sort of gave him until the end of the week because he paid us enough to make the payroll last Friday," Jacqui told him.

"It wouldn't hurt to call," Kyle suggested slowly, gently encouraging.

"Kyle," Jacqui said, not wanting to have anything to do with Christopher in the mood she was in at the moment.

"Look, I know that you are as hung up on him as I am on Alaine," Kyle said, "but business is business."

Jacqui consulted her watch. "He usually isn't even up at this time of day, especially on Monday."

"Uh-huh!" Kyle nodded, then reached out and

swung the door to the hallway closed. "I've kept my mouth shut for weeks about something...."

Jacqui sat back in her chair, feeling her defenses go up.

"That little scene in the hall, the night we were at the hotel—"

"All very innocent," Jacqui told him, trying not to let the memory rattle her.

"That's for you to decide," he said. "I have meant to apologize for... interrupting. I have a feeling that Christopher was not too happy with my showing up. Some loud noise awakened me, and I thought I ought to check it out, just in case you needed me."

Jacqui set her attention on the desk before her. "Maybe everything happened for the better," she sighed.

"I've gotten to know Christopher lately," Kyle went on. "He's not a bad sort of guy. I think we might have gotten a wrong impression of him at first."

"That could be true," Jacqui agreed. *Don't ask me about yesterday,* she thought, holding her breath.

"Jacqui? Is something wrong?"

"Darn it, Kyle, let's get back to this. What I really want to bounce around is the idea of advertising out of the area," she said, heading back to more comfortable ground. "We should advertise somewhere where the winters are cold. Pittsburgh or Grand Rapids or Buffalo."

"Jacqui, that sounds good, but I don't think the timing is right," Kyle said, shaking his head. "The time for that is in the fall and winter, it would seem to me."

"But if we tell people that if they come down now to contract for a house, they will be sure of having it finished to move into by the time the weather turns cold—"

"No, no. I still don't go for it," Kyle said. "Maybe in September, but not now."

Jacqui sighed and drew her hand through her hair. "All right, we'll shelve that idea," she sighed.

"But I do think you are on the right track," Kyle went on, unfolding himself and getting to his feet. "We need advertising that will get us the most attention and return for the money, and I think I know of a way...."

"What?" Jacqui asked, eagerly, intrigued by the spark that seemed to glimmer again in Kyle's blue eyes.

"Let me check it out first," he said.

Yvonne Halpern came to the door of the office with a handful of messages. "Jacqui, Ted Marks wants to talk to you about a house that Osprey built a number of years ago that is up for sale. He wants a date and figures on it," she said.

"You could handle that," Jacqui said, glancing at the slip of paper Yvonne handed her.

"But you know that Ted always prefers talking to you," Yvonne said playfully, then chuckled to herself. "Besides, he always wants to try to sell you some lots."

Jacqui laughed. "That's right, and I need to ask him for his latest list. I lost my copy around here somewhere."

"I can't for the life of me see how you can lose a thing in this office," Kyle said, his eyes suddenly looking very innocent.

Jacqui gave him a withering look. "What else?" she asked Yvonne.

"There was a site that had a lot of things stolen over the weekend," Yvonne said. "One of Empire Homes' sites."

"Now what?" Kyle asked.

"Lumber and roofing, according to the rumor," Yvonne stated.

"They are starting over again," Kyle mused. "Jacqui, when you talk to Chris today, tell him he might want to double the security on Egret. We have all the electrical supplies lying around over there and not enough room to lock them all up."

"And Thomas Plumbing called to say that they can

get to the Egret Island project Wednesday, so they want everything delivered to the site today or tomorrow," Yvonne summed up.

"That's strange," Jacqui said, grabbing the slip of paper from Yvonne's hand. "Phil Thomas usually just comes in on his lunch hour. Sure it was him?"

"It sounded like him," Yvonne said. "But I couldn't swear to it."

"We're nowhere near ready for plumbers, are we, Kyle?"

Kyle shrugged. "Maybe in the service area."

"Double check that with them, Yvonne," Jacqui suggested, handing the note back to her. "See if you can contact him where he eats lunch. These subcontractors who work out of their trucks are hard to find sometimes."

"What if he confirms it?" Yvonne asked.

"Then call the supplier and light a fire under him," Jacqui ordered. She sank back in her chair. "This gets so darned hectic sometimes! I'm so glad that you are going to take some of it over."

"Are you going to be happy sitting behind a desk all day?" Kyle asked. "I thought you liked jumping into the Beast and trouble-shooting the sites."

"Oh, I do," Jacqui admitted. "But you know more about construction now, so I guess that is your job. Maybe now I can wear decent clothes to the office, huh, instead of jeans and chambrays?"

"If that is what you want," Kyle said. "We can finish all of this nitpicky stuff after lunch. I really should see the houses that are being built so I'll know where they stand."

"Good idea," Jacqui said, grabbing for her plans and hard hat. Suddenly, she felt the need to get out of the office and away from the telephone. She dreaded having to talk with Christopher about money, and the longer that she could put it off, the better.

"WHAT about those three lots over on Admiralty?" Jacqui asked Ted Marks, having found her lot list by some stroke of luck.

"I sold one and have an option on the other two," Ted told her, and his pride was apparent even over the phone.

"Well, I guess that made your week," Jacqui teased. "That house you wanted to know about..."

"All I wanted to know is how many square feet," Ted said. "We got the date and original cost from the owners' papers, finally."

"No problem," Jacqui said, finding the information in the records before her. No, the only problem was going to be talking to Christopher Warden, the memory of yesterday still causing a fluttering in the pit of her stomach.

But there was a moment the inevitable could not be put off any longer. Jacqui reluctantly dialed the number that she had committed to memory long ago, biting on her thumbnail while she waited for an answer.

"I'm sorry, Miss Belpre," his secretary said, in an unemotional voice, "Mr. Warden is on a conference call and can not be disturbed. Shall I have him return your call when he is free?"

"Yes, please," Jacqui said, feeling her heartbeat slow to normal. "I'll be in my office until five."

Yvonne Halpern came to the door again. "I'm trying to follow up on this plumbing thing, Jacqui, but Thomas is a hard man to find."

"On second thought," Jacqui said, "let Kyle handle this. Construction is his end of the business now."

Kyle pushed past Yvonne into the office, his face lighted by some excitement. "Jacqui! Wait until you hear this idea. I called the company that has that blank billboard down the road by the gas station, you know? We can get that billboard very reasonably for a year, and they will put a picture of this house on it, and directions to the office. It will cost a little more than newspaper advertising, but I think it will be much more effective.''

"I never thought of that!" Jacqui said. "Let me see the figures on it while you get back to work on the plumbing situation. Whoa! Do we have to pay this all at once, or can it be broken into installments?''

"The owner says that we have to pay for the cost of doing the initial installation when it's done," Kyle explained, "and the rest on two-month leases. Then if we only need it for ten months or so, it's not tied up for two months after we have a new model.''

"That's great, Kyle!" Jacqui approved, smiling up at him as she handed the figures back to him. "How soon can they get to work?''

"Next week, and it will be up the week after," Kyle told her.

Jacqui was pleased to see him so lively again, his mind off Alaine's impending departure. "Give them the go-ahead, then make a decision on this plumbing mix-up. Oh, Yvonne, see if you can make an appointment with our lawyer about naming Kyle vice-president of Osprey Builders. And he'll have to go over to the bank and make out a signature card so he can sign checks. I had his name put on the account when I took over three years ago, but just never told him.''

Suddenly she felt the twinge in her shoulder more acutely than she had ever felt it before.

"What's wrong?" Yvonne asked, studying Jacqui's face with some alarm.

"A pain in my shoulder," Jacqui explained, trying to downplay the reaction she had felt to it. "It comes and goes. Now that Kyle can take over some of my work, I can have it looked into. But it is very important that we change the corporate structure to give him authority and have him sign a card at the bank. Today. As soon as he straightens out the matter with the plumbers.''

Yvonne nodded and backed away, her expression telling Jacqui that she was not totally convinced by protestations that Jacqui's shoulder was not something to be gravely worried about.

Jacqui took a deep breath and reached for the telephone directory to look up the number of a doctor whose office might not be too far from her own. She was just about to decide between two names when her phone buzzed.

"Mr. Warden is on the line," Yvonne announced.

Pushing the telephone directory aside, Jacqui picked up the receiver. "Christopher? How did you survive the picnic?" she asked.

"Wonderfully!" he said, his Bostonian accent unusually enthusiastic. "Just what I needed to get my mind off this place. And Red Key is really beautiful."

"I'm glad you enjoyed yourself," Jacqui told him, trying to sound more cheerful than she felt. "I have a few things to talk over with you."

"I'm pressed for time," he said. "I have to interview a prospective employee who's waiting only about half as nervously as I am. Company policy on security guards is really stiff. Anyway I have to work tonight because I played hooky last night, so perhaps you would be my guest for dinner here?"

A red-penciled note on her calendar caught Jacqui's eye. "Sorry, Chris," she told him. "I have a Builders Association meeting tonight."

"Why don't you send the boy-wonder in your place?" Christopher asked.

"That's the best idea I've heard all day," Jacqui brightened.

"Then let's say—oh, seven-thirty or eight o'clock, huh?" Christopher proposed. "Believe me, I have something in the works that is going to solve a big part of your problem."

"You mean you are going to give me a check for

what you owe us on Egret Island as of tomorrow?"
Jacqui said, hopefully.

"You think incredibly small for a dynamic business-
person," Christopher laughed.

"Oh, by the way, another site was raided over the
weekend," she told him. "Can you increase the security on Egret Island?"

"By the weekend, dear, I promise. But we always
check our applicants very thoroughly," Christopher explained. "Good security people don't just come out of
the woodwork."

Jacqui relaxed against the back of her chair. "All
right. I understand. We all have our little crises."

"I'm going to be a walking crisis until I see your
smiling face tonight," Christopher chuckled.

Jacqui laughed uninhibitedly for the first time in a
long time. "I'll see you at seven-thirty, then."

"Make it seven," Christopher said. "I'm already
getting anxious."

"I COULDN'T TRACK DOWN Phil Thomas to verify when
he is going to start on the plumbing," Kyle was ex-
plaining, as he piloted the Beast homeward at the end
of the day, "but the suppliers told me that they had
already sent a delivery to the site on someone's order.
There is quite a bit of confusion about it. By the time I
found out that the materials had been delivered, there
wasn't anyone left on the site to see that everything
was locked up. There isn't much room left in the site
trailer anyway. I hate to mess up like this on my first
day. Are you going to fire me, sis?"

Jacqui laughed. "Not if you promise not to fire me
when you're president of the company. Things like this
happen, but this one seems a little fishy, if you know
what I mean."

"I'd go over there now and check on things if you
weren't so bullheaded about my going to this meeting."

"The meeting is more important than going over to the site to see that everything is locked up," Jacqui told him. "I'm going down there for dinner with Christopher, so I'll look in on it. Sending you to the Builders Association buffet once a month will insure that no matter how tough things get at home, you'll be able to fill up on the expense account!"

Kyle laughed, then turned serious. "What is this about my being president?"

"When you reach twenty-one, if you show enough business savvy," Jacqui said, "I plan to step aside in your favor. I don't see myself doing this for the rest of my life."

"Besides, when you marry..." Kyle grinned.

"Hush your mouth!" Jacqui ordered, embarrassed.

Kyle raised his eyebrows. "Dinner with Chris tonight?"

"Just so I can get out of the Builders' meeting," Jacqui told him. "They tend to be a bore after a while if you aren't making deals."

"Don't try to sidetrack me on this," Kyle cautioned playfully. "I have seen how you react to Christopher."

"Come on, Kyle. You can't think Christopher Warden would want to marry me," Jacqui said, "even if I did want to marry him."

Kyle shrugged. "Maybe he just wants you to live with him," he said, with less humor than Jacqui would have thought he would inject into such an outrageous statement.

"That's ridiculous!" Jacqui said. "I could never live with a man without marrying him."

"Never say never," Kyle cautioned, but there was a twinkle in his eye.

"And I'd hope that you would never think of living with a woman without being married to her."

"You lose," Kyle laughed. "I've already thought of it."

"You're terrible!" Jacqui laughed, not able to control herself.

"No, I'm human," he countered. "And so are you. One can not always control one's thoughts. Would you think I was so awful if I did something like that, if I really loved the woman and couldn't avoid it?"

"Couldn't avoid it?" Jacqui demanded. "Ha! Kyle, what would you think of me?"

"Sis, if that was the only way you could be happy, I would think it was your business and none of mine," Kyle told her.

"You know that I could never do that," Jacqui said firmly.

"Jacqui, look at it this way," Kyle interrupted. "People were living together long before they decided that they had to have some piece of paper and some special ceremony to make it acceptable. Now if Chris wanted you to live with him, but didn't want to get married, would you?"

Jacqui bit her lower lip. "I'm glad we're almost home, because you are beginning to make sense, Kyle. But I just know that the question is never going to come up in the first place."

"Wanna bet?" Kyle growled as he geared down to enter the driveway.

WITH her good blue satin robe wrapped around her, and her hair rolled up in Janice's electric curlers, Jacqui sat at the breakfast table giving herself a quick manicure.

"Since when do you get so dressed up for the Builders Association meeting?" Janice asked, watching Jacqui apply nail polish to a freshly filed thumbnail.

"She suckered me into going to the meeting," Kyle called out from his bedroom. "She's having dinner with you-know-who."

Janice smiled and shook her head sideways a few times. "Well, well, well! Two dates in a row!"

"It's business," Jacqui explained, dipping the brush

into the polish she had liberated from Janice's room.

"Sure it is," Janice agreed, slyly. "Maybe I should call Alaine and see what she thinks about this."

"Leave her out of this," Jacqui ordered, then tilted her head toward Kyle's room. "I just got his mind off of her."

Janice grimaced. "Sorry. I forgot. I guess I'm pretty much preoccupied with thinking about Denny."

"You should be studying for your final exams," Jacqui told her. "With both of us out tonight, this gives you a perfect time to get a light dinner and hit the books. No phone calls, and nobody coming over to the house, understand?"

Janice groaned. "If you say so."

"Christopher was saying that you seem to show an interest in resorts and hotels, and he has some ideas of where you might study."

"I thought it might be best just to get a job at Leisure Discovery," Janice said, perching on one of the stools at the kitchen counter.

"You have to be eighteen or nineteen, depending on what you will be doing," Jacqui told her. "He can't even have Alaine work for him."

Janice made a face. "That shoots down that summer job."

"You can still work for Dorothea," Jacqui reminded her, shaking her fingers to dry the polish. "She's going to be busy this summer, she tells me, especially if I succeed in getting her to decorate Egret Island."

"I will be so glad when I never have to hear those words again!" Janice spouted.

"Not half so glad as me!" Jacqui told her. If it had not been for that project, she never would have been so involved with the Warden family, and certainly not caught up in these unfamiliar feelings she had every time she thought about Christopher, to say nothing of the pain of actually seeing him.

Thoughtfully, Jacqui blew on her fingernails, then carefully capped the bottle of polish. "Well, Jan, what do you think I should wear tonight? My blue dress or the yellow one?"

"Blue!" Janice said, decisively.

"The yellow!" Kyle argued, strolling into the kitchen, loosening his necktie as though he was not satisfied with the knot he had made. "Jac, help me with this thing."

"My nails are wet," she said. "Besides, you don't need a tie for the Builders Association."

"Are you sure?" Kyle asked.

"Positive!" Jacqui told him, and laughed when he sighed with relief and pulled the tie from under his collar with a sharp jerk. "Sometimes I think the men hardly get out of their work clothes for those things."

"Good. Now, wear the yellow dress," he said, forcefully.

"You'd allow him to tell you what to wear?" Janice asked. "The guy who is wearing white socks to dinner?"

"I'm sorry I asked," Jacqui giggled, cinching her robe at the waist and getting to her feet.

"I know! Wear the white pants and the silk blouse," Janice contributed.

"Yeah," Kyle agreed. "You look really nice in that."

Jacqui rolled her eyes heavenward. "Whose side are you on?" she asked.

"Yours," Janice and Kyle chorused.

"Have a good time," Kyle said, checking to see that he had his wallet in his hip pocket. "Think of me having to sit there and listen to dull speeches while you're eating lobster or something."

OUT OF THE CORNER OF HER EYE, Jacqui noted nothing unusual over on Egret Island as she drove into the parking lot at Leisure Discovery. There was still plenty of light in the sky, and even if dinner with Christopher took an hour, there would be enough light to check on the plumbing supplies when she was leaving. She had to admit that she was more comfortable wearing the white pants and red silk blouse that Janice had insisted upon than she would have been wearing a dress. The evening was going to be muggy, with little breeze coming in off the Gulf of Mexico and only a scattering of clouds after a shower late in the day.

It seemed that every encounter with Christopher was more of a chore than the last. Jacqui was becoming increasingly suspicious of his motives. Silently she vowed that if he was playing a game with her, she would retaliate by being untouched by it.

Alaine was talking on the phone at the front desk when Jacqui entered, and replaced the receiver as soon as she spotted Jacqui coming into the lobby. She smiled a little sheepishly, as though being caught at doing something slightly naughty.

"Chris wanted me to watch for you," she said in explanation. "He'll be right here. How is Kyle?"

Jacqui swallowed. "Frankly, he's taking your leaving very hard," she divulged, feeling slightly traitorous.

"I was afraid of that," Alaine said. "But there is nothing to be done. He knows I want to come back down here after I finish college."

"That's a long time away, and I don't think he quite believes you will," Jacqui said, giving voice to her own doubts as well.

Alaine smiled confidently and picked up a school book from the counter. "He'll see. Jacqui, I have to study for one last test. Have a nice evening."

Before Jacqui could say anything, Christopher appeared from his office. It seemed to Jacqui, when she saw him, that everything else in the world fell away, and there was just the two of them. She was not even conscious of Alaine taking her books into the office or of the desk clerk coming from behind a partition to check on a reservation.

Nor did she perceive the melting of the firm resolve that she had constructed just moments ago.

"I hope you weren't expecting me to dress formally," Jacqui said, when she noticed Christopher's cream-colored suit and pale blue shirt. He looked incredibly handsome, yet unconcerned for anything but her. "I was talked out of wearing a dress."

"You always look beautiful to me," Christopher said, smiling and taking her hand as he led her toward the wide curving stairway that led to the second floor. "I have some very exciting plans to explore with you tonight."

She did not dare to tell him that all she wanted to know was that he had come up with the rest of the payment for Egret Island. He led her along the second floor corridor to his suite. In the center of the parlor was a small table draped with a linen tablecloth, linen napkins folded to stand at attention. The table held a burning candle in a lantern, and there was a single red rose in a bud vase. To the side was a service cart on which were shiny dome-covered platters, piquing Jacqui's curiosity.

"What I have to discuss is too important to go over in the dining room," Christopher said, closing the door behind them. "I hope you'll be patient with me. It's been a while since I waited on tables myself."

Jacqui smiled at the shadow of uneasiness she saw in his eyes. "I'm sure it's like riding a bicycle or driving a nail," she assured him. "You always remember how."

"I didn't see much of Kyle today," Christopher said, as he held her chair for her.

"Vice-presidents have more important things to do than walk around making electricians nervous," Jacqui told him.

"I just realized that that makes Kyle and me equals,

doesn't it?" Christopher said with a grin as he placed a basket of hot dinner rolls on the table. "Now I will have to watch my step."

"He'll be Osprey's president when he's twenty-one," she said, not completely able to cover the slight regret in her voice with the pride that she felt also.

"And by then I'll be Leisure Development's president," Christopher countered.

"Then you will outrank him," Jacqui said, unfolding her napkin in her lap as Christopher served her tossed salad.

"Don't be too sure, young lady," Christopher said, his smile turning to a very serious expression. "I have some interesting ideas to discuss with you tonight. But first things first. I ordered steaks and baked potatoes. Not the most elegant of our cuisine, but I hope you don't mind."

"I don't think I've ever turned down a steak," Jacqui told him, smiling at him as he placed a salad on his plate and sat down opposite her.

"You are very reasonable this evening," he complimented. "I admire that. Now, I was talking to Alexis today, and she was asking about the plans for her house, so I relayed the discussion we had about it Friday. She thought that was very reasonable and said that she would be coming down to negotiate everything with you within the week. Since the house will be in her name, there is no reason for Uncle Charles to be involved. She has first and last say on everything."

"I envy her," Jacqui laughed, thinking of the major conflicts she had witnessed in couples planning custom homes, which she had feared might lead to divorces.

"And she tells me she envies you," he was saying, "to be in charge of your own life at such a young age. She says that she would like to be starting out again and have your advantages."

"Advantages?" Jacqui asked with a slight laugh. "I rarely look at them that way."

"Be that as it may," Christopher brushed that part of the discussion aside, "she says that she does have second thoughts about the house she was planning on. After we hung up, I got to thinking of the plans that you have for your dream house, and I was wondering—well, you mentioned the studio. You see, Aunt Alexis was a concert pianist, and I'm sure she would like a room big enough for a grand piano, with room for people to sit around and listen to her play. And she has so many friends who are musicians."

"That does give me ideas!" Jacqui said, excitedly. "That could be a bi-level room very easily, especially if the site would accommodate it. If I can't build my dream house for myself, I certainly would love to see it built for someone else, especially your Aunt Alexis."

"Then you can count on a contract for it within the next ten days," Christopher said. "But don't be too generous in giving your dreams away. Maybe you ought to save a little bit of it for yourself."

The look he gave her under partially lowered lashes caused Jacqui's heart to thump once before she tore her attention away. "I'll discuss that with Alexis," she told him, tearing a warm roll apart carefully, trying not to ruin her manicure. "I like her very much."

"It's obvious how much Alexis admires you. Next matter," Christopher said, unfolding his linen napkin and spreading it in his lap. "I think we can make that payment tomorrow if a few things work out. I had a conference call with Uncle Charles and my father, and I think things are fairly well worked out. Father's coming down tomorrow. Jacqui, how much do you want for your property on Red Key? I've checked with the man who owns the adjoining fifteen acres, where the natural marina is, and he wants five thousand an acre for his land. Now, does that sound reasonable?"

"For what you want to do with that land, that sounds like a steal," Jacqui breathed, surprised by the boldness of his actions. "I'm not going to let my land go for less than . . . eight."

"For that you can keep it," Christopher said firmly, as he salted his salad.

"Are you serious?" Jacqui asked, wondering if this was just a continuation of his pipedream from the day before.

"I'm serious," he assured her.

"Just let me figure this out," she said. "How can you think of planning something like this when you are having trouble covering your obligations for the Egret Island project?"

Unflustered, Christopher barely looked up at her. "The Egret Island project, as it was set up, was being financed exclusively out of the profits of Leisure Discovery. To meet this payment, we are having to dip into more general funds, which are being taxed right now because we are opening some of our places that are closed during off-season in Maine and Connecticut. If we develop Red Key, it will be out of our capital fund."

"I suppose that makes sense," Jacqui said after thinking it over.

"Is eight a firm figure?" Christopher asked, returning to the matter at hand.

"Come on, Chris!" Jacqui scolded. "You spring this on me and expect me to have a figure to quote you! Of course eight isn't a firm figure, but if I say yes to five and try to split fifty thousand three ways, I end up with sixes to infinity, don't I?"

"I didn't think of that," Christopher said, looking over at her with a shadow of a smile. "How about six?"

"How about seven-five?" Jacqui ventured, not really bartering with him as much as she was playing a game to see how far he would pursue this impractical idea.

"How about six and an interest in the firm?" Christopher countered.

Jacqui stared at him. "I—ah—would have to think that over, and discuss it with the vice-president."

"You would be able to put Janice through just about any school she wanted to go to," Christopher reminded her.

"Don't oversell, Chris," Jacqui cautioned, lowering her voice. "You know, with Kyle in the picture now, I cannot just wheel and deal the way I used to. His presence complicates things. He might decide that if you are so eager to buy our land, someone else might be even more eager."

"Well, then why isn't there more activity on Red Key?" Christopher asked. "You see, it takes real perception to look at that land and see what I see. Now, it goes without saying that we want you to design and build the place."

"No, it doesn't go without saying, Chris," Jacqui corrected. "I know nothing about building a marina."

"But I'll bet you could find someone who does," Christopher said, dismissing her comment by pointing to her salad. "I think we have talked enough business for me to write off this dinner. Now, eat."

Jacqui looked up at him and laughed. "You know that once we get started talking about business, we can never stop."

"Oh, I think we might find something to keep our minds off the bottom lines, later," Christopher said. "I—ah—have something in mind."

"I'll just bet you do," Jacqui said, flirting with him. "But when I finish dinner, I have to go out to Egret Island and check on a delivery of plumbing supplies that was brought in about two days too soon, and we don't have a place to lock everything up."

"Jacqui, what do you think I have security men for?"

"Just the same I'd like to look around myself."

Chapter Twelve

Too interested in Christopher Warden's company and the delicious food before her, Jacqui lost track of the time, and when she glanced out the window to admire the glorious bloodred sunset, she suddenly remembered that she should have checked the building site at Egret Island before the sky became so dark. She would have only a few moments left now.

"I really must get out to Egret Island, Chris," she told him, dabbing at her mouth with the heavy linen napkin.

"What could possibly go wrong?" Chris asked, replacing his coffee cup in its saucer. "My men make regular rounds, and I shouldn't think it would hurt plumbing supplies if they get rained on tonight."

Jacqui looked out at the sky, then turned a sheepish grin toward Christopher. "I suppose you are right," she said, willing to be talked into staying with him awhile longer.

Christopher got up from his chair slowly. "Since you're so fascinated by that sunset, let's go out on the balcony and get a closer look," he suggested, holding her chair for her. As she stood up, he put his arms around her and drew her close to him. Their lips met by mutual consent, and Jacqui found herself clinging to him.

Just then the telephone rang, one little lighted button flashing from across the room. Christopher sighed, kissed her forehead lightly and let her go. She watched him as he walked across the room to answer the phone, his posture telling her that he was very disappointed at being interrupted.

Not wanting to eavesdrop on what would undoubtedly be business, Jacqui turned back toward the window and slid the glass door open, thinking that she would go out onto the balcony. The door stuck slightly, and she looked back at Christopher for help.

"What do you mean, not until Thursday?" he asked heatedly into the phone, starting to come back toward her, carrying the phone.

Suddenly the door gave and opened easily. Jacqui took a step onto the balcony and looked out toward Egret Island and the color-drenched sky. A breeze was beginning to kick in off the Gulf, relieving the heat and mugginess.

Jacqui was about to reach back and close the door behind her, mindful that the air conditioning was on in the suite, when she saw the flash of headlights through the palm trees as a vehicle crossed the little bridge to Egret Island, briefly lighting the side of the structure.

Frantically, she turned to Christopher and pointed to what she had seen. His brow furrowed and he bit his lower lip, but he did not seem to be doing anything.

"Is that one of your vehicles?" she demanded, going back into the suite.

Christopher shook his head.

Jacqui grabbed up her purse from the couch where she had thrown it and took her keys from it, allowing it to drop on the floor, then she ran out of the suite through the balcony doors, down the cement steps to where the Beast was parked, in a pool of light from the streetlamp.

The Beast growled into action, and glancing around her, Jacqui was dismayed that she did not see anyone coming to her aid. Her headlights stabbed into the darkness gathering around the bridge and across it, the big tires whirring competently, even as she steered with less control than she would have had if her heart had not been racing.

Once across the bridge, the headlights washed unevenly on the rough structure ahead. Two men scrambled out of their light. Muscling the car into neutral, Jacqui sounded her horn three deafening blasts with her left hand while she fumbled under the seat for the heavy flashlight she knew was there. First, she grasped Kyle's hard hat, and thought for an instant she might put it on, then discarded the idea as foolish.

At last she found the flashlight, just as her hand slipped from the standard auto horn onto the special horn Kyle had installed, and it sounded the first few notes of the Georgia Tech fight song on the still night air. Unaware that the switch had locked in the position to repeat the tune over and over, Jacqui closed her mind to the racket it caused.

Flipping on the switch of the flashlight, Jacqui pushed the car door open and jumped down onto the uneven ground, the heels of her sandals sinking in, disorienting her momentarily. Her first thought, as the light caught the side of the battered pickup truck, was that she should know who owned the vehicle, which she had seen many times on building sites of several companies, but she could not place it. For a moment she thought she should kick off her sandals, but she knew that she could not count on the sand being free of stray nails and other bits of metal.

She pursued the sounds of the men as they tried to avoid her. Even with the advantage of knowing the design of the building intimately, prudence told her not to venture inside. Being trapped in a room with cement-block walls and a cement floor could only lead to disaster, she reasoned.

Looking around her Jacqui took a deep breath to steady her nerves and clear her mind. No one seemed to be coming to her aid from the hotel. It was up to her to stop these men from dragging off the electrical and plumbing materials that lay about the site.

Her flashlight illuminated the face of one of the men near a door to the service area. "He must know that's where the supplies are," Jacqui whispered to herself between shuddering breaths.

Then to her left, she heard footsteps. Sweeping the light to that direction, she saw another man waving a length of two-by-four with both hands.

Instinctively, she raised her left arm to ward off the blow and keep the board from striking her in the head. As the board struck her upper arm, she heard a cracking sound, and knew that it was not the board which had broken.

Dropping the flashlight, she clutched her left arm close to her body and fell to her knees in pain. Taking another deep breath to settle the wave of nausea that assaulted her, Jacqui fixed her eyes on a patch of wall that was illuminated by the headlamps of the Beast.

"This was a mistake," she said aloud.

"Hold it right there!" she heard a male voice rumble from behind her. "I've got a gun."

Looking back over her shoulder, Jacqui saw the hotel security men scrambling from their golf cart, one with his revolver drawn. Behind them, Christopher screeched his cart to a halt, completely blocking off the service bridge. He was running toward her almost before the wheels of the cart had stopped turning.

Jacqui swallowed, unable to stay conscious another second. As she lowered herself sideways to lie down on the sand, keeping her broken arm uppermost, she felt strong but gentle hands on her shoulders, supporting her, comforting her. She knew it was Christopher.

It seemed like an instant later, but it had to have

been longer, because red lights were swirling and the site was illuminated with spotlights, and there seemed to be people everywhere.

"She's coming around," someone cried. "Miss? Can you hear me? Are you hurt?"

"I think my arm is broken," Jacqui said, trying to sit up.

"Just lie there," he said, opening a metal case on the ground beside her. "Joe! We need a stretcher."

Jacqui closed her eyes against the pain in her arm and the nausea that got worse by the minute. A hand stroked her cheek, then smoothed her hair away from her face.

"Jacqueline," Christopher's voice came through the flickering of her consciousness, his accent fighting to contain the fear that undermined his usual composure, "are you hurt anywhere else?"

"No," she told him. She forced her eyes to open, but before she could focus on his face, she closed them again, wincing in pain.

"We need to splint this arm," the paramedic was telling someone else.

"My security men cornered the thieves and held them until the police got here, darling," Christopher was saying. "Now, can you tell us where Kyle is?"

"At a meeting," Jacqui said, annoyed that he had not remembered.

"But where is the meeting?" Christopher demanded gently.

"At—at—" *Stupid!* she chided herself. *You've been there dozens of times!* But she still could not make her mouth form the name of the hall.

"Would Janice know?" Alaine's voice asked, solicitously.

"Yes," Jacqui replied, relieved that she didn't have to think anymore.

"Good. Now we're getting somewhere," Christopher sighed, some of the frustration leaving his voice. "Alaine, take my car, go get Janice and Kyle and take them to—which hospital?"

"Gulfside is closest," the paramedic told him.

"Right. Alaine, take your time, now. Jacqueline's in no danger, and there is no reason to alarm Kyle and Janice. She just needs them for moral support." Christopher's confidence grew by the second.

"I know. Jacqui, don't worry about anything," Alaine said, and Jacqui felt the girl kiss her forehead before hurrying away, jangling Christopher's car keys in her hand.

A very deep, authoritative voice said, "Mr. Warden, we need to get some information from you."

"In a moment, please," Christopher said, impatiently trying to put him off.

"Sir—"

Jacqui opened her eyes and looked up into Christopher's face, shadowed in the uneven light. His voice had been confident, but his face told her something else in the intensity of his gray eyes, the shock of dark hair that fell out of place unheeded across his forehead. She gritted her teeth and let go of her arm with her hand, reaching out uncertainly to smooth the forelock back into place.

"Go ahead," she told him.

"Mr. Warden, we're ready to splint her arm and lift her onto the stretcher," the paramedic said. "If you don't mind..."

Christopher threw the man a fierce look, then his expression softened as he looked down at Jacqui. "It's going to be all right," he said, then reluctantly moved aside, stood up, and walked away.

WANTING TO FORGET about the impersonal, yet too personal prodding of the emergency room personnel, Jacqui was relieved and bolstered by Janice's appearance in the examination cubicle. And living up to Jacqui's expectations of her, Janice reacted true to her usual form.

"They ruined your beautiful blouse," Janice complained, after giving the examination room of the hospital the once-over with her analytical blue eyes.

Jacqui nodded her head and tried to laugh. "Better that than my new yellow dress," she said.

"But they wouldn't have had to cut your dress," Janice reasoned. "It doesn't have any sleeves."

"Where's Kyle?" Jacqui asked.

"That doctor wanted to see him before he came in," Janice said. "He stopped him in the hall, waving X-ray pictures around. Jacqui, I wouldn't be surprised if—"

"Miss Belpre," the orthopedic surgeon interrupted Janice, coming into the cubicle, followed by a very concerned-looking Kyle. "May I show you something on this X-ray?"

Jacqui took a deep breath and turned her head to look at the viewer on the side wall, which Dr. Packard slipped the X-ray plates into.

"You will see here the fracture of the arm," he said, pointing it out with a tap of his finger. "However, it appears that there is something in your shoulder joint—a bone fragment, perhaps, or a calcium deposit, which was jarred loose by the blow. Your brother tells me that you have been troubled off and on by a sore shoulder."

Jacqui lay her head back and nodded.

"We cannot rule out the possibility that it is a small tumor, either," Dr. Packard went on. "Therefore, your brother thinks it is best that we open up and see what it is."

"Kyle," Jacqui complained.

"Jac, you know that shoulder has been hurting for much too long," Kyle argued. "What difference would it make to have it taken care of now? Get all the pain out of the way at once."

Jacqui groaned, unable to find a reasonable chink in

their logic. "When will you do it?" she asked Dr. Packard, pushing to the back of her mind the question of how this incident was going to be paid for.

"First thing in the morning," he said. "Then I'll set the arm and put a cast on it."

"Will you leave much of a scar?" Janice asked, always practical and typically somewhat vain.

Dr. Packard looked at her then smiled. "I promise I will leave just as little scar as possible."

Janice seemed pleased, but Jacqui felt apprehensive even as she signed the release form. When Kyle and Janice had left her for a moment, she turned to Dr. Packard. "May I ask you a question?" she asked.

"Of course, anything," he said, looking up from a chart he was studying.

"Is there really a chance that it is a tumor?" she asked.

"Oh, one, maybe two chances in a hundred," he said. "And if it is, four chances out of five it is benign— no problem at all. But still there is that chance, and it can not be ignored."

"I fell on that shoulder one time when I was playing volleyball in high school," Jacqui admitted. "I was much heavier then."

"Hm!" the doctor said, his chin puckering momentarily. Then he closed the chart, took off his glasses and folded them into his pocket. "Now, we have made this decision in a bit of a hurry. If you want to reconsider, to get a second opinion, we could tear up the consent form."

"But that would put off setting the arm and putting the cast on it?" Jacqui asked.

"I'm afraid so."

"No, it would be best to get it out of the way now," Jacqui decided. "This afternoon I was at the point of looking up a doctor in the yellow pages and making an appointment. I had thought of the twinges it gave me as a reminder of conscience. Then it just sort of went hay-wire.''

Dr. Packard chuckled. "Let me show you why," he said, pointing again to the X-rays. "When you are tense, your muscles contract and press this object, whatever it is, against the nerve. When you were heavier, it did not matter quite so much as now, when there is less room for it to move around in. You say it went haywire? That may be significant."

Jacqui felt a little foolish, but with the painkillers she had been given, she was not as prone to exercise her usual reserve. "It began to torment me when I was in the company of, or thinking about, a certain man."

Dr. Packard grinned and switched off the light behind the X-ray plates. "Well, you see, that is probably a sign that you should have been taking very seriously, Miss Belpre! When one is in love, one tends to straighten the shoulders, stand, or sit taller." He smiled as though she should know all the additional consequences of being in love. "If all goes well, you will be going home Wednesday morning without the annoying sensations of this wonderful emotion and able to enjoy it without the pain."

"I'll have to see about that!" Jacqui laughed nervously.

When Kyle and Janice had gone for the evening, after helping her settle into a room with one other unoccupied bed, Jacqui lay in the unfamiliar bed in the darkened room, trying to put some stray bits of memory into proper order. The strange way the order for plumbing supplies came. A battered pickup truck which she thought she should have recognized. Faces grotesquely illuminated in the harsh light of the headlamps, the uncertain beam of the flashlight. They were two men she had seen working for one subcontractor after another, neither skilled nor reliable enough to hold a job for long. They must have been desperate for money, with the trade so slow.

She breathed easier now, having put that much together, knowing that it really had nothing to do with her personally.

THE ROOM WAS FILLING with flowers, bunches of them, in little bouquets and big arrangements. Still groggy from surgery, Jacqui tried to keep track of all of them as the nurse read the little cards to her. "From the Builders Association. The Realtors Association. Mr. Ted Marks. And the plant is from Interiors by Dorothea."

"She would send a plant," Jacqui said.

"And this single rose is from a young man who delivered it in person while you were in surgery," the nurse said, moving the three-quarters open red rose in its bud vase to the table which stretched across her bed. "He seemed to think you would know who it was from."

"I do indeed!" Jacqui said. It was the same rose which had been on the table the night before, between Jacqui and Christopher as they ate dinner.

Kyle, coming into the room gingerly, teased her about opening a flower shop, but Jacqui could see through his bantering. He was covering up.

"Is everything all right at the office?" Jacqui asked. "I realize it's still early, but—"

"We've been open three hours, and the place has gone to pieces!" Kyle told her, with exaggerated movement. "Phone ringing, people dropping by from all over the place."

"It's because I'm not there that they are coming," Jacqui said.

"You have everyone thinking you are so brave and selfless to go after those guys," Kyle teased. "You and I know that it was just plain foolish."

"Just plain foolish," Jacqui repeated. "That's the truth!"

Kyle pulled a handful of pink message slips from his

pocket and riffled through them. "Alaine told me that she would see you after school today. She gets out at noon; today's her last day. Janice wanted to come after school, but Dorothea needs her to look after the shop. Cletus Garwood said: 'You done Ol' Jack right proud,' and that is an exact quote. Oh, here, you just go through these on your own."

He put the notes down on the table beside the rose, and then drummed his fingers on the railing of the bed.

"No one has been in to ask me any questions about what happened," Jacqui told him.

"That's because I asked that no one bother you, at least until after your ordeal was over," Kyle told her.

"I've been trying to place those men," Jacqui said. "Who are they?"

Kyle took a deep breath. "A couple of men who have bounced around the trade for a couple of years, mostly in framing and roofing. They learned the ins and outs of construction, a few key words here and there. They could tell that we had electricians working on our site, so they made some calls to have the plumbing supplies delivered, and they counted on everyone who knew what was happening to be at the Builders meeting. They did not know about my getting my license, nor of your romantic connection with Christopher Warden."

"Neither did I," Jacqui laughed.

Kyle smiled indulgently. "They are clever, but just too lazy to make a real go of construction. And when they got to jail, they just spilled everything."

"Who were they working for?" Jacqui asked. "I mean, was someone telling them what to take?"

"So far as anyone knows at the moment, they were completely on their own," Kyle told her. "But they only account for a little over half the pilferage."

Jacqui shook her head. "What about Christopher?"

"He's a nervous wreck," Kyle laughed. "As nearly

as I can piece the events together, he was on the phone talking to his father when you discovered the activity on Egret, so he put his father on hold and called the police, who just happened to have a squad car cruising two blocks away. He also alerted the security men and then went out after you himself. He was hoping that you would just stay in the Beast and let the thieves know they'd been discovered. As it was, you panicked them."

"It would have been smarter to stay in the car," Jacqui agreed, "but I'd still have something in my shoulder, twinging every time I told a lie."

Kyle laughed, then became very serious. "When I went over to get the Beast last night, Chris was pacing the floor, berating himself for not taking you seriously about increasing security. He was tied up with his company's policy on doing very close checks on guards, although he thought he could fill the job by the weekend. The thieves just broke their pattern."

"All right," Jacqui sighed, feeling one last knot of apprehension unravel inside her. "It was irrational to think that Christopher had anything to do with—"

Kyle stared at her in surprise. "How could you possibly think that! First of all, he knows nothing about construction except what he has learned from us. Secondly, he was in such a state last night! If you had seen him, Jac, you would have known—"

"You're right, of course. He would never have suggested we go out onto the balcony to watch the sunset."

"Hm." Kyle tilted his head and smiled teasingly. "Sounds very romantic, if not very original. I'll skip over what I think of you having dinner in his suite and go right on to asking if the doctor has told you what was in your shoulder."

"Not yet," Jacqui said, straightening the sheet over herself. "I am a little worried about it."

"Well, whatever it was, it's not there now," Kyle brightened. "I was hoping I could talk to the doctor before I had to go back to work."

"Maybe I should ask one of the nurses if he is still around," Jacqui suggested, reaching for the call button.

"Don't bother just yet," Kyle said. "Is there anything that has to be done at the office that I don't know about? It seems as though everything is running smoothly, but that is when things are most likely to go wrong."

"Ha! You have gotten a grasp on the construction business after all!" Jacqui laughed.

Kyle laughed with her, then straightened up again as Dr. Packard, having changed from surgical pajamas back to street clothes, entered the room.

"Aha!" Dr. Packard said, putting on his glasses, then taking them off again. "You're looking much better. Your color is returning. Nothing to that bit of surgery, dear."

"What was in my shoulder?" Jacqui asked cautiously.

Dr. Packard fished a glass vial from his coat pocket and placed it on the table. "A piece of bone which was picking up calcium crystals," he explained. "Nothing too dangerous, but it was not going to get any better by your ignoring it."

Jacqui picked up the vial and studied the chip of bone for a long moment. "So small a thing to be causing me so much trouble," she mused. She handed the vial to Kyle, who looked at it briefly and handed it back. "Here," she said to Dr. Packard, extending the vial toward him.

"You could keep it," the surgeon said.

"Absolutely not!" she said, decisively.

He smiled at her and pitched the vial into the wastebasket. "Now, if you get too uncomfortable, the nurses can give you something for the pain. I'll be back around seven o'clock tonight, if you want to ask any questions. And I'll see you again tomorrow morning before you go home. You, son, take good care of this lady when she goes home.''

"Count on that, sir!" Kyle pledged cheerfully.

Kyle's departure, although she knew he had to leave, left Jacqui depressed and having to face her own thoughts which had been suppressed for the last few hours by induced sleep. The unreality of the bare hospital room presented nothing to catch her imagination, and she fitfully tried to become interested in the television talk shows that glared down at her from a set mounted from the ceiling across the room. But finally she turned off the set with the remote switch and turned her head toward the blank wall.

A rather dismal lunch did no more to cheer her, nor to help her dredge something from the back of her mind that was bothering her.

Jacqui had just given up on the gelatin and iced tea on her lunch tray when Alaine appeared, wearing a bright pink sundress, her long black hair arranged up off her neck and tied with ribbons.

"I borrowed Christopher's car to come see you," she said, pleased with herself. "But I have to get right back to the hotel. Poor Chris! Everything seems to have come apart at the same time!"

Jacqui opened a paper bag Alaine handed her and peeked inside, only to groan when she saw its contents. "Pastries! You certainly know my weakness."

"It was Chris's idea," she said. "He wanted to come up with something different. You certainly have enough flowers."

"I wish you had come a little earlier," Jacqui told her. "Then I would not have filled up on this so-called lunch. But I'll save these for later, for an afternoon snack."

"Chris didn't get any sleep last night," Alaine went on, seeming to know the topic Jacqui most wanted to hear about without being prompted. "The police were there for hours, and he had to call Father and Uncle Charles. Then this morning things started to fall apart in the hotel. We had a plumbing backup on the third floor. And just before I left to take my very last final test in school, Father called and said that he was at the Tampa Airport, and Chris had to go collect him."

"I see," Jacqui said, trying not to be distracted by the pastries.

"But Chris doesn't know that there is going to be an even bigger crisis," Alaine said, her gray eyes widening, "and when he finds out, he's going to kill me."

"I hardly think so," Jacqui tried to console her.

"Ha! Wait till you hear!" Alaine went on, lowering her voice. "Mom called yesterday and said that she would be coming down this afternoon, instead of to-morrow, because she thought she would need an extra day or so to get used to Florida before my commence-ment Friday night. Can you imagine what is going to happen when Mom sees Father? I had no idea he was coming!"

"No," Jacqui said, with a shake of her head. She had heard enough of the Warden family's problems, how-ever, to know that there would be fireworks. She had conscientiously avoided uttering anything that would let Alaine or Christopher know that she had formed a negative opinion of Merrill Warden, based on their first encounter. She had a nagging feeling that she should not have been so hasty in her conclusion, but he had not gone out of his way to conceal what he thought of a woman functioning in the construction business, so she felt in part justified.

"Chris tells me that I'm too much of an optimist, hoping that my parents will discover that this divorce is not what they really want," Alaine confided. "Everyone can see how miserable they are without the other. They were together for thirty-five years, and it seems to me that if there was not something really good between them, they would not have been together that long.''

When Alaine looked to Jacqui for some support, all Jacqui could do was smile weakly, and pat her hand. ''It's up to them, you know,'' she said. ''You and Chris will just have to accept what happens.''

''Well, so much for my problems,'' Alaine said. ''When are you going home?''

''Tomorrow morning,'' Jacqui said, inwardly hoping that she would feel stronger then and that some of the fogginess in her mind would evaporate.

''Kyle must be up to his chin in work,'' Alaine said, grinning.

''And he will be for a while,'' Jacqui agreed.

''I could have cried for him last night,'' Alaine said. ''He was so concerned about you, even after he had been here and talked with the doctor. He's still upset about my leaving.''

''You'll have to be patient with him,'' Jacqui told her.

For the first time, Alaine looked away from Jacqui. ''You've been like a big sister to me since I have been here, and I really have to tell someone who will understand. Jacqui, I think I love Kyle more than anyone I have ever met. At first, I know, he did not feel the same way about me, but now he tells me he does, after I had given up and decided to go back home. My plans are made, and on an intellectual level, I know that they are going to be the best thing for me in the long run. I'll be close to my parents again, for whatever that is worth. And I'll know some of the people in college. But part of me doesn't want to leave Kyle. He is making it hard for me to go.''

Jacqui was at a loss for something to say in the face

of Alaine's confession. She swallowed then reached for Alaine's hand. "It would be nice if everything would work out," she said at last. "But so many things could go wrong over the years it will take to resolve all the problems."

"Tell me, do you know of anyone who has waited three or four years to get married after they met?" Alaine asked.

"My parents," Jacqui said. "Actually, they waited almost five years."

Alaine brightened. "Well, then, since there is a precedent, maybe there is hope! Look, I have to get back to the hotel and see if it is still standing. I know Chris wants to come see you, but with everything that is happening, he might not have the time."

"Tell him that I understand," Jacqui said, making a cheerful mask of her face. "Tell him that I appreciate the rose and the pastries." She wanted to say that she was anxious to see Christopher, but there was something holding her back.

What a strange turn of affairs, she thought when Alaine was gone, and in the lazy buzzing of the hospital, she tried to resist the pastries in the paper bag. Her shoulder ached but not unbearably. At least it no longer twinged when she thought of Christopher, and she was doing that more and more.

She could not quite identify what the change in her feelings was, or why it had occurred. All she knew was that every time she heard sure, measured footsteps in the hallway, she hoped that it would be Christopher coming to see her. And when she thought of how she had dreaded seeing him before.... Jacqui laughed at herself and grabbed for the bag of pastries. Maybe just one, to help her survive until dinnertime.

Chapter Thirteen

"Ready to go home?" Kyle asked, coming into her room Wednesday morning and swinging a small suitcase up onto the side of her bed. No matter how cheerful he sounded, though, Jacqui noticed a certain firmness in his lean jaw that sent a warning through her that something was not right.

"Darn right!" she told him, getting out of the bed carefully, trying not to disturb her shoulder. "This place is boring. What did you bring me to wear home?"

"Jeans and one of my chambrays," he said, snapping the lid of the suitcase open. "I thought it would be more comfortable than one of your own."

"It wouldn't be that no one has done a laundry, would it?" she teased, pulling the shirt from the suitcase and laying it out on the bed. "That looks like it will go over the cast, all right. Kyle, you didn't tell me last night if Christopher Warden made that payment yesterday like he promised."

Kyle placed a fresh red bandana on the bed table, then closed the suitcase. "No, he didn't," he said, lowering his voice and averting his eyes.

"He said he was going to."

"You gave him until Friday, technically."

"But he promised!" Jacqui said, striking her fist on the bed table. The force of her blow caused the petals of the red rose in the bud vase to plop dismally to the surface of the table and onto the sheet of the bed until only the stem and its bare calyx stood in the vase. Jacqui swore so softly only she heard. "I can't even leave that place for a day and it starts to fall apart!"

"It does not," Kyle argued, and she could see that he was angry with her. "I understand Christopher had some real problems yesterday. I'm sure he'll bring us the check today when I take him and his father out to Red Key."

"If he doesn't, we'll close down the site until he pays," Jacqui vowed, feeling her teeth clench.

"But you gave him until Friday, Jacqui," Kyle reminded her. "A verbal contract, dear, which you can not break lightly. Besides, it is not a matter of life and death to the firm as it was last week."

Jacqui groaned and pounded her fist on the bed table once more. A nurse came into the room on almost soundless feet. "What's all the commotion in here?" she asked.

"My sister is trying to run our business from here," Kyle said, not completely nonchalant.

"Jacqui, you're going to need some help getting dressed, aren't you?" the nurse said, securing her stethoscope in the pocket of her uniform. "Kyle, why don't you go down to the business office and sign her out, and I'll have her all ready to leave in five minutes." She tactfully nudged Kyle out of the room and then drew the curtains around the bed.

"Your rose seems to have gone the way of all roses," the nurse said, picking petals up off the bed and dropping them into the wastebasket.

"Just symptomatic of the romance, I guess," Jacqui sighed.

"It can't be that bad," the nurse said, tilting her head to one side as she picked up on the desolate note in Jacqui's voice.

"I have learned something in the last few days that I should have learned long ago," Jacqui lamented. "You can't mix business with love. It just doesn't work."

Deftly, the nurse supported Jacqui's left arm while she slipped the sling aside. "Now, I've seen a lot of life go through this ward, Jacqui, and I'm going to tell you a little about my observations. Things always look very bad from a hospital bed. You are used to running your own life, and suddenly, temporarily, you can't control much of anything. That is as much a shock to your system as the broken bone or the surgery. But once you are out of here, home, and adjusting to what has happened, everything will fall into place again."

"Sure," Jacqui groaned. "I should never have trusted that man! I knew from the moment I laid eyes on him! He is too suave, too educated—"

"I saw him yesterday when he brought that rose, Jacqui," the nurse interrupted, smiling coyly. "He is also a very handsome man. But more importantly, at that time he was very, very concerned about you. So wait until you are out of here and feeling better before you make any judgments."

Saddened, Jacqui held her breath and braced herself for the pain she would feel when the sleeve of the chambray shirt was eased over her arm. At least her shoulder did not twinge.

THE FLORIDA SUN beat down too hot to tolerate for very long, but Jacqui lay on her reclining chair on the patio and sipped her iced tea, trying not to think of all the things that Kyle could do wrong in the office.

Then she shook her head, remembering how excited and pleased she had been that he was getting his certificate early, how she had anticipated his taking over some of her responsibilities, relieving her of some of the strain of running Osprey Builders alone. Now, when he was doing just what she had wanted him to, she had little justification for finding fault.

If she should find fault with anyone, it should be with herself, for giving Christopher Warden more time to come up with his payment. She should have stood firm, demanded payment by the end of business yesterday, in order for his check to clear by the time the payroll had to be met Friday. What was she thinking of to give him the extra time!

She set her iced tea aside on a table and pulled her straw hat down further over her blue eyes. She knew what she had been thinking of. She had been thinking too much of Chris, the man who had held her in a passionate embrace outside her bedroom at the Leisure Discovery hotel, who had eagerly sought her lips on the sands of Red Key, not Christopher Warden, the tough, Harvard-educated businessman, who knew how to get what he wanted any way he could.

In the beginning, way back when she had first met Christopher Warden, she had known exactly what he was. But then she had allowed herself to get close to him and had allowed him to get much too close to her. She had only herself to blame.

She braced herself for the twinge that her shoulder would have given her in agreement, but it did not come. There was only a dull ache in her shoulder, echoed by a dull ache in her heart.

She heard the motor of a car in the driveway and the slamming of car doors. Inwardly, she groaned, not wanting to see anyone.

"Jacqui!" Janice called out, coming through the house. "Where are you?"

"Just getting some sun," Jacqui told her. "How did you get home?"

"Denny brought me," Janice bubbled. "You remember Denny."

Jacqui pushed her straw hat back on her head and looked up into the freckled face of Denny Behrensen, who stared down at her from a height which was vaguely startling. "Denny," she acknowledged.

"Sorry to hear about your—accident," he stammered.

Without batting an eyelash, Janice forged on. "You shouldn't get too much sun when it is so hot," she said. "Is there any soda pop? Denny, would you like something cold to drink? Jacqui, I thought I'd fix something for dinner before I go to work, then it would be all ready when I get home."

"Sounds like a good idea," Jacqui agreed, trying to get to her feet from the lounge without jarring her shoulder. Denny reached down and helped her with amazing gentleness. "Thank you," she said to him, reassessing her opinion of the demise of chivalry.

The house was cool and dark, and Jacqui breathed in the cooler air gratefully.

"What I really wanted to make was a macaroni salad," Janice was saying, handing a can of pop to Denny while her head was still in the refrigerator. "But we don't seem to have any cucumber. Can you make a macaroni salad without cucumber?"

Jacqui lowered herself to a chair at the breakfast table. "If you have to."

"I could take you over to the fruit stand," Denny offered, popping the top of the can.

"No, no. I don't have that much time," Janice fretted, laying a stalk of celery on the counter. "I have everything else."

While Janice fussed around the kitchen, setting water to boil for the macaroni and the hard-cooked eggs, Jacqui watched with amusement as Denny pitched right into the job, getting her box of macaroni down from a high shelf and then scrubbing vegetables. When he began to criticize the way Janice was cutting the carrots, Jacqui had to laugh.

She could not imagine Christopher getting involved

this way, remembering how he had hung back from helping with the cookout on Red Key, except for holding tools and passing plates around. Well, another strike against him.

Impatiently, Jacqui got to her feet and walked into the living room. Why did all her thoughts have to circle back to Christopher Warden? she demanded of herself.

The phone rang in the kitchen, and Janice answered it. "Jacqui, Alaine says she wanted to get over this afternoon, but she can't make it. She'll come over tomorrow."

"No," Jacqui responded. "I'll be back at work."

"What! You can't go back to work tomorrow!" Janice protested sharply.

"Yes, I can!" Jacqui said, more firmly. *If I don't go back to work, I'll sit around here mooning about Christopher Warden,* she thought to herself, *and that won't do anyone any good.*

KYLE SPRINKLED SALT on his portion of macaroni salad and looked up at Jacqui. "Merrill Warden is all for buying that land up on Red Key," he said.

"Good!" Janice exclaimed. "Then I'll never have to go there again."

"I can't think why Pop Kelly would want to sell his land adjoining ours," Jacqui said, thoughtfully.

"He needs the money to keep his charter boats going," Kyle told her. "From what I understand, he thinks it is a great idea, building a resort out there, thinks it will be great for his business. And it might be too."

"I hate to think of what they were talking about doing to the place, though," Jacqui said.

"I think this is where I came in," Janice teased. "Only the topic was Egret Island."

"Well, according to what I could piece together," Kyle confided, "the Red Key development is going to have to wait awhile. The company is slightly overextended with Egret Island as it is. That is why there has been such a mad scramble for funds—"

Jacqui slammed her fork down on the table. "Cletus Garwood and Dorothea Grace warned me that this would happen! But I was so blinded by revenge and greed—"

"To say nothing of Christopher Warden's straight white teeth," Janice interjected, not passing up an opportunity to tease Jacqui.

"It's not as bad as all that!" Kyle interrupted. "You have to remember that this is just the beginning of the season for the resorts Leisure Development holds in the north. At least, they seem to think that in a few weeks their cash flow situation will ease up. That is exactly why they have diversified to having resorts all along the coast, to stabilize their money situation. Pop Kelly wants cash on the barrelhead for his land, but I told the Wardens that we would have to talk the matter over between us to agree on the particulars. After all, Jacqui, you know the business better than I do, and you know what is coming up in the near future."

"I'm glad you acknowledge that," Jacqui said, some of her hurt feelings of the morning mollified.

"Now, I heard a rumor that you're going to work tomorrow," Kyle said.

"Where did you hear that?" Janice asked, looking critically at Jacqui.

"Alexis Warden made an appointment with Yvonne to see you about her plans for her house tomorrow afternoon," Kyle explained. "She came down from Boston with Alaine's mother." Suddenly he laughed. "From what I hear, the family suite at Leisure Discovery must be like a grade-B comedy from the thirties. Christopher is trying to keep his mother and father apart, and Alaine is trying to get them together."

"My money is on Alaine," Janice wagered.

"Christopher had the inside track on this one," Kyle told her, with a discouraging wave of his hand.

"Shame on both of you!" Jacqui scolded. "It is not our business to inspect other people's lives. It's all their own affair."

"Well," Janice said, slowly, leveling her blue eyes at Jacqui across the table, "if I were going to marry into a family, I'd like to know that the in-law situation was stable, so that I wouldn't have to watch my step all the time and not have to worry about breathing too hard."

"Who is marrying into the Warden family?" Jacqui asked.

"I see two likely candidates sitting at this table," Janice said, with a waggle of her honey-blond pony tail.

"Janice, please!" Jacqui spouted, and expected to feel her shoulder twinge. When it did not, she looked at the bulky cast on her arm, then at Janice again. "I think Christopher Warden is out of the picture, so far as I am concerned."

"You're kidding!" Janice exclaimed, almost wailing. "After all he has done? I'm sure this deal he's making for our land is really going to benefit us a lot more than it will him, personally. I mean, if Leisure Development wants to build another resort around here, it doesn't have to be on that piece of land we just happen to own. And Alexis doesn't have to give you the contract for her house either."

"I know all that," Jacqui said, "but—"

"I just don't understand you!" Janice complained.

"Jan, leave her alone," Kyle intervened. "Jacqui, I'm sure you'll feel better about Christopher when you've had time to rest and sort things out."

"I've had enough of resting and sorting things out," Jacqui said, leaning back in her chair and crumpling up her paper napkin. "That's what has got me so depressed in the first place. I need to get back to work."

"Dr. Packard warned me that you would be this

way," Kyle told her, "but I just didn't think it would happen so soon."

"Well, he was right, wasn't he?" Jacqui asked.

Kyle sighed. "All right, go back to work tomorrow. I can always bring you home if you get too tired."

JACQUI SPENT THE MORNING working in the office, pacing herself, resisting the urge to dash off to one site or another and pitch into the heavy work. Kyle had made it plain that she was not to be driving the Beast, a practical consideration based on the lack of power steering and the necessity to take one hand from the wheel to shift gears. Yvonne was in her glory pampering Jacqui until Jacqui could hardly stand it and holed up in her office.

Shortly before Alexis was scheduled to appear for her two o'clock appointment, Jacqui relented on the self-imposed exile and had Yvonne help her prepare to face Alexis by setting out some materials on the dining table of the model home, and as an extra precaution swallowed one of the pain pills Kyle had gotten for her at the drug store.

Entering the model home before Jacqui was emotionally ready for her, Alexis Warden took off her sunglasses and looked around the living room, smiling broadly. She wore a crisp yellow dress and chalk beads, looking every inch in charge of herself and everything around her.

"My, you made a quick recovery, Jacqui darling," she said, as though they were oldest and dearest friends, and at that moment, Jacqui would have loved for it to have been true.

But there was a certain apprehension deep inside her, as there always was when she was entering into a contract to build a particularly customized home for a client. Yet, it went further than that. She was uncomfortably aware of the reputation she had at stake not only as a builder but as a person. She did not know what had been going on with the Warden family; indeed, she did not want to know. Whatever it was could be none of her business, yet it could affect everything about Alexis's house.

"It's good to see you again, Mrs. Warden," she said.

"Alexis, remember?" she said.

Jacqui smiled a little uncertainly. "I thought we'd spread out all the plans on the dining table over here, so you could compare the plan you liked with something I found which might interest you."

"Oh, yes!" Alexis said, her inbred reserve cracking a little. "Chris said you have some outstanding ideas. You know, there isn't any reason that the house has to have a second floor. In fact, it might be better if it didn't. We're just so used to that style up North."

"What do you particularly like about the plan you chose?" Jacqui asked, motioning toward the plan that Yvonne had already helped her put on the table.

"The kitchen for one thing," Alexis said, tracing the lines with one well-manicured fingertip.

"That is exactly what Janice and I thought," Jacqui said. "Now, if you will look at this other plan.... This could be a bi-level studio for your grand piano, and you could have a built-in sound system in these bookcases."

"Marvelous! I hadn't thought of that," Alexis said, slipping gracefully into a chair without taking her eyes from the plans.

"I'm at a bit of a disadvantage yet to draw anything, but as soon as Kyle is off the phone, he promised to come help us combine the plans in a sort of preliminary sketch, then we'll have to go see the site."

"I love the idea of all this open space," Alexis said, putting on her reading glasses to get a more precise look. "You know, all my life I have lived in confined, formal spaces. This would be marvelous if we could have shutters between the kitchen and the studio, instead of a wall. Great for entertaining."

Jacqui swallowed. Her idea of the studio was for it to be a place that could be closed off from everything else, not open to the hubbub of a household. But once she redesigned the house for Alexis, it would no longer be her dream house. It would belong to someone else, and there was every possibility that she would never have her own place exactly the way she wanted it. Nonetheless, as the afternoon wore on Jacqui wrenched more and more of her cherished innovations that she had been hoarding in the storehouse of her mind away from her own dream and watched Kyle sketch them, deftly and cleanly, onto the floorplan.

"Now," Kyle said, when the plan had reached a critical stage, "the next thing is to go out to the site and see if we can fit all this into the topography and the landscape that is already there."

"Is there still time today?" Alexis asked. "It's only about a fifteen-minute drive from here, if you are up to it, Jacqui."

"What do you say, Jac?" Kyle said, putting his pencil down and running his hands through his tangled blond curls.

"Why not!" she said, trying to feel energetic and carefree. "We might as well get it over with. You don't mind riding in the four-by do you?"

"The infamous Beast? Oh, not at all!" Alexis brightened. "Promise me when we get out into the woods I can toot that horn I've been hearing about."

Jacqui and Kyle laughed. Building a house for Alexis was going to be an experience. She seemed game for just about anything.

The piece of land that Alexis Warden directed them to was in an area of rolling hills and sinkhole ponds, dotted with groups of oaks. A rough track led into the ten-acre portion of land, bumping and curving toward a grassy-banked pond large enough to be stocked with fish.

"This is beautiful," Kyle said in wonder, as he eased the Beast out of gear.

He helped Alexis out of the wagon, then gave Jacqui a hand down from the back seat, while Alexis looked on sympathetically. "You just never realize how much you use that left arm until you can't, eh, Jacqui?" Alexis observed. "I'll never forget a time I sprained my wrist falling on the ice. It seemed that every time I turned around, I was hurting it again."

Jacqui winced. "Is that what I have to look forward to?" she asked, trying for a lighter mood. She looked around the land with a practiced eye. It was beautiful, but presented some problems in placing the house to best advantage.

Kyle had returned to the car for the preliminary plans and now spread them on the hood of the Beast, weighing them down with his hard hat and a flashlight. "Where did you plan to place the house?" he asked.

"I've always thought it would be nice to watch the sun set over the pond," Alexis said. "And with this plan, I'd like these studio windows to look right out over the center of the pool."

Kyle turned the plans around to the opposite orientation and weighed them down again. "Like this, then?" he asked.

"Lovely," Alexis said, "but I suppose that you'll have to cut down that great tree over there."

"Not on your life!" Kyle exclaimed, directing his attention to a moss-shrouded oak tree that was easily fifty years old. "That is one of the guiding principles of our firm. We never lose a tree if we can help it. Jacqui, how can we offset this plan?"

"Could I suggest that instead of just offsetting it, like we did for Bushes' house," Jacqui said, pointing to the area of bedrooms, "that we angle this wing, and that way you would even improve the view from the bedrooms."

"How much will that add to the cost?" Kyle asked, scratching his forehead.

Alexis looked at each of them and smiled indulgently. "Have I mentioned cost? This is the house I am going to spend the rest of my life in, and cost is the last of my considerations. Now"—she went back to the plans—"would it be possible to angle the master suite also, so the house curves around the pond?"

Jacqui studied the plan carefully. "Instead of having the studio rectangular, it could be shaped like a wedge, and this outer wall could be rounded—"

"This is getting better and better," Alexis approved.

"I'm going to walk down by the pond and see if we are going to have any problems with the land." Kyle asked, "Jacqui, do you want to come with me?"

"No," Jacqui told him. "But if you see anything strange, I'll come take a look."

Alexis seemed to be waiting for Kyle to be out of hearing range, watching Kyle wade through the tall grass. Then she turned toward Jacqui. "Christopher is quite concerned about you," she said, without warning. "But so many problems have come up lately, that he has not had time to call on you."

"That's all right," Jacqui said, knowing as she said it that she was lying. "I understand."

"Of course Merrill decided to stay for Alaine's graduation tomorrow night," Alexis went on, apparently unaware that Jacqui really did not want to be privy to what was going on within the Warden family. "So Christopher and I decided to throw a little party in the suite afterward. All the Belpres are invited, by the way."

"I don't know," Jacqui said. "It sounds lovely, but—"

"You know, I never thought that Merrill and Dianna could have worked out their differences, but they seem to be making a real effort," Alexis went on, her voice somehow distant. "It may just be that they don't want to ruin Alaine's graduation."

Jacqui watched as Kyle walked to the far side of the pond and sighted back toward where the house would be positioned. He seemed to have found no problems in positioning the house so far, and Jacqui almost wished that he would, that he would beckon for her to join him so that she would not have to think about the Wardens any longer. Thinking about them led to thinking about Christopher, and it hurt too much.

"Are we going to have to drill a well?" Jacqui asked Alexis. "Even if there is an old one, it might be safest to put down a new one."

Alexis looked at her, mixed expressions on her face. There was a touch of annoyance that they would not be exchanging any juicy gossip, yet a respect for Jacqui's practicality. "Yes, of course. I'm sure you know more about working out the details than I do."

"And will you need a decorator when the house is finished?"

"Well, yes, I suppose so," Alexis answered. "I've a lot of antiques, and sometimes a decorator knows the best refinishers and so on."

"You should drop by to see my friend Dorothea," Jacqui suggested. "I think you'll get on well with her. She can keep an eye on things for you while you're up North."

Jacqui relaxed, in control of herself and the situation once again. She was a professional woman going through the long-established routine of her business with a client. It did not matter that the client was the relative of someone she loved.

Chapter Fourteen

"Why aren't you up?" Kyle demanded, coming into Jacqui's room and finding her still in bed the next morning.

"I can't face it," Jacqui groaned, trying to hide in the sheets. But it was already getting hot and muggy. She really should get up, close all the windows, and turn on the air conditioner.

"Can't face what?" he asked, disgustingly cheerful.

"Not getting that check from Leisure Discovery," she sighed.

"I'm sure Chris will bring it in this morning," Kyle told her, tugging at the corner of the sheet. "Or else he'll give it to me when I go over to Egret Island this morning. Everything will be all right."

"I'm glad you think so, because I don't," she told him.

"I'm going to chalk this up to post-op depression," Kyle said, giving the corner of the sheet a stronger tug. "Come on. You can't give in to it!"

"I can and I have," Jacqui told him, turning her face away.

"Okay! Be that way!" Kyle sat down on the edge of the bed. "It's going to be a long day, with Alaine's graduation party tonight. Maybe you ought to take the day off. I can do the rounds, see that everyone gets paid, and work up the floorplan and the cost figures for Alexis Warden's house.

You know she wants the plans this afternoon and the figures before she goes back to Boston on Tuesday."

Jacqui groaned. "All right, all right! I'll get up."

Redrafting the plans for Alexis Warden's house was going to be an all-day job, considering the handicap Jacqui was working under. Coming up with a cost estimate was going to be worse.

"No, no," Kyle tried his reverse psychology. "You just lie there and feel sorry for yourself, and I'll run the business."

"I said I'm getting up," Jacqui told him, inching her feet toward the floor. "You don't have to threaten bankruptcy!"

"Oh, there you are!" Janice said, coming into the bedroom. "About this party tonight, do you think we should each take Alaine a gift or give her something from the family?"

"Jan, could this wait until I'm awake?" Jacqui asked, reaching for her robe.

"What do you think, Kyle?" Janice went on, ignoring Jacqui, except to hold the left shoulder of the robe for her.

"I wanted to get her something special," Kyle confessed, "but I don't know just what. A necklace, I guess, but she has that one she wears all the time."

"I know just the thing!" Janice told him, nonchalantly going to Jacqui's dresser and starting to lay out clothes for her without consulting Jacqui. "I'm working at Dorothea's from nine until one today, so why not come by at one and we'll go to that jewelry store in the plaza. I promise you, it's the perfect gift!"

"That's what Jacqui said about her magnificent plan to get Alaine off my case, and look what happened," Kyle said, his note not totally free of irony.

"Don't blame me," Jacqui said.

"As for us, Jacqui," Janice was going on with her usual maddening disregard for anything else that was going on, "I saw a darling wrap-around skirt with embroidery on it—"

"Those are terribly expensive!" Jacqui cautioned, starting into her own bathroom.

"You forget I'm a working person," Janice told her. "I have been saving my money."

"That'll be the day!" Kyle spouted, and Jacqui heard him leaving her bedroom.

"I have been!" Janice protested. "When Dorothea gave me my first pay, she sat down with me and told me what she had learned over the years about budgeting her money. And she was right. I was skeptical at first, but she was right. I put some in my bank account, and some aside for daily expenses, and some for what Dorothea calls 'gifts and investments.'"

"Very interesting," Jacqui said, digging a clean towel and washcloth from a drawer.

"Dorothea may have some old-fashioned ideas," Janice said, "but some of them are more practical than you might think."

Jacqui looked at herself in the mirror, then back at Janice, who was coming into the bathroom. She was never going to tell Janice that it had taken her a little longer to adjust to Dorothea's ideas when she had begun working for her, a fact that Jacqui had conveniently forgotten two months before when she had gotten Janice the job.

"Your shoulder is going to need a fresh dressing this morning," Janice was saying calmly, taking a pad of gauze from a pile on the counter. "We may as well take care of it first."

SLAPPING her metal ruler down on the drafting board in front of her, Jacqui sighed and wiped perspiration from her upper lip with the cuff of her sleeve.

"What's wrong?" Yvonne asked, turning from the filing cabinet.

"A little of everything," Jacqui told her.

"Need a cup of coffee?"

"No, I'd probably spill it on these plans," Jacqui said. She got to her feet slowly and flexed her back.

Yvonne Halpern studied the plans on the drafting board for a moment. "This is one house I'm going to have to see myself," she said at last, then whistled through her teeth.

"It's going to be beautiful, all right," Jacqui agreed.

When Yvonne had left the room to go back to her own office, Jacqui looked back at the plans, then out the window. This one house had so many of her dreams in it that she almost regretted building it, tucked back in the hills where no one would see it. What Osprey Builders needed desperately was more contracts. This one house and the promise of a juicy contract for the construction on Red Key could not possibly be enough to keep the company going.

"I wish Kyle would get back here," Jacqui said aloud, sitting down on the stool at the drafting board again. Just as she reached for her pencil, she heard the familiar growl of the Beast. Setting her jaw firmly, she braced herself for some tale of woe that Christopher Warden had had to ask for another extension on his payment.

Kyle strode into the office with more than his usual speed and intensity. "Well, now we're getting somewhere!" he said, reaching into the pocket of his shirt and pulling out a folded check.

Jacqui looked at it, not able to focus her attention on more than the signature on the bottom.

"Chris stopped me on my way out of Egret Island," Kyle said. "This is the rest of the payment he owed us. Is the amount correct?"

"It looks all right," Jacqui said, blinking. "Check it with Yvonne."

"He also gave me a copy of the sixty-day option Leisure Development wants to take on our property on Red Key. I took it straight over to the lawyer to have him go over it. Merrill Warden wants signatures by Monday afternoon at the latest if we are going to accept. I thought that project would just fall through once they started going through the zoning books and tried out the idea on the county commissioners up there, but everyone is so eager for fresh money, they are bending over backward."

Jacqui groaned. "You realize this means another set of builder's tests?"

"Thought you were going to retire, didn't you?" Kyle asked, taking the check away from her to give to Yvonne. "You're going to have to do that on your own, because I'm not going to ask for a waiver."

Jacqui stared at the place where he had been standing while he went to Yvonne's office a few steps away and then returned. "And when am I supposed to do that?" she asked him.

Kyle shrugged and grinned. "You're not good for much else right now, are you?" he teased. "You can't drive the four-by, and you can hardly manage your drafting tools."

Jacqui growled at him, more disconsolate because what he said in jest had the definite ring of truth. "I could try to push sales," she said.

Kyle sank his hands into his pockets and fixed her with an intent look. "I've been thinking of looking into more commercial construction."

"I'm afraid we're going to have to," Jacqui agreed reluctantly. She had to admit to herself that she saw a certain romance to building houses that was not present in the design of shopping plazas and office buildings.

Turning back to her work on Alexis's house, Jacqui was conscious of Kyle looking over her shoulder. "This is great, isn't it, Jac? This house. Egret Island, Red

Key, everything else. Just watch! We're going to make Osprey Builders everything Dad ever wanted it to be."

"I sure hope so," Jacqui said, part of his enthusiasm burrowing into a corner of her depression and nipping away at it.

"Did Alexis say what style she wanted for the house?" Kyle asked.

"She couldn't decide between our Elizabethan and Spanish."

"Why don't I move the other board in here from Yvonne's office," Kyle suggested. "Then I can work up the elevations in time to take them over to Alexis when I take the paychecks to Egret Island this afternoon."

"That's a good idea," Jacqui agreed.

JACQUI FELT GAUDILY OVERDRESSED in her floor-length white dress, but Janice had insisted that she wear it. It was all very logical, if one followed Janice's reasoning. The long sleeve of the blue dress would not go over Jacqui's cast, and the yellow dress would not lie properly across her shoulder over the dressing.

But the way Janice was acting lately made it plain that she was not going to be crossed in her plans. She had wheedled an invitation to the party for Denny Behrensen, capitalizing on Alexis's feeling that the more younger people who were at the party, the better for Alaine's sake.

As they neared the family suite from the elevator, Janice was the only one of the four of them who seemed happily excited about the party. She had tucked flowers into her hair and used more makeup than Jacqui would normally have approved.

Kyle, dressed in his good suit and looking over-poweringly immaculate, was nonetheless obviously uncomfortable.

Alexis Warden answered their knock at the door, her face lighting when she recognized them. Jacqui immediately breathed more easily, seeing Alexis in a simply elegant gown of flowing ecru chiffon.

"You certainly know how to throw a party, Aunt Alexis," Janice breathed, looking at the decorated room, the spread of food, and the number of young people, mostly young employees of the hotel, who were already there.

"I think you have just been adopted," Jacqui confided in Alexis.

"How marvelous!" Alexis beamed, drawing them into the room. "Alaine and the rest of the family aren't back from the high school yet, but we expect them any moment. Come in and make yourselves at home."

Janice and Denny immediately found some youngsters to talk with, while Jacqui and Kyle looked nervously around themselves then turned to each other for company.

"I feel a little out of place," Jacqui hissed through her teeth.

"Ha!" Kyle laughed, ironically. "As though I haven't the slightest idea what you're talking about! Should I put this gift with the others on that table over there, or should I wait to give it to Alaine if and when we're alone?"

"An astute engineer like you ought to be able to figure that one out all by yourself," Jacqui told him.

"This past week has taken a lot out of my self-confidence," he told her.

Nodding, Jacqui had to agree. In the office, he was a ball of fire, but anywhere else, he clearly was having problems. The long hours of concentration on studying for his tests could have been blamed for draining his energy and causing a letdown once he had achieved his goal. But the real cause was Alaine's leaving. It was time Jacqui admitted to herself that Kyle was in love with her, and that nothing was going to change that very soon.

There was a commotion at the door as Alaine entered, followed by her mother, a woman only a hairsbreadth taller than her daughter, with dark hair crisply coiffed and a slender figure clad sedately in a stylish black silk dress. Jacqui would have known Dianna Warden to be Alaine's mother in a crowd of thousands. Moreover, from the firmness of her chin, she would have know Dianna to be Christopher's mother, also.

Dianna Warden had an air of holding herself back, allowing Alaine to be the star of her party, whereas Jacqui suspected that a woman of Dianna's beauty could easily have stolen any moment she cared to, no matter what the competition.

When Jacqui glanced toward Merrill Warden, she was immediately taken by the subtle changes in his carriage and attitude since the one other time she had seen him. His forehead showed the furrows of recent worry, but the line of his shoulders was more relaxed. Without any apparent thought on his part, his hand reached to his wife's elbow and he drew her along with him into the room.

Anxiously, Jacqui looked past them, expecting to see Christopher enter behind them, but the door closed, sending almost palpable distress through her. It was as though the chip of bone had not been taken from her shoulder. Now the thought of Christopher sent a more generalized pain through her being, without justification. *Or was there?* she wondered.

Alaine, spying Kyle, immediately brought her mother to him to introduce them.

"You don't have to tell me," Dianna Warden was saying. "Jacqueline and Kyle, of course. I have heard so many nice things about the Belpre family in the last two months."

"I'm afraid that is us," Kyle said, instantly putting on his best sales personality.

"You have been a tremendous help to Alaine in

straightening her world around," Dianna said, offering them each her gracefully slim hand.

"I'm sure she would have done it on her own," Jacqui said.

"Perhaps," Dianna said, her gray eyes studying Jacqui slowly. "In time, no doubt. The point is, you and Kyle and Janice took the time, while Merrill and I were too involved in our silly squabble to see how desperately she needed us. By the way, Christopher said that he would be along in a few minutes. You know how he is, always having to check out one last detail before he calls it a day."

"Come meet all the kids who work here," Alaine urged Kyle, taking his hand and pulling him along behind her.

Dianna watched them, then turned to Jacqui. "Remarkable as it is that you are building the structure on Egret Island and the house for Alexis, what you have done for Alaine and Christopher is even greater. With sixteen years' difference in their ages, I thought they would never be close, but somehow you accomplished what I never could—to make them friends."

"I take no credit there at all," Jacqui said. How could she stand here and smile pleasantly, listening to Dianna Warden saying all sorts of things about her supposed great powers over the Warden family, when all she wanted to do was get out of this room! If Christopher was not going to be here, then there was no reason for her to be, either.

Luckily the music was getting too loud to talk over, and the champagne punch from the fountain on the buffet was livening the party. Alexis drew Dianna aside to discuss some detail, and Jacqui found herself unable to take her attention from the front door; even when she resolutely turned her back on it, she saw the door mirrored clearly in the reflection of the patio doors opposite.

Almost as if she had willed it, the door opened and Christopher entered, tall and straight in his blue blazer and white slacks, every hair in place as though it would not dare to be otherwise, much as he had looked that first time she had seen him.

Her heart fell when he did not even seem to be looking for her, but went first to where his father was standing, nursing a glass of something stronger than the champagne punch. They exchanged a few words, then Christopher took something from his pocket and pressed it into his father's hand. It looked like a room key.

Still not even glancing toward Jacqui, Christopher moved confidently across the room to where Kyle was standing, watching Alaine chatting excitedly with two girls. Kyle and Christopher drifted away from the group a few steps, talked for a few moments very earnestly, and then patted each on the shoulder and parted company.

Again Jacqui was disappointed when she thought that Christopher would look her way. When he stopped to talk to some young men, while obviously on his way across the room to confer with his mother and Aunt Alexis, Jacqui had had enough.

Gritting her teeth, she let herself out onto the balcony, carefully sliding the door closed behind her. *Well, you made a fine mess of this,* she said to herself, leaning against the railing at the top of the steps that led down to the pool.

She was at a loss to know what had gone wrong. The last time she had seen him, she was lying on the sand of Egret Island, barely conscious, in excruciating pain with her broken arm throbbing, and they had been surrounded by strange people, swirling lights, and whining sirens. What had she done wrong? She could not have told him that she loved him then, because she had not known it herself then, not until—

Not until that last moment, before the paramedic

had shouldered him aside, and Christopher had looked down at her for a moment, the reflected light glinting, catching something on the lower lid of his left eye. A single tear.

She clutched at the cast that encased her arm, feeling a phantom of pain course from her shoulder to her fingertips. So that was it! That was the one thing she had been searching for, a touch of vulnerability in Christopher Warden's perfect facade, some evidence of caring.

And knowing Christopher, it was the one thing he had not wanted her to see, just as it had embarrassed him to tell her that his parents were getting a divorce, almost as though it was a great failing in himself.

She knew now that he felt emotions more deeply than he had wanted to admit, and they presented new problems.

Whether she looked back at the sliding door behind her before or after she heard it start to open, she did not know, but Christopher was there carrying two glasses of punch and opening the door with his toe, a trick he must have had some practice at.

"As I was saying before we were so rudely interrupted," he said, unhurriedly handing a glass to her, then turning to close the door behind him.

"What?" Jacqui asked, trying to keep her hand from trembling as she took the glass.

"It's been a long week, hasn't it?" Christopher said. "I'm going to apologize for not being able to spend any time with you, and if you don't accept my apology, I'll understand. Besides, you're partly to blame."

About to take a sip of her champagne punch, Jacqui glared at him over the rim of her glass. "I beg your pardon?"

"You should not have gone back to work so soon," he told her, stating something her fatigue had already been trying to tell her.

"I had to," she told him, suddenly defensive, forgetting the conclusions she had come to only moments ago.

Christopher drained his glass and set it down carefully on the umbrella table. "A lot has happened since Monday night," he said, leaning against the railing beside her. 'I've had to deal with the sheriff's men, the insurance adjustors who were arguing over how liable we are for your hospital expenses, and on top of that, my parents and Aunt Alexis descended on me!"

"I've heard a few of the echoes," Jacqui teased, unable to restrain herself.

"I suppose you have," he chuckled sheepishly. "I have to admit I even tried looking for courage where I should have known better than to expect to find it. Dad and I got drunk together Wednesday night. Maybe we should have done that ten years ago. Anyway, he started telling me what a shame it was that he had let a perfectly wonderful woman fall out of love with him. Then—well—it hadn't taken long for the word to reach me that you thought it was over with us before it really had gotten started—"

"What?" Jacqui asked, her face flushing in disbelief. "That gossip Janice!"

"Kyle confirmed it," Christopher said, "so I took it as truth."

"Chris, I think I know what they thought they heard," Jacqui tried to explain, "but—I—I just don't know—how I feel about anything right now."

Turning toward her, Christopher took the champagne glass from her hand and placed it on the table beside his own. The expression of his eyes burned into her until she felt almost naked. "Perhaps I can help you put things into perspective," he said, starting to put his arms around her, then looking down at the cast on her arm and back at the glass doors to the suite.

"On second thought," he said, "I'm afraid that party

is going to spill out here any moment. What do you say to a walk on the beach?''

Jacqui nodded, unable to say anything around the lump in her throat.

Confidently, Christopher put his arm around her waist and began to guide her down the steps to the long promenade which ended on the sands. ''I think my parents' divorce is about to bite the dust,'' he told her, his voice hushed. ''Alaine was right; thirty-five years is too much to throw away.''

''So that was why you slipped him a room key?'' Jacqui dared to inject.

Christopher chuckled. ''You saw that? There are advantages to being boss. There are also disadvantages, you know?'' He sighed, and his hand on her waist drew her closer to him.

''Such as?'' she asked.

''I have to go to Tallahassee next week to see what the environmentalists are going to say about the Red Key project, then I'm going to have to make trips to Boston and New York to see about some financing. You realize I wouldn't have to be doing all of this if Dad hadn't decided to try to win Mom back? He'd be flying all over the place meeting with people so that he could avoid thinking about how lonely he was.''

''I have to admit I was afraid of him when I first met him,'' Jacqui said.

''You had a right to be,'' Christopher laughed. ''He was a bear without Mom! I hardly think he would compare with those two men on Egret Island, though. I just had a glimpse of that ruffian when he hit you with that board. I cannot understand how a man could hit a woman—''

''Maybe he thought I was a man.''

''The way you looked that night?'' he said, chuckling, then sniffed. ''The way you smelled? God, the scent of roses gives me ideas!''

When they reached the uneven surface of the sand, Jacqui drew her attention away from Christopher and from the velvety darkness of the softly lapping waves of the Gulf to kick off her sandals and leave them on the top of the retaining wall.

"Can you move your arm at all?" Christopher asked her, as he removed his jacket and lay it on the wall.

"A little," she said, looking up at him, wondering what he was thinking.

"Where there is a will, there is a way," he philosophized, gently taking her left hand and placing it behind his back so that her fingers could rest on his belt. He drew her into his arms gently, but the kisses on her cheek and neck showed none of the restraint he exerted otherwise.

Jacqui gave herself up into his arms. There was no reason to deny that this man who held her so possessively, who was making her heart thump and her pulses race, was the only man she had ever loved, the only man she desired with every fiber of her being.

"Monday night turned into such a mess," Christopher said, his warm breath fanning her blond hair at her temple. "I had planned to take you out on the balcony to watch the sunset and—"

"Yes?" Jacqui encouraged, made impatient by a pause, during which he seemed intent on driving her insane by kissing her ear.

He raised an eyebrow and looked down at her, his eyes intent and smoldering in the random lights from the hotel. "I love you, Jacqui," he said slowly. "I know you didn't want to deal with this before Egret was finished—"

"Chris."

"What?"

"Stop talking," she ordered, pressing her mouth to his impetuously.

Christopher broke away after a moment and took a

deep breath. "I take it you have decided that it is not over between us," he said.

"Chalk it up to insecurity and—inexperience," she told him. He tilted his head to one side, coaxing her, encouraging her. "All right!" she conceded. "I love you!"

His arms around her were suddenly holding her so tightly, she was afraid she would not be able to breathe. "I promised Kyle I would see that you got home," he told her, seeming very matter-of-fact and more controlled than Jacqui thought he had any right to be.

"It's early yet, isn't it?" she asked.

"That, young lady, is why going to your house is the logical move at the moment," he said, then kissed the tip of her nose. "What is the one place you know of where there won't be anyone for at least two hours?"

"You have a thoroughly devious mind, Christopher Warden," she laughed, "and for that I admire you tremendously!"

FOR THE THIRD TIME, Jacqui tried to read an article in the Sunday paper, then threw it aside on the heap in the middle of the floor. It was not so much the paper she was disgusted at, but that she was alone, and had nothing to distract herself from the dissatisfied feeling she had every time she thought about Christopher. He was terribly busy, she knew, trying to juggle his family with his responsibilities and his plans for Red Key.

It seemed that Christopher separated the ideas of love and marriage and a lifetime of commitment, while they were inseparable in Jacqui's mind. Although he was now telling her how much he loved her almost constantly, he had yet to mention a word about permanent arrangements.

She should have known better than to expect a pledge of undying adoration from Christopher amid all the confusion in his life. Just because she had come to the conclusion that she was never going to love anyone but Christopher was no indication that he felt the same way toward her. She was just going to have to be patient, and patience was not her strong suit.

The Beast growled to a stop in the driveway, and Kyle burst into the house, waving a rolled-up set of plans at her. "You'll never guess what happened!" he exclaimed.

"Probably not," Jacqui said, and was immediately sorry for trying to dampen Kyle's high spirits.

"Not only did Alexis Warden come over to the model while I was there, and approve her plans and sign her contract, but"—Kyle took a deep breath and paused for emphasis, just as Janice would, to prolong some important tale—"another client came in, saw that preliminary we had done for her, and signed a cost-plus contract for us to build it—guess where?—on those two lots on Admiralty!"

"You're kidding!" Jacqui said, caught up in his elation.

"There are some alterations to be made in the plans, but we can handle that," Kyle said, handing her the roll of plans. "I thought we'd go out to the barbecue place to celebrate, then get to it for a few hours tonight."

"Who is crazy enough to sign a cost-plus on these plans?" Jacqui asked, unrolling the sketches and taking a cursory look at the list of changes Kyle had scribbled.

Kyle ignored her rhetorical question as he unbuttoned his shirt, preparing to change it to something more comfortable. "He's a bit of a weird duck. He really doesn't want you working on this house, except perhaps for the plans and maybe the decorating. You'll be busy enough with Alexis's house and studying for your tests—"

"Sounds like a..." Jacqui said, her voice trailing off as she studied the plans.

"Come on, change into something nice!" Kyle

yelled to her from his room. "With these two contracts and Red Key, you're going to have to throw your chambrays away and start dressing like a lady!"

"Just for that, Kyle Belpre, I'm going to order pecan pie for dessert," she called to him, putting the plans aside and getting to her feet. "And you're going to pay for it."

.

IT WAS THE FIRST TIME she had driven the Beast since her arm had been broken, and Jacqui's left elbow still felt a little stiff. The last six weeks had not been entirely fruitful, even though she was prepared to take her test in the next county, and Alexis's house was going along smoothly.

It had seemed that every time she had seen Christopher, he was preoccupied, and he refused to tell her what was bothering him. Their encounters had been mildly passionate, and yet definitely noncommittal. She had just about decided that she was, indeed, merely a diversion for him, and that he was just using her to further his own plans and those of Leisure Development.

The Beast settled into a pair of ruts in the barren front yard of the sprawling house, impressive even in its unfinished stage. Kyle had cajoled and coerced her to put almost every one of her favorite ideas into this house, and it was going to pain her more than her broken arm and worrisome shoulder ever had to see this house finished and inhabited by someone else.

The crowning touch had come when Kyle had told her that he had arranged an appointment for her to meet with the owner this afternoon to consult on the decorating. To the suggestion that he go to Dorothea for the finishing touches, Kyle had shrugged. "He says that he was impressed with the decorating of the model, and he wants you to handle it."

Jacqui switched off the motor and gathered up her

plans and her hard hat. She had only the worst possible feelings toward the snob who wanted Kyle to be responsible for the building of the house and her to have only the decorating.

Letting herself into the foyer, she looked at the house more critically than she had ever looked at a structure put together by Osprey Builders, because this was the first one, the only one so far, that Kyle had been solely in charge of. She had inspected the living room, dining room, kitchen, and part of the bedroom wing before she had found anything to call to his attention, and she was as annoyed as she was pleased.

Kyle was capable of taking over for her, she had to admit. Now the only Belpre who had to depend on her was Janice, and she could so easily look to Kyle for support, with her own part-time job and dreams of going to a modest college to study business.

Jacqui cleared her throat. Dust in an unfinished house is everywhere, unavoidable, no matter how tidy the subcontractors try to be. And in the mid-July heat, she felt suddenly stifled.

Leaving her purse and her plans on a relatively clear place on the unfinished floor, Jacqui let herself out the door of the vaulted-ceilinged studio onto the deck, and strolled across the uneven backyard to the shade of a majestic oak tree which dangled Spanish moss in long gray chains. The breeze from the Gulf made the spot bearable. And the view of the rolling waves and Gulf sky was nearly the best part of the site. She could not but envy whoever was going to live here.

Conscious of the sound of a motor behind her, Jacqui turned back to the house too late to see the car that drove into the yard and parked beside hers.

Sighing, she left the shade of the oak and picked her way back to the house, head down, being careful of her footing. As she slid the patio door open, she looked toward the door from the kitchen curiously, now anxious to know who was going to live in this glorious place that she had put so much of herself into.

He walked slowly into the studio, looking around at the structure while he dropped his car keys into his pants pocket. A slow smile spread from his gray eyes to the rest of his tanned face when he saw her.

"Chris," Jacqui said, her voice suddenly catching in her throat.

"Is it the way you wanted it?" he asked her, looking up at the high ceiling, and then out at the magnificent view of the Gulf framed by the broad windows and the gigantic oak tree beyond. When she could not answer, he went on. "I think Kyle has done a pretty good job, don't you?"

"Yes, so far," she managed to say.

"Has he proved to you that he's up to your standards?"

Jacqui swallowed and had to smile back at him. "I have to admit that he has, yes."

Christopher took a few steps and looked out the windows that were at the front of the house, toward the street. "And is it obvious to you that I'm not going to live with my work all the time?" he asked. "It would be foolish—totally against New England frugality—to build a house as beautiful as this is going to be and not enjoy it at least sixteen hours out of a day."

Jacqui chuckled. "Is that what you plan to do?"

Unexpectedly, he reached out and took her hand in his. "That is only the roughest sketch of what I plan to do," he told her.

He tugged her along behind him up the two steps that led to the master suite off the studio and waved his arm at the large expanse of the room, now dismally gray with gypsum-board walls. "I want this to be blue-gray just like your model, but I want white moldings on the walls and a white carpet. Would you like that?"

"That would look very nice," Jacqui agreed.

"You didn't quite answer my question," Christopher said, placing his hands gently on her shoulders and turning her to face him squarely.

"Um—what was the question?" she asked, flustered by the penetrating look of his gray eyes.

"I—ah—have been putting it off until the house was this far," he said, and she wondered if he would ever get to the point. "I know you've probably thought I'd never actually say the words. I—ah— Will you marry me? And live here—and have at least one little Warden for one of the bedrooms at the other end of the house?"

"Yes," Jacqui said, moving closer to him, "yes, and most definitely, yes!"

"It's not too much to ask of a career woman, is it?" he asked, encircling her with his arms.

"Of course not," she smiled up at him. "Chris, you're asking too many questions." She raised up on her tiptoes to kiss his chin, but he met her mouth with his.

"We're going to have to have some rules here," Christopher informed her between kisses. "We're both going to quit work at five-thirty every day, not a minute later. We'll come home and take a swim in the Gulf, or jog along the shore, or build a fire and drink hot chocolate. And never, never bring work home."

"But the reason I wanted a studio was to have a place to work on plans," Jacqui told him, snuggling close.

"You can take up watercolor," Christopher suggested.

"And what are you going to do?" she asked.

"I'm three years behind in my reading," he confessed. "And I like to play the guitar. Don't worry about me, I'll find plenty to keep myself busy."

"Somehow I think we'll find something to keep *each other* busy," Jacqui teased, kissing him with growing passion.

Chapter Fifteen

The reception had filled the Magellan Room and had overflowed out under the palms around the patio and the pool. Unusual for a day on the Gulf coast, there seemed little possibility of an afternoon shower to dampen the spirits of the guests or the principals of the wedding.

Alaine had flown down to be bridesmaid between the end of summer session and the start of the fall term at her college. She and Kyle had maintained an active correspondence, and if anything, they seemed more in love with each other than when she had left in June.

Kyle, formally resplendent, had given Jacqui away with every bit as much dignity as she might have expected from their father had he been there. Janice seemed to have acquired new stature, having helped Dorothea decorate the units of Egret Island and plan the Belpre portion of the wedding.

The Wardens, both senior couples, had arrived in Florida in enough time to play golf and appreciate the final stages of the construction of Alexis's dream house.

Personally, Jacqui was looking forward to a few weeks of honeymoon. She had just finished the designs for the resort at Red Key, which was becoming more of an installation than even Christopher had first anticipated. It was getting so that Jacqui held her breath every time Kyle or Christopher reached for the tube of plans marked "Red Key."

Christopher was being maddeningly secretive, however, about part of the plans for their honeymoon, and no amount of coaxing on her part would gain Jacqui a bit of information about where they were going to spend their wedding night. Since she had not been able to get their house finished by this first Saturday in September, they could not possibly spend the night there. The only thing she could figure out, up until the time she was about to throw her bouquet to the waiting mass of unmarried women, was that he had intended them to spend the night in his suite—and she was not ecstatic at the prospect.

With a squeal of delight, Alaine grabbed the bouquet of white roses from the air and clutched it to her.

"Well, I guess that's that!" Christopher said with finality. "Come on! Time to leave!"

He grasped Jacqui's wrist so tightly that she was afraid that he would tear the froth of white lace that was the sleeve of her story-book gown. Unexpectedly, he dragged her through the wide doors that led to the patio, to a streamer-decked golf cart that sported a giant JUST MARRIED sign.

"What on earth?" Jacqui demanded, when he made her sit in the cart, then threw it into gear and circled out onto the cart path.

"It must be obvious by now," Christopher said, as the little machine whirred toward the bridge. "We are going to be the first couple to ever use Egret Island. I thought it was only fitting."

"I should have known!" Jacqui laughed, snuggling closer to him. "You are just a great big romantic!"

Christopher chuckled. "So are you!"

He parked the golf cart under the carport roof and led her up the stairs to the highest unit, overlooking the palms and oleanders, the rioting bougainvillea and hibiscus. It was quiet except for the breeze fluttering the palms, and the constant lapping of the waves on the sandy beach. It was more beautiful than Jacqui had imagined it could be in her wildest dreams.

"It's fantastic, isn't it?" Christopher asked, pausing just a minute before unlocking the door and carrying her over the threshold.

"Marvelous," Jacqui agreed, reveling in the strength of his arms. "But isn't this just a little too close to your work?"

"Normally, it might be," Christopher said, putting her down on the couch and dropping the key to the table. "But I conveniently forgot to have the phones connected. You know, sometimes even an executive like me might forget a detail...."

"I should have known!" Jacqui said, giggling.

JACQUI SAT AT THE DRESSING TABLE, trying to calm her self-consciousness with vigorous strokes of her hairbrush through her blond hair. She moistened her lips and adjusted the tiny strap of her filmy blue nightgown on her left shoulder, tracing the tiny scar there with her index finger. Each day it grew less noticeable, especially since she was taking a little time now and again to work on her tan.

Christopher emerged from the bathroom, clad only in white pajama bottoms which had settled low on his slim hips, his tanned chest gleaming here and there where his towel had missed a few droplets left from his shower. He barely glanced at Jacqui before a bolt of pink lightning surged through the room, even through the closed drapes. When it was followed by almost instant thunder, Jacqui dropped her brush to the polished top of the dressing table and got to her feet.

"That was close!" she gasped, going to the window of the bedroom and moving the drapery aside.

"I'm still not quite used to Florida thunderstorms,"

Christopher confessed, following her to the window.

"You never will be," Jacqui said, looking up at him. He drew her close to his side, the warmth of his body searing through the thin gossamer of her gown.

When another jagged tongue of lightning flashed through the sky, Christopher took a deep breath. "When I said that our love would light up the sky," he chuckled, "this is not what I had in mind."

Smiling at him encouragingly, Jacqui let the drapery fall back into place and wound her arms around his neck. "You're not afraid of a little storm, are you?" she asked.

Christopher kissed her shoulder and the curve of her throat. "Not with you here—to protect me," he said with mock seriousness. "Should I turn the lights out?" There was a flash of lightning and the lamps dimmed.

"I think there isn't going to be a choice," Jacqui chuckled as the lights went out completely.

"What a shame!" Christopher said, lifting Jacqui into his arms and carrying her the few feet to the opened bed. "I won't be able to appreciate the way you look in this blue gown."

"Oh, some other time," Jacqui said, unconcerned, stretching out on the cool sheet and waiting for him to lie down beside her. As they explored each other's bodies, their nightclothes cast aside, she kissed Christopher's wonderful mouth and drew aside just a little. "I'm beginning to think your shyness was just an act," she accused him playfully.

"Not completely," he chuckled, "but you have to admit, it helped you over your shyness to think I was afraid of the storm."

"You're terrible!" Jacqui said, pretending to batter his shoulders with her fists, but stopping the blows short.

He caught her hands and kissed the insides of her wrists. "Now, now!" he murmured. "Let's not get into that!'' He released her hands and kissed her. His hands gently explored the round fullness of her breasts, the firm strength of her thighs.

When she sighed in surrender to him, and she cradled him with the first full passion she had ever known, the room was suddenly lit with pink lightning, shaken with a roll of almost simultaneous thunder. Quivering, Jacqui took a deep breath and held Christopher tightly to her.

Christopher kissed her shoulder, then looked across the room toward the window. ''You've been enough help, thank you!'' he said.

Jacqui started to laugh just as the lights flickered and came on, and the forgotten radio wafted romantic violin music through the room. As Christopher disengaged himself from her arms, and tried to find his pajamas, she was tempted to reach out to him and try to keep him close to her.

When he had turned out the lights and the radio, he lay back down beside her, snuggling her to his side so that her head rested on his shoulder. ''I think I'm over my fear of storms,'' he said, as rain began to pelt the roof. He kissed her forehead.

''Christopher,'' Jacqui said.

''What?'' he asked.

''I love you,'' she murmured, with the feeling of one who had finally found her true home.

Chapter Sixteen

With a sense of finality, Jacqui placed the lid on the enamel roasting pan and dropped her tea-towel to the broad white counter beside the stainless-steel sink.

"Is that everything?" Christopher asked.

"I think so," she told him, with a sigh.

Effortlessly, he lifted the roaster to the top shelf of the pantry cupboard, then closed the door, brushing his hands together. "I don't think I'll ever forget our first Thanksgiving in this house," he told her.

Catching her hand, he pulled her along into the studio, where he had turned on the stereo and built a fire in the great stone fireplace.

"I don't think anyone is going to forget this Thanksgiving," Jacqui laughed, dropping to her knees on one of the floor cushions Christopher had placed close to the hearth. "Alexis and Charles showing up in their jeans and sneakers, for one thing."

"Dorothea walking around saying, 'I wouldn't change a thing!'" Christopher laughed, sitting down beside her and draping his arm around her shoulder.

"The greatest moment, though," Jacqui said, looking at him adoringly, "and you've got to agree, was when that hotel limo drove up and Alaine got out. I thought Kyle would explode from happiness."

"Well, didn't she sound lonely when she called last Sunday?" he asked.

"You're still a big old romantic," Jacqui teased him, snuggling closer.

"It gave me another idea, though," Christopher said, reaching to a table where two glasses of wine waited for them. "Since the trade closes down during the week between Christmas and New Year's, I thought it would be nice to send Kyle and Janice up to Boston for a week. They've never really seen snow, have they?"

"No," Jacqui said hesitantly, taking the glass of wine from him.

"Well, then, I'll order snow."

"I'm sure the people of Massachusetts will be very thankful. Why do I have a feeling that there is an ulterior motive somewhere in your largess?"

Christopher paused before taking a sip of his wine to look down at her with exaggerated innocence. "It's just that I'm taking that week off, too," he said, "and since a certain sister-in-law of mine seems to think you need so much help with your housework, and is over here every time she has a day off—"

"Oh, I see," Jacqui murmured. "It's not so much Kyle you're getting rid of as Jan."

"We could just let the housework go for a week," he suggested.

Jacqui giggled and put her glass of wine aside. "Sounds like heaven."

Christopher shrugged. "No more than every day around here," he said.

Jacqui watched as Christopher took another swallow of his wine, then she took the glass away from him, putting it aside with her own. Dorothea would be proud of her, Jacqui thought, looking back at him. She had allowed Christopher to fill every moment of her life away from her work, and there were even times when thoughts of him distracted her from things she should have been doing.

When their lips met, it was by mutual agreement,

something that seemed so natural and right, so complete but with an exciting freshness. Jacqui knew in her heart that there would never be an end to this building passion.

ROBERTA LEIGH

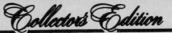

A specially designed collection of six exciting love stories by one of the world's favorite romance writers—Roberta Leigh, author of more than 60 bestselling novels!

1 **Love in Store**   4 **The Savage Aristocrat**
2 **Night of Love**   5 **The Facts of Love**
3 **Flower of the Desert**   6 **Too Young to Love**

Available in August wherever paperback books are sold, or available through Harlequin Reader Service. Simply complete and mail the coupon below.

Harlequin Reader Service

In the U.S.
P.O. Box 52040
Phoenix, AZ 85072-9988

In Canada
649 Ontario Street
Stratford, Ontario N5A 6W2

Please send me the following editions of the Harlequin Roberta Leigh Collector's Editions. I am enclosing my check or money order for $1.95 for each copy ordered, plus 75¢ to cover postage and handling.

☐ 1   ☐ 2   ☐ 3   ☐ 4   ☐ 5   ☐ 6

Number of books checked_____ @ $1.95 each = $_____

N.Y. state and Ariz. residents add appropriate sales tax $_____

Postage and handling $_____.75_____

                                                    TOTAL $_____

I enclose_____

(Please send check or money order. We cannot be responsible for cash sent through the mail.) Price subject to change without notice.

NAME_____
                        (Please Print)
ADDRESS_____APT. NO._____

CITY_____

STATE/PROV._____ZIP/POSTAL CODE_____

Offer expires January 31, 1984   30756000000

**For a truly SUPER read,
don't miss . . .**

SUPERROMANCE

EVERYTHING YOU'VE ALWAYS WANTED A LOVE STORY TO BE!

Contemporary!
A modern romance for the modern woman—set in the world of today.

Sensual!
A warmly passionate love story that reveals the beautiful feelings between a man and a woman in love.

Dramatic!
An exciting and dramatic plot that will keep you enthralled till the last page is turned.

Exotic!
The thrill of armchair travel—anywhere from the majestic plains of Spain to the towering peaks of the Andes.

Satisfying!
Almost 400 pages of romance reading—a long satisfying journey you'll wish would never end.

SUPERROMANCE